THE LAST SEASON

THE LAST SEASON

ROBERT JOSEPH

Library of Congress Control Number:

Paperback ISBN 978-0-9962160-3-6
Electronic Book ISBN 978-0-9962160-4-3

Cover by SelfPubBookCovers / Daniela

This book was printed in the United States of America.

Acknowledgements

The following people have been helpful in the development of this book:

Sheila Lowe

Jeanne Rejaunier

Marguerite Johnston Arno

Robert T. Joseph, Jr.

Steven W. Johnson

Jag Mundhra

The Santa Barbara Screenwriters Association

Carl Belfor

Gayle Sherman

David Jackson

and, most of all,

Shauna Shapiro Jackson

Books by Robert Joseph

Long Ago and Far Away

The Raff Rafferty Mystery Series

    Deadly Desire - #1

    Ominous Obsession - #2

    Dangerous Deception - #3

    Sinister Secrets - #4

    Lethal Legacy - #5

    Curse of the Cobra - #6

    Perilous Pilgrimage - #7

Diva

The Brazen Baroness

Reading Runes

Chapter One

The sound of an automobile roaring up the circular drive to Stags-bridge awakened Lady Mary Ashmore. Jumping out of bed in her nightgown, her ash blonde hair tousled from sleep, she ran to the open window of her second story bedroom. As she shoved the heavy brocade drapes aside and peered out, her eighteen year old heart pounded with excitement.

Can it be Andrew? she wondered, but she was disappointed to see that it was his younger brother Nicholas who stepped out from behind the wheel of the open automobile, a Delahaye 135 MS painted a brilliant shade of turquoise. She knew very well that the more modest Andrew would have never chosen a car of that color. Although it was early morning, Nicholas was still dressed in rather rumpled formal evening clothes, the starched white shirt wilted and badly wrinkled from the August heat, the black bow tie at his throat askew.

Hardly an outfit for someone who is about to join a shooting party, she thought.

Dunsmuir, the Ashmore family's gray-haired, rosy cheeked, middle aged and perennially deferential butler, dashed out the front entrance to greet the new arrival.

"I'm afraid that you're a bit late, Lord Buckford," Mary heard Dunsmuir inform him. "The other gentlemen departed some time ago. It is the 'Glorious Twelfth' you know, sir, and his lordship was eager to begin the day's shoot at sunrise."

"Sorry I'm late," Nicholas apologized, stepping out of the car and brushing his thick, raven's wing black hair, ruffled by the wind in the open vehicle, from his forehead. He was generally considered handsome, even with a nose whose bridge was somewhat deformed. "I attended a party in London until quite late, and then there was the drive down here to Surrey. My shotgun and shooting clothes, however, are in the rear of my car. It will only require a moment or so to change, and then I'll be off to join Lord Ashmore and the others."

"You may change in the house if you wish, sir" Dunsmuir offered, indicating the five hundred year old, three story manor house behind him. Its honey-hued stone had at one time formed the walls of the Catholic abbey which had originally stood on the site.

Nicholas tore off his formal black evening jacket and formal shirt and threw them in the car. He was stepping out of his black trousers with their shiny satin stripe down the sides as he replied, "No need for that. I'll just change right here. No one in the house who might be offended by my state of undress is up and about at this early hour."

With a disapproving frown, Dunsmuir said, "As you wish, sir," and returned into the great house.

From her bedroom window Mary was now wide awake, her deep blue eyes focused on Nicholas as he prepared to step into the pair of wool tweed trousers of his shooting outfit. She was startled when her sixteen year old sister Lucy, who occupied the adjoining bedroom, burst in without knocking. She was still in her nightdress as well.

"I heard you stirring," Lucy said. "What has caught your interest?"

"Nothing," Mary snapped, turning away from the open window.

"Something has," Lucy said, squeezing in beside her older sister. "You're watching Nicholas down there, aren't you?"

"No, I'm not," Mary protested indignantly.

Lucy gasped. "My goodness! He's undressed!"

"No, he's not – not completely," Mary said defensively.

Hearing their voices from the second story above him, Nicholas, buttoning the fly of his trousers, looked up.

"He's nicely proportioned," Lucy mused. "Like one of those Greek statues in our garden."

"He boxed when he was at university in Edinburgh," Mary explained. "One of his opponents fractured his nose in a boxing match."

"Broken nose or not, he is rather good-looking," Lucy remarked.

"I much prefer Andrew," Mary replied with a sigh.

"Yes, we know," Lucy said with a smirk. "It's too bad he doesn't prefer you."

Taking offense, Mary responded, "How do you know?"

"Anyone can tell from the way he looks at Fraulein Herzog."

Mary frowned. "Don't be silly. Andrew would never be interested in someone like her."

"Oh, no?" Lucy retorted. "Charles and I were out riding the other day, and we saw them in the meadow by the river under a great oak tree."

"I don't believe you," Mary snapped. Then, reconsidering Lucy's words, she asked. "What were they doing?"

"Reading poetry to one another."

"Andrew has no interest in poetry."

"Perhaps he does now."

"Ridiculous," Mary sniffed.

The two sisters continued to watch as Nicholas, now properly attired in his shooting clothes, reached for the shotgun in his car. With a mischievous grin, he raised his shotgun and fired into the air, startling Mary and Lucy.

Laughing, Nicholas hopped back into his turquoise sports car and sped down the long drive to join the other men who were stalking grouse somewhere in the vast acreage surrounding Stagsbridge.

Eventually sighting his father and brother Andrew as well as Lord Arthur Ashmore in a distant field, Nicholas pulled over to the side of the narrow dirt road, raising a cloud of dust, and climbed out of his car.

In the field, Lord Arthur Ashmore's game-keepers were directing the 'beaters', a group of farmers whose job it was to flush the grouse, to form a semi-circle in front of the shooters. Since grouse were known to fly downwind, the 'beaters' were armed with cloth flags to indicate the direction of the wind for the benefit of the shooters.

Just as Nicholas was approaching the trio, a flock of grouse flew into the air before him, vigorously flapping their wings, their croaking – a cry peculiar to grouse – sounded an alarm.

Arthur Ashmore, Andrew and Simon Buckford raised their shotguns in unison and prepared to shoot, but when they spotted Nicholas in the vicinity of the fleeing birds, they were forced to hold their fire. Nicholas, on the other hand, fired and downed a number of grouse. Pumping the shotgun, he fired again, adding more grouse to his total.

The excited spaniel dogs retrieved the fallen birds and dropped them at the feet of the game-keepers who gathered them into a burlap sack.

"Nice shooting, Nicholas," Arthur Ashmore complimented him as he joined the group.

Disgruntled, Andrew muttered, "He was just lucky – like always."

Under the watchful eye of butler Dunsmuir, the kitchen staff, aided by some of the footmen, scurried about the spacious formal dining room preparing the long table for that evening's dinner party. Beneath the gilded ceiling, designed to reflect the light of the three ornate crystal chandeliers, Dunsmuir was using a yardstick as a measuring device to determine the placement of the silver dining utensils, china and crystal goblets to be certain that they conformed with Lady Ashmore's precise standards.

Lady Celia Ashmore entered the room. Her svelte figure and pale complexion were complimented by a summery lavender silk dress. The staff acknowledged her presence with a deferential bow and, then, in response to a silent signal from Dunsmuir, returned to the kitchen, leaving the butler and the lady of the house alone.

Surveying the table, she smiled. "Very nice, as always, Dunsmuir."

"Thank you, my lady."

"All that's lacking are the floral centerpieces." Flowers were important to Celia, a dedicated gardener. "Later I shall gather some roses from the garden. The blooms in the walled garden are especially lovely this year."

"They are indeed, my lady."

A puzzled frown creased her otherwise smooth, ivory brow. "Do you think I should have the cook roast a lamb just in case?" she asked.

"In case of what?"

"In case there is an insufficient number of birds for our guests."

Dunsmuir chuckled. "I'm sure that, with Lord Nicholas in his lordship's shooting party, there will be plenty of birds for all. That young man is an expert shot, even if he was late in arriving for today's shoot."

"Nicholas Buckford is a bit of a gadabout, " Celia quipped as she slowly circled the long table, fingering the strand of pearls at her throat. "Now then, we must discuss the seating arrangement for tonight. Have you prepared place-cards from the guest list I gave you?"

"I have." With his gloved hand he passed her a pack of white cards.

Celia looked over the cards one by one. "Your calligraphy is excellent, as usual."

"Thank you, my lady."

"I would like Lord Simon seated on my right. As a member of the House of Lords at Parliament I should like to hear his opinion on our prime minister's recent dealings with Germany's Chancellor Hitler."

"Very good," Dunsmuir said as he inserted Lord Simon Buckford's place-card in the sterling silver holder before the place at the table indicated by Celia.

"His wife, Lady Antonia, can be seated at Lord Arthur's right at the opposite end of the table. Lord and Lady Knightsgate will also be at dinner. It's uncertain whether their son Trevor will be with us tonight or not. He's salmon fishing in Scotland with a group of chums from Oxford this week and may not arrive back in England in time, but set a place for him just in case. His sister, Lady Jane, will be here, of course. She spent last summer in Paris with Mary. The girls got on very well when they studied French with Mademoiselle Fourchet. Put Lord Philip on my left and Lady Alice on his lordship's left."

"And Lady Jane?"

Celia considered a moment. "Seat her next to Lord Nicholas with Lucy on his other side. His charm and wit will keep both young ladies entertained. Those two Buckford brothers could not be more dissimilar – Andrew so upstanding and serious, and Nicholas a bit of a rake."

With the sun beginning to set and the day's shooting concluded, Arthur, Nicholas, Andrew and Simon Buckford headed across a meadow of grazing sheep toward Stagsbridge.

The game-keepers carried sacks of grouse, and the 'beaters', some of whom were also laden with sacks of birds, followed. The pack of springer spaniels, panting from the August heat, ran in circles ahead of the shooters.

Arthur Ashmore, his once fair complexion now ruddy and deeply lined from life as a country aristocrat, turned to his contemporary Simon Buckford, whose days were spent legislating in London at Parliament's House of Lords. "Tell me, Simon, what is the latest news these days regarding our country's relations with Chancellor Hitler's Germany?" he asked.

"Prime Minister Chamberlain persists with his policy of appeasement despite growing opposition from such prominent individuals as Sir Winston Churchill," Simon replied. "Churchill has been warning us about Nazi Germany and campaigning for Britain's re-armament for years."

"Chamberlain's appeasement is nothing but sheer cowardice," Andrew remarked, a note of disgust in his voice as he brushed aside a lock of his auburn hair which was poking out from beneath the edge of his tweed hunting cap. "I say that war is inevitable, so let's take on those blasted Nazis and get it over with." He mopped beads of perspiration from his freckled forehead.

"One must be realistic, Andrew," Simon cautioned his son. "At the present time, Britain is no match for Hitler's Germany from a military standpoint. They've got us outnumbered all around. Germany is not going to try a land invasion of Britain. If they do decide to come after us, it will be by air, and the Luftwaffe has 2,600 planes to the RAF's 640. Their strategy would be to bomb us into defeat."

"Don't use a word like 'defeat' when you speak of this country, Father," Andrew reproached. "Especially when the RAF has planes like the Spitfire and the Hurricane."

"I'd give anything to fly either of those aircraft," Andrew continued enthusiastically.

"Are you planning to join the RAF, Andrew?" Arthur asked.

"I've been giving it serious consideration," the elder Buckford son replied.

Nicholas, who had been listening, spoke up, "What good are those planes if we can't get them into the air in time to stop German bombers? Britain needs a good air warning system."

"A rumor is circulating about Whitehall that the Nazis have developed a secret weapon called the 'Death Ray' which is capable of destroying aircraft," Simon said. "It's just a rumor, mind you, but let's be honest, right now Britain doesn't stand a chance against the German war machine. That's why Chamberlain believes our only option at the moment is to appease Hitler. He knows that if we fought the Germans now, we wouldn't have a prayer of winning. If we were to lose, our whole way of life would be completely destroyed. That's why many in this country favor the present policy, hoping that will make Germany leave Britain alone."

"I'm not among those who favor appeasement," Arthur staunchly declared. "Chamberlain and even that ex-king of ours and that American divorcee wife of his can fraternize all they want with that Hitler fellow, but they don't represent me and how I feel."

"Nor me either," Simon said. "I lost a leg fighting against the Kaiser for our country in the Great War."

"We need Churchill for Prime Minister – someone with military prowess and leadership ability. He's dead set against appeasing the Nazis. Like Churchill, I say: let's stand up to the Nazi bastards," Andrew declared.

Turning to Lord Buckford's younger son, Arthur asked, "What about you, Nicholas? Do you agree with your brother?"

Before Nicholas had a chance to reply, Simon said, "Nicholas is too occupied with breeding a new strain of polo ponies by crossing Scottish strains with those from Argentina – a rather frivolous venture in my estimation."

"My brother has been mad for polo ever since a broken nose convinced him to give up boxing," Andrew said.

"I think it's far more likely there may be a young lady in Suffolk he's keen on," Arthur said jovially. "Is that why you're spending so much time in East Anglia, Nicholas?"

"Nicholas made no reply, responding only with a subtle grin.

At Celia's request, Mary joined her in the rose garden. Along the smoothly raked gravel path, Mother and daughter were followed by a footman with a large wicker basket containing a pair of clippers to a section where pink hybrid roses called 'Tea Sunset Celebration' flourished. This lush, fragrant variety of rose was Celia's special favorite.

"I think these particular roses will do very nicely on our table this evening," Celia said, stopping before a bush with abundant blooms.

Turning to the footman, she requested the clippers which he silently passed into her gloved hands. Carefully selecting the best roses on the bush, Celia began clipping them and placing each rose in the footman's basket.

"You know, Mary, we really should begin planning your debutante ball. Your father and I favor a date in early April, either shortly after or just before your presentation to Their Majesties. That's the month I had my ball when I was eighteen," Celia said.

"I think April would be a lovely month for the ball, Mother," Mary replied, knowing full well that she would ultimately have very little to say in the matter; the decision would be her parents'.

"We'll hold it, of course, in our London residence. The ballroom there is quite large and, therefore, suitable, although it might mean trimming the guest list a bit. Hotel ballrooms can accommodate more guests, but their atmosphere is so impersonal," Celia said. "The house will have to be re-decorated, of course. I shall select the colors. I'm presently favoring a shade similar to these roses with some gray trim and splashes of silver here and there. What do you think?"

"Pink and gray with a touch of silver sounds lovely," Mary agreed. "I can't wait for the Season to start. It's something to which I have been looking forward so very long – my presentation at court, the many lovely balls, the week-end house parties, the Ascot races, so many wonderful, exciting activities!"

"Lady Alice informed me last evening that she and Lord Philip are planning a wonderful ball preceded by a week-end house party for Jane during the Season," Celia informed her daughter.

"I'm sure it will be a lot of fun," Mary said. "London is so exciting, but it's also lovely here at Stagsbridge, especially with Andrew nearby. Without his presence, I'm afraid that country life would be quite dull."

"Yes, Andrew is a fine young man. It's fortunate for the Buckfords that he will be the one to inherit Lammersley and not his brother. Nicholas is quite handsome and can be amusing at times, but Andrew has a more highly developed sense of responsibility. He'll be a fine master for Lammersley after Lord Simon has passed on. At least Nicholas gave up boxing and developed an interest in polo instead. He is a fine sportsman, and polo is far more appropriate for a young man of his station than boxing. It's such a vulgar sport – two men pummeling one another. I don't consider it a 'sport' at all. Lord Simon was disappointed when Nicholas chose to attend university at Edinburgh rather than Oxford, as Andrew did. Andrew developed a love of German romantic poetry such as Rilke and Schiller at Oxford while, oddly, Nicholas seemed to prefer the sciences. Edinburgh appealed to him for that reason. I suppose that as the 'second son' he will eventually go off to Australia or South Africa -- or even America – to seek his fortune. According to his mother, Nicholas seems to be spending a lot of time in Suffolk lately, although he's rather secretive about his activities there. He claims that it has something to do with breeding polo horses, although Lady Antonia fears that he might be seeing a young lady of whom she and Lord Simon would not approve. I certainly hope that is not the case."

At that moment Ruth Herzog opened the garden gate and was making her way toward them.

"Pardon me, Lady Celia," Ruth began. The young woman's dark eyed, brunette beauty was complimented by a certain charisma which seemed to spring from her intelligence and ability to relate to others in a compassionate, yet sensible, way. Although Celia herself was not an admirer of highly educated women and regarded most of them with suspicion and disdain, she, nevertheless, hired Ruth because of her superb command of English and her experience in teaching that language at the university in Berlin where Ruth had earned a graduate degree. She felt that Mary, who had been educated entirely at home by a series of governesses, needed instruction in German, as well as French, for social reasons. Celia's cousin Anne had achieved what was generally considered a brilliant marriage with the German count and banking expert Kurt von Rohrsbach, and they now lived in Berlin. Celia and Anne were very close, and the Ashmore and von Rohrsbach families visited one another with some degree of frequency.

"Yes? What is it, Fraulein Herzog?" Celia asked brusquely without diverting her attention from the roses.

"It is now time for Lady Mary's German lesson," Ruth announced, gently tapping her wristwatch for emphasis. Her spoken English was remarkably fluent and had almost no trace of a German accent.

"Mrs. Dougherty was looking for you earlier in the day and was unable to locate you. She had some chores for you to do," Celia said, referring to Stagsbridge's housekeeper. "Where were you?"

"I'm very sorry," Ruth replied. "I was out walking."

"When you are not engaged in instructing Mary, you are to assist Mrs. Dougherty and the household staff. Is that clear, Fraulein?"

"Yes, of course. Perfectly clear," Ruth answered.

"It's such a lovely day, Mother. I would much prefer to remain here in the garden with you than study German," Mary protested. The thought of dealing with a language which required three different genders for nouns was unappealing to Mary. Spending the afternoon with a young woman she was beginning to suspect might be attracting Andrew's attention – at least according to Lucy – made it even more so.

"You will please go with Fraulein Herzog now. I don't want you visiting Cousins Anne and Kurt in Berlin without knowing at least a little of the language," Celia ordered, dismissing her daughter with a wave of her gloved hand and returned her attention to her roses.

<hr />

In the vast library at Stagsbridge whose walls were lined from floor to ceiling with leather-bound books and large oil portraits of Lord Ashmore's ancestors, Mary and Ruth sat side by side at a long table, notebooks and German texts spread out around them. The summer afternoon sun poured through the windows, several panes of which were stained glass.

"This is all rather maddening," Mary complained. "Some German prepositions take the dative case and others take the accusative. Some even take both. Why can't it be simple like English? Or even French? I much prefer French."

"Because it is German," Ruth replied in a matter-of-fact tone. Ignoring Mary's protests, she continued, "Let's review: I'm going to say a simple sentence in English which you must then translate into German. Is that clear?"

"Go on," Mary said impatiently.

"Can you tell me where the train station is?"

"That's a ridiculous sentence," Mary reproached. "I would never have to ask that to anyone in Germany. Count von Rohrsbach's chauffeur will drive me anywhere I want to go."

Restraining herself from getting into an argument with Mary, Ruth ignored her complaints and repeated the sentence to be translated: "Can you tell me where the train station is?"

As Mary was about to capitulate to Ruth's request, male voices were heard outside.

"That must be my father and his shooting companions returning," Mary cried excitedly. Anticipating seeing Andrew in the group, she jumped up she ran to the window without first asking Ruth's permission. "They've got sacks and sacks of game! Come and see!"

Reluctantly, Ruth rose and joined Mary at the window.

"How absolutely splendid Andrew looks in his shooting clothes!" Mary exclaimed.

"Yes ... yes, he does," Ruth agreed somewhat hesitantly, although her dark eyes were bright with admiration. Then turning away from the window, she resumed her role as tutor. "Again, Lady Mary, can you tell me where the train station is?"

Chapter Two

The soft candlelight from the trio of crystal chandeliers above the long, highly polished dining table with its bowls of fragrant roses flattered the faces of the Stagsbridge guests.

Mary was delighted to be seated next to Andrew who, like all the other men, had changed into formal evening wear. The place next to Lucy, which had a place-card bearing the name of Trevor Knightsgate, was vacant.

"What's happened to Trevor?" Antonia Buckford asked, turning to Philip Knightsgate who was seated beside her.

"He's traveling by motorcar from Scotland today with his friend Oliver Longwood and another chum from Oxford. He warned his mother and me that he may arrive late," Philip explained.

"Or not at all, given the rain that's been falling in Scotland today, according to the radio weather reports," Nicholas remarked. "It's a bloody awful climate in Scotland."

"Oh, dear! I do hope Trevor is able to join us," Celia said, glancing at Lucy whose attention was focused on Nicholas at the moment.

"It would be a shame for him to miss this special dinner," Simon commented. "The results of our hunt today."

At a silent signal from Celia, Stagsbridge footmen began to serve the guests unobtrusively under the watchful eye of Dunsmuir. When one of his favored footmen appeared with a huge silver platter of roasted grouse, the assembled dinner guests cheered and applauded.

"Although I'm rather reluctant to admit it once again, Lord Nicholas is our champion shooter," Arthur, at the head of the table, announced.

Dr. Lyme, the local veterinarian, extended his arm and patted Nicholas on the back and said, "Good man."

"It's no small accomplishment when one considers the condition my brother was in when he arrived this morning," Andrew remarked snidely.

Everyone laughed except for Antonia who was not amused by references to her younger son's reputation for heavy drinking and general carousing.

"Driving here in my open automobile rendered me completely sober by the time I arrived," Nicholas declared.

"Dr. Lyme tells me, Mary, that you have a new horse," Mr. Davis, the village banker and avid fox hunter, said.

With a proud smile, Mary replied, "I do indeed, Mr. Davis."

"A fine filly, she is," Dr. Lyme said. "I would venture to guess from my examination of the animal that she will be a superb jumper, excellent for fox hunting."

"I've also seen this filly, and I must say that I wouldn't mind having a fine animal like that in our stable block at Lammersley," Simon said.

Andrew, who had a keen interest in livestock, raised his wine glass in a salute to Mary and toasted, "Congratulations, Mary. May you enjoy this horse for many years."

Thrilled by being the focus of his attention, Mary smiled and replied, "Thank you, Lord Andrew."

"Have you selected a name for your new horse yet?" Jane Knightsgate, who was seated on Nicholas' left, asked.

"I've decided to call her 'Blue Bonnet'." Mary answered.

Jane's father, Lord Philip Knightsgate, a polo player in his younger days, directed a question at Nicholas whom, he noticed, had been casting repeated admiring glances at his vivacious, red-haired daughter during dinner. "I understand that you're doing a bit of horse breeding yourself these lays, Lord Nicholas."

"One might say that," Nicholas responded.

Philip appeared skeptical. "But crossing Scottish ponies with Argentine o mounts seems a bit odd, don't you think?"

"Not at all, Lord Philip," Nicholas responded. "We're trying to develop ier polo ponies which can last more than a season or two."

"Well, I wish you luck, sir," Dr. Lyme said, looking skeptical.

More curious about Nicholas' romantic status than polo ponies, Jane's mother Lady Alice asked, "Who is this 'we', if I may ask?"

"A Scottish gentleman with whom I became acquainted while at university in Edinburgh," Nicholas answered.

"And he's in Suffolk now?" Alice questioned.

"He is," Nicholas said.

"Where exactly?" Lord Philip asked.

"Near the coast," Nicholas answered.

Celia decided to enter the interrogation of Nicholas. With a playful tone, she asked, "Are you sure that there is nothing or nobody else occupying your time in Suffolk?"

"Possibly," Nicholas admitted with a Cheshire Cat grin.

"Are you not going to enlighten us further?" Celia persisted.

"I shall, but at the proper time," Nicholas replied.

At that moment, Ruth entered the formal dining room and passed a note to Celia. She waited beside her ladyship's chair with a pencil in hand in case her employer wished to write a response.

"It's a telephone message from Trevor," Celia announced. "He's been delayed in Scotland by rain and won't be arriving tonight."

"Unfortunately, he's going to miss these wonderful grouse," Andrew said and then suddenly added, "Since Trevor is unable to be with us this evening, why don't you sit down in his place and join us, Ruth?"

A look of surprise was reflected on the faces of those seated around the table. They were stunned that Andrew invited the tutor to join them at the table without first consulting Celia.

As shocked as everyone else at Andrew's impulsive invitation, Ruth quietly replied, "Oh, Lord Andrew, that is very kind of you, but it wouldn't be proper for me to do that."

"Oh, come on," he urged, oblivious to the reaction his invitation had produced among the other guests.

Observing Celia's censuring frown, Ruth shook her head and said, "No, no ..."

Andrew shoved his chair back, rose to his feet and went to the vacant chair beside Lucy. He pulled it out and ordered Ruth in German, *"Sitzen sie sich."*

Flustered and aware of Celia's displeasure, Ruth hesitated.

"Sit down," Andrew repeated in English. "I insist, and I refuse to take 'no' for an answer."

"Yes, Ruth, join us, won't you?" Nicholas chimed in, sensing Celia's disapproval, but savoring a chance to not only support his brother but also to express his basically rebellious nature.

With a quick glance at Celia, Ruth hesitantly answered, "Well … if it's all right with Lady Ashmore."

Realizing that all eyes were upon her, Celia, although seething with anger, opted for graciousness in the situation. Forcing a reluctant smile, she nodded toward the empty chair, signifying her approval for Ruth to take a seat as she said, "Yes, of course," with as much genuiness as she could muster.

Mary was relieved that at least her tutor was seated on the opposite side of the table from Andrew and not next to him.

A young footman approached Ruth's place at the table with his tray of grouse. After accepting the roasted fowl, Mary noticed that Ruth slid the bacon-wrapped bird to the edge of her plate with her fork and concentrated on the vegetables instead.

Strange, Mary thought.

"Tell us, Mary, how is your study of German progressing?" Andrew asked, still basking in the glory of securing Ruth's presence at the table despite Celia's displeasure.

Mary, pleased by his unexpected attention directed at her by Andrew, hesitated a moment, wishing he had asked her about an aspect of her life which did not involve Ruth.

"Perhaps you should ask my tutor Fraulein Herzog," she replied.

Focusing on Ruth across the table, Andrew said, "Well, Fraulein Herzog … ?"

"Lady Mary is quite capable of learning German when she applies herself to the task," Ruth replied with a benevolent smile. "Perhaps she will find the language more easily acquired when she is actually in Germany."

"At Oxford we read some of the German romantic poets such a Rilke and Schiller – in English translations, of course. I became exceedingly fond of them," Andrew said, his hazel eyes, bright with enthusiasm.

"You must read them in German in order to savor their true essence, Lord Andrew," Ruth replied.

"Unfortunately, I don't know the language well enough," he admitted. "Just a few phrases here and there."

Lucy, who had been quiet so far, spoke up. "Then you must get Fraulein Herzog to tutor you, Andrew."

Mary glared at her younger sister.

"Yes, I should like that," Andrew agreed enthusiastically, smiling at Ruth whose only response was to lower her eyes.

Surprised, solicitor Dangerfield, who wore a Teddy Roosevelt-like pince-nez attached to his vest by a black ribbon, looked from Arthur to Celia. "So will Lady Mary be going to Germany in the near future to improve her language skills?"

"Actually, it would be nice for her to visit our cousins, Graf Kurt and Graefin Anne von Rohrsbach," Celia replied, pleased by Dangerfield's suggestion. "Kurt studied at Cambridge with my husband. In fact, it was Arthur who introduced Kurt to my dear cousin Anne. After their marriage, Kurt returned to Berlin with Anne. He is engaged in banking there. Kurt and Anne visited Stagsbridge with their only son Karl-Heinrich often when relations between our two countries were more amicable."

"Yes, I remember that Karl-Heinrich chap," Andrew said. "Nicholas and I both played tennis with him on several occasions."

Nicholas rolled his eyes and groaned. "Karl-Heinrich – or 'Heinzi', as we called him – was an utter disaster at the game and a bit of a hot head besides."

Alice addressed Ruth. "I understand, Fraulein, that there is considerable turmoil in Germany at the present time. Is that a correct assessment?"

Looking suddenly somber, Ruth replied, "Unfortunately, it is."

With a look of concern, Antonia asked, "Do you think Lady Mary would be safe in Germany if she were to go there?"

"I am certain of it," Celia replied. "Graf Kurt and Graefin Anne will look after her. Cousin Anne considers Mary almost as if she were her own daughter."

"And God will protect her as well," plump Vicar Stouthammer felt compelled to add.

"Yes, we must never forget God," the vicar's wife Eugenia added.

⁓

After dinner, the male guests retired to a drawing room of leather easy-chairs and dark wood paneling decorated with fox hunting prints. Footmen circulated among the men with silver trays of brandy and a humidor of cigars.

It was not long before current political issues dominated the conversation.

"I must confess that I find the popularity of Germany's Hitler positively shocking," banker Davis said as he leaned forward to light his cigar from a burning candle.

"It's as though he wields some kind of demonic power over the German people," the Vicar Stouthammer mused, swirling brandy around in a snifter.

"To go from a rabble-rousing inmate in an Austrian prison to Chancellor of Germany seems absolutely astounding to me," solicitor Dangerfield said, shaking his head in dismay as he exhaled a long stream of pungent cigar smoke, the black ribbon of his pince-nez fluttering.

"Well, I think the secret of the man's popularity is that he's hell bent on giving the German people what they've been yearning for," Andrew speculated.

"And what is that?" Dr. Lyme, perhaps the most apolitical of the men in the group, asked.

"The Germans have been licking their wounds for a long time, ever since their humiliating defeat twenty or so years ago," Andrew continued. "Hitler has restored their national pride by building up the military and thereby improving the country's economy."

"By flooding the country with worthless currency lacking any sort of backing at all, such as gold," banker Davis interjected.

Andrew went on, "Hitler also has his sights set on areas in Poland and Czechoslovakia with ethnic German populations which were taken away from Germany in the Treaty of Versailles."

After listening attentively to what was being discussed, Nicholas decided it was time to speak up. "What worries me most are the genuine strides German scientists have been making with regard to weaponry and technology," he said as he reached for a second snifter of brandy.

"We suffered such severe financial hardships in the last war – not to mention the terrible losses of life and limb. I, myself, have to wear this blasted artificial leg," Simon knocked on the prosthesis beneath his trouser leg with his knuckles. Hence, I can understand Prime Minister Chamberlain's wanting to keep Britain out of another war," Simon paused a moment, then added, "That doesn't, however, mean I necessarily approve."

"Frankly, I find Chamberlain's meeting and negotiating with Hitler in Munich appalling," Dr. Lyme commented. "It seems to me that Britain has been spiraling downward ever since Edward the Eighth's abdication."

"I feel that war between Britain and Germany is inevitable," Andrew said with a shrug. "I can't speak for my brother, but I intend to do my utmost to defend my country if called upon. A Prime Minister with any backbone would march right in and eradicate those Nazi brown-shirts before they cause any further trouble."

Raising his hand, Arthur pleaded, "Gentlemen, gentlemen, please, let's not spoil a splendid day's shooting with talk of war. Why don't we all have one more brandy, finish our cigars and then rejoin the ladies?"

Later, in the music room, the Ashmore guests patiently endured Lucy's playing of a Mozart composition on the piano.

As Andrew was about to slip quietly out of the room, Mary caught him by the sleeve of his dinner jacket and whispered, "May I have a word with you before you leave?" She suspected that he might be going to secretly meet with Ruth who had dutifully disappeared as soon as dinner was finished.

"If you wish," he replied.

Knowing Andrew's fondness for strolling about the immaculately landscaped grounds of Stagsbridge, she said, "Shall we walk outside a bit?" She hoped this would sabotage any clandestine rendezvous he and Ruth might have planned.

With an indifferent shrug, he replied, "All right."

Mary would have preferred his response to have been more enthusiastic, but was sufficiently satisfied that he was willing to spend time with her away from the others.

Side by side, they headed out the door and strolled toward the splashing fountain in the center of the circular drive.

Struggling to conceal the excitement she felt in his company, Mary said, "Dr. Lyme informed me that you have accepted the chairmanship of the Agricultural Council."

"I have," he responded.

"I think that's splendid, Andrew," she gushed. "Simply splendid."

"Do you?" He smiled, amused by her enthusiasm. "Well, it's traditional for a Lammersley male to serve as chairman of the Agricultural Council."

"It's also traditional for someone from Stagsbridge to serve as one of the livestock judges at the county fair, and, since my brother Charles will be away at boarding school, I'd like to volunteer for that position."

Her offer surprised Andrew. "What? Serve as a livestock judge? You, Mary?"

"Why not? In past fairs, as you may recall, several of my horses have won blue ribbons. I'm quite knowledgeable about all animals."

Andrew stopped, looked at her dubiously. "Really?"

"Besides, it would be quite pleasant working with you," she added.

Andrew's only response was an amused chuckle.

When they reached the fountain, Mary perched on the raised edge of the splash basin and dipped her hand into the water.

"I adore this fountain," she said. "When I was a child – perhaps seven or eight– I would come here and make wishes."

"Oh? And what did you wish for?"

"I can't tell you. If one reveals one's wishes, they won't come true."

Skeptical, Andrew remarked, "I assume then that some of your wishes are yet to be fulfilled?"

"That's correct."

"Then, you're still hoping?"

"I am," she replied. "Fervently."

Moments later, much to Mary's chagrin, Ruth appeared from the house and was heading in their direction. She had been savoring the time alone with Andrew and now, with her tutor's appearance, it had terminated abruptly.

"His Lordship sent me to tell you to come into the house now, Lady Mary," Ruth announced.

Defiantly, Mary protested, "But it's still early."

"I am only delivering your father's message," Ruth informed her.

"Perhaps you'd better do as you father wishes, Mary," Andrew urged.

His words confirmed to Mary that he wanted her to leave so that he could be alone with Ruth. Feeling disappointed and hurt, she rose from the fountain's edge and prepared to return to the house.

"Are you coming with me, Fraulein?" Mary asked, determined not to allow a possible rendezvous to go forward.

Ruth exchanged glances with Andrew, as if seeking his silent approval for what she planned to say. "I will be along shortly. First, there is something I wish to discuss with Lord Andrew," she said. "But you must go now."

In the house, Mary hurried straight up the vast staircase, its walls lined with still more family portraits, to her bedroom instead of joining her parents and their guests still in the music room.

Going to the window which overlooked the drive and the fountain, she observed that Andrew and Ruth were now strolling across the vast lawn in front of the great house.

"Damn!" Mary swore, stamping her foot.

At that moment, Lucy entered Mary's room. "What's the matter?" she asked.

Abruptly turning away from the window, Mary snapped, "Nothing."

Lucy joined her in staring out the window. "Can that possibly be Andrew and Fraulein Herzog that I see walking together out there on the lawn?"

"Yes, unfortunately," Mary replied. "I was having a lovely chat with Andrew when Fraulein Herzog came out and spoiled everything."

"What were you chatting about?"

"Andrew asked me to help him with his duties as chairman of the Agricultural Council."

Lucy made a disagreeable face. "Do you really fancy mucking about with pigs and sheep and cattle and such?"

"Why not?"

Lucy narrowed her eyes suspiciously at her sister. "You're really keen on Andrew, aren't you?"

"So what if I am?" Mary snapped.

"It seems foolish to me."

"'Foolish'? Why?"

"I don't think Andrew cares for you. He seems smitten with Fraulein Herzog, especially after what occurred at dinner tonight."

Mary bristled. "Why do you say that?"

Indicating the two distant figures now strolling together in the darkness, Lucy replied, "Just look."

⊰⊱

As Andrew and Ruth walked beside a meticulously trimmed boxwood hedge, he stopped suddenly, took her by the shoulders and gazed into her dark eyes.

"Will I see you again tomorrow?" he asked.

Ruth shrugged. "I don't know."

Andrew took hold of her arms. "I must see you," he said, his voice imploring, almost desperate.

"I don't think it's a good idea. It's very difficult for me to get away, and we shouldn't be seen together. Lady Celia is already suspicious. She must know that we've been secretly meeting one another."

"It's time for us to be seen together – openly," Andrew asserted. "I don't like the way we've been sneaking around, hiding from everyone. It's not the way I prefer to do things."

"It's different for you than it is for me," Ruth attempted to explain. "You're English. This is your country. You're a British subject. You have a legal right to be here. I do not. I am in this country illegally without the proper documents. I must not to be forced to return to Germany."

"Listen to me, Ruth," he said. "My father is a member of Parliament with powerful friends in high places. If the need arises and there is a danger of your being deported, he can secure the proper papers for you which will permit you to stay in Britain."

"Neither your mother nor Lady Ashmore would not want that."

"What has my mother got to do with it?"

"Can't you tell? She would prefer someone else for you. She and Lady Celia are already conspiring to arrange a match between Lady Mary and you."

"That's absurd," he said with a laugh. "I regard Lady Mary as a child – a little sister. Besides, neither Lady Celia nor my mother makes my decisions for me. I do. You are the woman I want in my life. That's the only thing that matters to me."

Looking him squarely in the eye, Ruth took a deep breath and announced, "There's something you must know about me."

"I know all I need to know."

"No, you don't. There's something else that's very important.

Puzzled, Andrew frowned. "What's that?"

"I am a Jew."

"So what?" He shrugged indifferently. "Your religion makes no difference to me."

"It does to others such as Lady Celia and your mother. You must understand, Andrew, that it is now a dangerous time for Jews in Germany. The Nazis terrify me. Before I left for Britain, I begged my father to also leave, but he refused to accompany me. He's a physician who would not allow himself to abandon his patients, and, honestly, he hasn't been the same since my mother died. He doesn't understand the danger we Jews are in. He foolishly believes that because he is a well trained and highly regarded surgeon, the Nazis will leave him alone," Ruth said. "He's wrong, and I believe that he doesn't fully realize the peril of our situation."

In the darkness, a dog suddenly began barking loudly, startling the two and interrupting their conversation.

Alarmed by the dog which reminded her of the Gestapo and their German shepherds, Ruth said nervously, "I really must go inside."

"I want to see you this week-end," Andrew said.

Without replying, Ruth turned and began to walk away toward the great house.

"I am unwilling for us to go on hiding from everyone," he called after her. "Do you hear me? We're not going to hide any longer. No more!"

Chapter Three

Mary rose early the following morning, determined to exercise her new horse Blue Bonnet, hoping that a long ride would help her to recover from the disheartening sight of Andrew and Ruth together the previous night.

She headed outside to the stable block by way of the kitchen, avoiding the dining room where her parents and sister Lucy were having breakfast.

In the stable, she proceeded to Blue Bonnet's stall where Hogan, a young Irish stable boy, was finishing the filly's daily grooming.

Tipping his cap to her, he said, "Good morning, my lady. I'll have your horse ready for you in a couple of minutes."

"Thank you, Hogan," she replied, playing with a litter of kittens recently born to one of the stable's resident cats.

When he finished, Hogan led Blue Bonnet out of the stall and transferred her reins to Mary and helping her into the saddle.

"She's a fine filly," he said, stroking the horse's neck affectionately.

Mary rode across a fenced meadow where a flock of sheep were peacefully grazing. Approaching a gate in the wooden fence, Mary urged the horse over it instead of dismounting to open the gate. Blue Bonnet instantly responded, smoothly executing the jump.

Horse and rider then proceeded through a series of pastures, some enclosed by similar wooden fences, others by stone walls and still others by hedgerows. Blue Bonnet deftly executed a series of jumps over all. Pleased by her mount's ability to clear all manner of hurdles and her own skill as a rider, Mary found herself feeling better.

Seeking relief from the increasing heat of the summer day, Mary decided to abandon the open fields for a stretch of woods along the narrow river which separated Stagsbridge from Lammersley where horse and rider could benefit from the cool shade of ancient oaks.

On the meandering trail through the great trees, Mary and her horse unexpectedly encountered a fallen oak whose giant trunk blocked their path. Encouraged by Blue Bonnet's previous jumps, Mary urged the filly over the obstacle. Although the tree trunk was only slightly taller than most of the fences, walls and hedges the horse had surmounted, Blue Bonnet balked and refused to jump. Deciding not to force the issue, Mary relented and allowed the filly to circumvent the dead tree.

When they reached the bank of the river, Mary heard the sound of another horse's hoof-beats in the woods on the Lammersley side. She stopped and waited for the approach of the rider through the trees, hoping that it might be Andrew. She now felt ready to forgive his attention to Ruth the previous night.

When the rider came into view, Mary realized, much to her disappointment, that it was Nicholas and not Andrew astride a sleek black stallion. From the shotgun slung across his saddle, she assumed that he was hunting.

Seeing Mary on the opposite side of the river, he raised his hand and waved to her. Although she would have much preferred that it was Andrew mounted on the stallion, she returned Nicholas' greeting with a reciprocal wave.

Fearlessly, he urged his stallion into the fast-moving water. Horse and rider splashed their way across the relatively shallow river and joined Mary and Blue Bonnet on the opposite bank.

"Out for an early ride are you, Lady Mary?" Nicholas said, smiling sensuously, displaying his white, even teeth.

"Good morning, Nicholas," Mary replied coolly.

In the presence of Mary's mare, the stallion began to prance about in an agitated fashion which forced Nicholas to pull hard on the horse's reins to restrain him.

"Your filly has this old boy excited. He thinks it's rutting season," Nicholas remarked with a laugh. "How do you like your new horse?"

"She's a splendid jumper," Mary answered. "Perfect for fox hunting."

"Where are you going?" Nicholas asked.

"Nowhere in particular," Mary replied.

"Just trying out the new horse, are you?"

"I suppose one could say that."

"Good. Then, in that case, I'll join you," Nicholas said.

Together Mary and Nicholas guided their mounts along the wooded trail beside the river

As they approached a bend in the river, Mary thought she heard voices rising from the water. Peering through the trees and thick brush, she observed a small skiff, similar to those she had seen on the river at Cambridge, with two individuals, a man wearing a straw 'boater' style hat standing at the stern and moving the craft forward, gondolier style, with a long pole. A young woman holding a silk parasol, which she recognized as belonging to Antonia Buckford, lounged on a pile of cushions in the bow of the boat.

Mary slowed Blue Bonnet, lagging behind Nicholas, so that she could have a closer look at the couple. Much to her dismay, she recognized Andrew and Ruth. She found it odd that Ruth had apparently been granted free time. Usually when she wasn't occupied with tutoring Mary or, on rare occasions, her younger siblings, she was assigned by the housekeeper to assist the household servants with various chores. Mary speculated that Andrew had been instrumental in obtaining this free time for Ruth, perhaps by asking Celia if Ruth could assist in some way at Lammersley.

Deception, she said angrily to herself.

Impulsively, Mary yanked hard on Blue Bonnet's reins and turned the horse around, spurring her into a gallop in the opposite direction, eager to leave the disturbing scene.

Nicholas twisted around in his saddle and watched Mary rapidly disappear among the trees.

Galloping through the woods, Blue Bonnet gracefully navigated deep ravines, boulders and rushing streams until they were once again confronted by the giant trunk of the fallen oak, and, just as before, Blue Bonnet balked at jumping over it. This time, however, Mary refused to allow the horse to circumvent the obstacle. Repeatedly, she prodded the filly's flanks with the heels of her boots but to no avail. Finally resorting to a series of sharp slaps with her riding crop, Mary forced the horse to attempt the jump.

The attempt proved disastrous for both horse and rider. Blue Bonnet failed to clear the trunk and landed in such a way that a loud cracking sound indicated that the mount had fractured a bone in one of her legs. For her part, Mary went flying out of the saddle and landed in a clump of briers, ripping her jodhpurs and blouse. Dazed and in pain, she was unable to move for a few minutes.

Nearby, Blue Bonnet, lying on her side, was writhing frantically in agony. Her shrill, piercing equine cries of pain shattered the stillness of the woods.

With great difficulty and pain, Mary managed to crawl slowly toward the injured animal.

Moments later, galloping to the scene, Nicholas arrived. Quickly dismounting, he tied his horse to a tree and rushed to Mary's side.

Alarmed by her state, he said, "You're hurt."

"Please...don't concern yourself with me," Mary pleaded. "Look after Blue Bonnet. I think she's badly injured. Go and summon Dr. Lyme right away."

Nicholas hurried over to the writhing filly and, bending over her, gently stroked her neck, attempting to calm the horse. Cautiously, he inspected her right front leg, the angle of which was badly distorted; an exposed bone had pierced the skin. He shook his head in despair.

"Your horse has fractured her right front leg," he informed Mary moments later. "There's nothing Dr. Lyme can do for her."

Mary burst into tears.

Nicholas then went to his stallion and took his shotgun from the saddle.

Observing him, Mary, although in great pain, managed with difficulty to rise to her feet. Apprehensive, she demanded, "What are you going to do?"

"I'm not going to do anything. You are. She's your horse," he answered, shoving the shotgun at her so forcefully that she nearly lost her balance.

Confused and bewildered, Mary said, "What are you talking about?"

"You are going to put this unfortunate animal out of her misery."

"What do you mean?"

"I mean that you are going to shoot her."

Mary was horrified. "I can't!" she protested.

"The animal is suffering. Pull the trigger and dispatch her quickly," he ordered.

"No! Please ... !" Mary cried.

"It's time you learned that sometimes you must consider something beside yourself," he said. "Now, end her suffering."

Mary sobbed louder. "I can't! I can't!"

"Yes, you can and you will. Stop blubbering and do what's best for your horse."

Nicholas positioned himself behind Mary and, reaching around her waist, placed his hand over her hand forcing her index finger onto the trigger of the shotgun. "Aim at her head and fire. It's a shame this wonderful creature must pay with her life for your foolishness and stupidity. "Pull the trigger and get on with it. Go on, pull it!"

"Oh, please, Nicholas, no! I can't."

"Do as I say, damn it, and pull the trigger!"

"Don't ask me to do such a dreadful thing."

I'm not asking you. I'm ordering you. Pull the trigger now!"

Writhing on the ground, Blue Bonnet's cries of pain grew louder.

Exasperated, Nicholas shoved his index finger over Mary's and forced her to pull the trigger. The initial shot instantly stifled the stricken animal's cries and ended her suffering.

Mary collapsed and was about to slide to the ground when Nicholas promptly swept her up into his arms and carried her to his stallion. He carefully placed Mary on the horse's back in front of the saddle, where he could attend her, as need be, on the ride back to Stagsbridge.

Untying the stallion from the tree, he swung himself into the saddle and, together, they rode away.

Mary continued sobbing uncontrollably.

Chapter Four

In an upstairs sitting room, Celia prepared to have tea with Antonia. Her personal maid, Flora, entered with the tea service on a silver tray and placed it on the table before the two women.

"Will there be anything else, ma'am?" Flora asked.

"Not at the moment. I'll ring if I need you," Celia responded, reaching for the teapot, which was enclosed in a hand-crocheted cozy, as Flora departed.

Celia poured the tea into two delicate china cups and passed one to Antonia. "It was kind of you to visit Mary today," she said.

"What a dreadful accident that poor girl has suffered," Antonia replied, shaking her head sympathetically. "And to lose her favorite horse in such a tragic fashion."

"Yes. Mary has been taking it all rather badly, I'm afraid," Celia lamented. "Fortunately, she suffered only some minor cuts and scratches and a few bruises, but no broken bones. She's been in bed, confined to her room with all the curtains tightly drawn for the past three days."

Antonia frowned. "Really? Doctor's orders?"

"No, it's Mary's own choice," Celia replied. "The doctor said that it would be perfectly all right for her to be up and about, but she refuses to leave her room. She's quite heart-broken about the whole thing."

As she reached for a tiny diamond-shaped watercress-and-cream cheese sandwich, Antonia speculated, "Perhaps something else may be bothering her."

Celia frowned for an instant. "What are you suggesting, Antonia?'

"I'm sure that you are aware that Mary is quite fond of Andrew."

Celia smiled. "I am indeed."

"As his mother, I regard this as favorable," Antonia said.

"As do I," Celia agreed.

Antonia continued, "It has come to my attention lately, however, that Andrew has become somewhat smitten with Mary's tutor."

Celia raised her eyebrows in surprise. "'Smitten' with Fraulein Herzog?! Really? Surely, you must be joking!"

"No, I'm perfectly serious," Antonia assured her. "They've been observed by the servants and others together on several occasions: sitting on a bench right here in your garden beneath the shade of a yew tree reading German poetry to one another."

"I can't believe it!"

"Yes, and they've been seen taking long walks together."

"On the grounds of Stagsbridge?"

"Yes, and boating on the river as well."

"I had no idea," Celia fretted, raising her hand to her cheek in surprise. "I had no idea at all. I assumed that when she wasn't with Mary or the younger children, she was assisting the housekeeper, although I must admit that on more than one occasion lately, Mrs. Dougherty informed me that she had gone missing and could not be located."

"I'm not at all surprised," Antonia said. "I must tell you quite frankly, my dear, I find the current situation between Andrew and this young German woman most unsuitable."

"As do I," Celia concurred.

Antonia reached out and placed her hand on Celia's. "Then it's time we must do something about it, mustn't we?"

Looking bewildered, Celia replied, "Yes, of course, but what?"

"You must dismiss this young woman, of course," Antonia declared.

Uncomfortable with such a solution, Celia repeated, "Dismiss Fraulein Herzog?"

"I see no other recourse," Antonia said with an indifferent shrug. "I realize that in Germany, at the present moment, unrest prevails, although I'm sure that in time things in that country will change for the better."

"I hope you're right," Celia responded. "This talk of possible war with Germany worries me."

"With two sons of military age, I am worried as well, especially since Andrew has expressed interest in joining the RAF as a pilot. He's always been keen about airplanes and aviation. I'm not as concerned with Nicholas. He seems so much more preoccupied with the breeding of polo ponies and indulging himself in the pleasures available to young men rather than more serious pursuits. He seems to have no interest in affairs of state and rarely participates in political discussions with his father and brother," Antonia said, reaching for a cracker spread with caviar and capers. "Simon still suffers from the wound he received in the last war twenty years ago which resulted in the loss of his leg."

Refilling Antonia's teacup, Celia said, "A war we all believed would bring lasting peace to Europe, but I fear we were badly mistaken."

"With regard to Fraulein Herzog," Antonia said, determined to return to the topic which was the true purpose of her visit, "Andrew has revealed that this young German woman is here without the proper papers. My worry is that she may take advantage of Andrew's feelings for her and appeal to him for help, knowing full well that Simon is a member of parliament with important connections. Therefore, Celia, you must act quickly and dismiss her as soon as possible."

With a look of concern, Celia replied, "Yes, Antonia, I suppose you're right."

———❦———

In her overly warm and airless bedroom, Mary lay in her great canopied bed gazing at the tightly drawn drapes when Lucy, followed by Charles, bounded into the room.

"It's as dark as a tomb in here," Lucy commented.

"And all hot and stuffy," Charles added.

"I'm going to open these curtains whether you like it or not," Lucy declared, shoving the heavy brocaded drapes aside to reveal bright sunshine outside. Then, opening the window, she permitted a breeze to freshen the room's stale air.

Mary raised her hand to shield her eyes against the brilliant light.

"Dr. Patterson told Mother that three days in bed is quite enough for you," Lucy said. "You must get up and go outside for some fresh air."

"Lucy and I have just positioned the proper wickets in the lawn for croquet," Charles informed his sister. "We were hoping we might coax you to play."

"Not today," Mary listlessly replied.

"At breakfast this morning Mother and Father were talking about sending you to visit our cousins in Berlin," Lucy disclosed. "They feel you've been moping much too much over Blue Bonnet and that a change of scene might be beneficial.""

"Of course I'm 'moping'," Mary snapped. "Blue Bonnet was a marvellous horse."

"We could go riding if you're not keen on croquet," Charles suggested. "There are other horses in the stable, you know. Blue Bonnet wasn't the only one."

"But none as fine as Blue Bonnet," Mary retorted as she crawled out of bed.

Lucy's face brightened. "Are you going to dress?"

"I am," Mary answered.

"Shall I ring for Polly to help you?" Lucy asked.

"No. You can help me, Lucy," Mary said as she ducked behind a colorful Chinese screen in a corner of the room.

As Charles gazed out the window, he called to Mary behind the screen, "Are you expecting Andrew this afternoon?"

"No. Why do you ask?" Mary responded.

"He just drove through the gate at the end of the drive in his yellow Adler Trumpf Junior and has the top down," Charles, who already had a keen interest in automobiles at age thirteen, announced.

Mary's mood instantly brightened as she threw a dressing gown over her silk slip and dashed to the window with Lucy close at her heels. The three of them observed Andrew pulling up to Stagsbridge's front entrance. Mary's expression promptly changed from one of joy to one of dejection when she realized that Ruth was in the car with him.

Andrew hopped out and opened the door on the passenger side of the automobile for Ruth who

dashed to the the door of the great house. Before entering, she whirled around and blew Andrew a kiss as he was driving away.

Much to her chagrin, Mary could see that he was smiling happily as he departed down the long driveway.

Mary was not smiling.

Chapter Five

Simon Buckford brushed his hand over his neatly barbered silver hair as he sat at the desk in his private study at Lammersley poring over official documents from Whitehall which had arrived by special courier that morning.

In the hall outside Nicholas rapped on the door. "May I come in, Father?"

"Of course," Simon responded.

"I hope I'm not interrupting anything important," Nicholas said as he entered.

"Not at all," Simon replied, reaching for a box of cigars. "It's time for a rest from all these papers. Would you care for a cigar? They're from Cuba."

"No thanks. Not right now."

Simon clipped off the end of the cigar and lit it. "This is the one room where we can smoke without your mother's objecting. What's on your mind, son?"

Nicholas glanced at the official-looking papers spread out before his father, some of which were stamped 'Confidential' and others 'Top Secret'. He was surprised that his father made no effort to conceal them.

"Are you sure I'm not disturbing you?" he said.

"It's government business. I know you well enough to be aware that their content – political topics and international matters – is of no interest to you." Simon took a drag on his cigar and emitted a long plume of pungent smoke.

"Not entirely, Father," Nicholas objected.

"Actually, one of these documents is quite interesting. It's a top secret report from the Air Ministry," Simon said as he shuffled through some of the papers on his desk.

Nicholas' interest was suddenly aroused. "Oh? Can you tell me what it's about?"

"Only if you promise not to disclose anything I say."

"I promise," Nicholas agreed.

Simon picked out the paper from the pile and read the title aloud. "It's entitled 'Detection of Aircraft by Radio Methods'."

Nicholas nodded. "That topic was touched upon when I was at university in Edinburgh in a lecture by James Clerk Maxwell, the noted Scottish physicist and expert in electromagnetism."

"Yes, I've heard the name bandied about in parliament," Simon commented, tapping his cigar's ashes into an ashtray.

"It was a fellow by the name of Heinrich Hertz, a German – and a Jew, by the way – who first discovered at the end of the last century that radio waves can be reflected by metal objects," Nicholas said. "The Nazis destroyed a lot of the reports on his research as part of their campaign against the Jews, but it's rumored that one of his daughters managed to salvage some of that information."

Simon sat back in his chair and looked at his son in amazement. "Just when I think you're becoming a hopeless playboy, you astonish me with some bit of obscure knowledge, although I must admit that when you were at university in Scotland you did display considerable interest in the sciences and technology," Simon paused a moment and sighed wistfully. "Unfortunately, all of that seems to be in the past."

"Not entirely, Father," Nicholas replied. "Recently I have developed a renewed interest."

Simon raised his bushy eyebrows which were as black as his hair was silver. "Oh? And what is that?"

"It's something which would require a loan."

Simon scowled. "A loan?"

"A small one, Father."

"What for this time? Please don't tell me that this new interest of yours involves gambling."

Nicholas laughed. "No, no, nothing of the sort."

"Trouble with a woman?"

"Not this time."

"Then what?"

"Business – an idea and a very good one, I believe," Nicholas replied. "One which will ultimately serve our nation well."

Still somewhat skeptical, but eager to hear more, Simon said, "Well, what is this idea of yours?"

"It involves selling British scrap metal to Germany," Nicholas disclosed.

Simon rose to his feet awkwardly because of his prosthetic leg "Are you mad?! Selling British scrap metal to Germany?! I don't like the sound of it. The Germans will use that metal for weaponry – tanks, planes, guns and whatnot that could be used against us someday."

"Don't you see, Father, that with the profits from the scrap metal sales – which could be considerable – we could develop and strengthen our defenses," Nicholas said, his dark eyes bright with enthusiasm. "Right now we are in a very vulnerable state, especially with regard to German air power. We've got to do more to protect ourselves."

"I could not agree more," Simon said. Relaxing a bit, he seemed to be reconsidering his son's proposal.

Nicholas' tone was hopeful as he ventured to ask, "Then, you would be willing to consider helping me to finance my scrap metal business?"

"Tell me, son, what does your brother Andrew think of this idea of yours?" Simon responded, reaching for a crystal decanter from a nearby cabinet and pouring himself a glass of brandy. "Would you like some?"

"No, thank you, sir."

Simon chuckled. "I can't believe you're refusing a drink."

"Quite truthfully, I must confess that Andrew doesn't favor it," Nicholas admitted. "He disapproves of my doing business with the Germans."

"I'm not surprised," Simon said. "Have you approached Lord Arthur with your idea? He could possibly be interested in your proposal."

"I intended to discuss it with him a few days ago, but that incident with Mary and the horse occurred, and I felt it was not the proper time."

"Rightly so," Simon agreed, swirling the brandy around in his glass. "I will consider your idea."

"Good!" Nicholas was delighted that his response was encouraging and not negative as he had expected.

Simon glanced out the window. "It's a splendid day for tennis. I'm surprised that you and your brother are not out there on the court playing."

Andrew went off to Stagsbridge." Nicholas answered, reluctant to mention that his brother was probably spending the afternoon with Ruth who seemed to be occupying a substantial portion of his free time lately.

"Unfortunately, it's not to see Lady Mary," Simon said with a note of regret in his voice. It was apparent from that remark that he knew of Andrew's interest in Ruth. "It's more likely that it's that young German woman Lady Celia hired as tutor for her daughter."

"Possibly," Nicholas conceded. He had no intention of elaborating further with either parent on a subject which he knew was a delicate one.

"She's an attractive young woman and quite intelligent, but your mother believes that she is not at all suitable for your brother."

"What about you, Father?"

"I leave those matters up to your mother," Simon said as he gathered together the various papers on his desk and locked them in a drawer.

⁂

A few days after Antonia's visit, Celia interrupted her letter writing at her French provincial desk in her upstairs sitting room to ask Flora to summon Ruth.

"She's not in her room, ma'am," Flora informed her.

"Then, where is she?"

"After she helped me straighten up the children's rooms, I saw her in the garden," the maid replied.

"What was she doing?"

"I don't know, ma'am," Flora replied.

"Was she alone?"

"No, ma'am."

"Well, who was she with then?"

Flora took a deep breath before sheepishly replying, "Lord Andrew."

Celia slammed down her pen. "Go and fetch her for me at once," she ordered.

"Very well, ma'am," Flora responded and left.

⸻ ⸻

In the walled Stagsbridge garden, the air fragrant with blooming roses, Andrew and Ruth lounged on a blanket spread out on the grass in the shade of a yew tree. Andrew was lying on his back with his head in Ruth's lap as she rested against the trunk of the tree running her fingers through his auburn hair and reading to him from a book of German poetry.

"Wenn du es wisstest/ Was Traumen heisst von brennenden kussen/ Von Wandern und Ruhen mit der Geliebter/ Auge in Auge..." Ruth paused for a moment.

"That's so beautiful when one hears it in the original German, even though I don't understand a single word of it," Andrew mused. "I studied Rilke and Schiller and the other German romantic poets at Oxford, but in English translations, of course."

"It's not the same," Ruth said, bending forward and tenderly kissing his brow.

"No, it's not," Andrew agreed. "When one hears that beautiful poetry or listens to Beethoven, one cannot help but wonder how such a creative, sensitive people could tolerate a leader like Hitler."

"There are many theories," Ruth said, reluctant to elaborate further.

Taking her hand, he pressed it to his lips. "I love it when you read to me. In fact, I love everything you do."

"Oh, stop it, Andrew," Ruth scoffed.

"No, I do! I really do. You must believe me, Ruth," he protested. "And I'm so glad you brought that little book of poetry to England with you."

"I had to hide it under my clothes," she said. "Otherwise the Nazis would have confiscated it for their book burnings."

Andrew shook his head in disgust. "How stupid that is – burning books."

41

"Of course it is, but books have ideas in them which the Nazis are frightened of," Ruth replied. "Especially books by Jews or books with ideas about individual freedom and tolerance."

"What a repulsive bunch those Nazis are," Andrew said.

"They're full of hate and intolerance which makes them dangerous," Ruth added.

"Don't worry, I'll protect you," he assured her.

When Ruth started to laugh, Andrew reached up and drew her face down to his, kissing her tenderly.

At that moment Flora appeared, cleared her throat audibly and delivered the message that Lady Celia wished to see Ruth right away.

Somewhat startled, Ruth gently pushed Andrew aside and rose to her feet, brushing the grass from her skirt. "I'm sorry, Andrew, but I must go," she apologized and prepared to follow Flora into the house.

⚶

Standing nervously before Celia, who was seated at her desk, Ruth asked, "What is it that you wished to speak with me about, Lady Ashmore?"

"Why don't you sit down?" Celia said, indicating the antique French Provincial chair upholstered in fine silk nearest the writing desk.

"Thank you, Lady Ashmore," Ruth replied, seating herself.

"I'm afraid I have some rather bad news for you," Celia announced, striving to sound matter-of-fact rather than apologetic.

Alarmed, Ruth repeated, "'Bad news'?"

"Your services will no longer be required here at Stagsbridge."

Ruth was stunned. "I don't understand ..."

Instead of telling her the truth, Celia chose a less harsh option, hoping it would soften the blow. "There's nothing to understand. It's all quite simple. Mary and I will be going to our London residence for a while so that Mary can prepare for her presentation to Their Majesties at court. She will be making her debut to society during the upcoming Season. Lucy and Charles will be returning to their respective boarding schools so there's really no need for you to be here any longer."

"I could tutor Lady Mary in London," Ruth said, feeling suddenly desperate.

"Lord Arthur and I have decided that she should visit my cousin, the Graefin von Rohrsbach, in Berlin before the Season begins. Mary can continue her German studies in Germany, if she wishes."

Puzzled, Ruth said, "This is a very turbulent time in Germany, especially in Berlin. Are you not concerned about your daughter's safety, Lady Ashmore?"

"I see no reason to be. The von Rohrsbachs will take good care of her, I'm sure."

Shaken by Celia's dismissal, Ruth said, "If I have no employment, I shall be forced to return to Germany. Conditions there are very bad for Jews like myself."

"I'm sure your family will welcome and protect you," Celia assured her.

Ruth, tears beginning to form in her eyes, said pleadingly, "I have only my father, and I was hoping that he might join me soon here in England. If I do not have employment, here in Britain, there is no hope of getting him out."

"Come now, Fraulein, I'm sure that a clever girl with your university education can find another post," Celia said with a dismissive wave of her hand.

"Every issue of *The London Times* is full of notices by many German Jews, such as myself, who are desperately seeking employment here in Britain. They are willing to do any manner of work. University graduates have accepted positions as servants. Physicians are driving taxis. Lawyers are sweeping the streets. Symphony conductors are now farm laborers. I am simply asking you to try and understand my situation," Ruth pleaded.

Unaffected by her protest, Celia calmly opened a drawer in the desk and extracted an envelope. "This envelope contains funds with which you may pay your passage back to Berlin. Your bags are being packed by Flora as we speak. Jamison will deposit you at Victoria Station this afternoon."

Ruth gasped. "This afternoon?! That's impossible!"

Celia continued to ignore Ruth's objections. "There is an extra month's wages in this envelope as well. That should tide you over until you can obtain employment in your own country."

"Don't you realize what is happening to Jews in Germany now? I am terrified of going back."

Celia shrugged her shoulders indifferently. "Graf von Rohrsbach and his wife have not mentioned any particular difficulties."

"Of course not." Ruth responded. "Not for them. They are not Jews."

Celia was beginning to be irritated by Ruth's protests. "I think you're exaggerating. Conditions can't be as bad as you say."

Increasingly emotional Ruth said, "The Nazis have taken everything away from us, our homes, our property, our bank accounts, our businesses – everything we possess. They force us to work as slave labor. Those who are weak or ill or too old to work are shot, and their bodies tossed into muddy trenches for burial. There are even rumors of gas chambers. Don't you know about *Judenrein* – Hitler's own policy to rid Germany – and soon all of Europe – of Jews?"

"As I just stated: I think you are exaggerating the situation to gain sympathy and coerce me into reversing my decision," Celia said. "Something I have no intention of doing."

Struggling to regain her composure, Ruth boldly looked Celia straight in the eye, something she had previously refrained from doing, and asked, "Has this decision of yours, Lady Ashmore, resulted, by any chance, because of my present friendship with Lord Andrew Buckford?"

Unfazed, Celia met her gaze squarely. "Not in the least," she lied without flinching. "Goodbye and good luck, Fraulein."

Distraught, Ruth left the room, and Celia calmly resumed her letter writing.

Weeping, Ruth sat in the rear seat of the Ashmore's BMW 335, her luggage stowed in the trunk and the family's chauffeur Jamison behind the wheel. As they were exiting the high, wrought iron gates of Stagsbridge, Andrew, in his open car, was driving in, apparently returning to be with Ruth.

Observing that she appeared to be crying, Andrew sensed that something was wrong. He thrust his hand out the window and signaled for Jamison to stop, but the Ashmore's chauffeur ignored him and continued on, disappearing quickly around a curve in the narrow Surrey country road.

Chapter Six

At the Ashmore's city residence in London's elegant Regent's Park, a small army of painters and scurried about the mansion's ballroom, climbing up and down ladders to scaffolding high above the polished hardwood floor to reach the domed ceiling which was studded with crystal chandeliers.

All work was closely scrutinized several times a day by Celia who threaded her way cautiously among the forest of ladders, buckets of paint and protective drop-cloths. Casting a critical eye on the proceedings, she was never hesitant about pointing out the slightest deficiency or imperfection that she observed to Miles Crachton, head of the refurbishing crew who respectfully removed his painter's cap in her presence.

"You and your crew are doing a fine job, Crachton," Celia commented, fingering the strands of pearls at her throat as she surveyed the room with a critical eye.

Crachton respectfully removed his cap in her presence and replied, "Thank you, ma'am," pleased by the compliment. "Your ladyship's choice of colors -- pink, gray with touches of silver here and there -- was excellent."

"Things seem to be coming along nicely," Celia said. "Do try to see that when your men paint the mezzanine, they don't allow paint to drip down onto this lovely floor," she said, referring to the elevated balcony-like structure which surrounded and overlooked the ballroom and was reached by a sweeping staircase from the dance floor.

"Yes, ma'am," Crachton promised.

Since leaving Stagsbridge for London, Celia found herself wishing that things were going as well with her elder daughter as they were with the re-decorating of the house. Mary was spending most of her time moping alone in her room, refusing to go on shopping trips to Harrods or Selfridges with her mother and reluctantly attending the preparation classes for her presentation at court. The classes were held at the home of Lady Cargill, a dowager who had fallen on hard times.

In addition, Mary had shown little interest in the swatches of various fabrics among which she was to choose the ones from which a number of ball-gowns would be fashioned for her by Mrs. Kazanjian, a designer and seamstress greatly favored by the London aristocracy.

As a perceptive mother, Celia suspected that her elder daughter's melancholy state, characterized by withdrawal and obstinacy, was undoubtedly caused by Andrew's interest in Ruth.

Hopefully, Antonia and I have taken care of that situation." she said to herself.

Unfortunately, the preparation for Mary's upcoming debutante season was not proving to be the distraction that Celia had hoped it would be.

"If Mary doesn't soon recover from this present melancholy state she's in, we're going to have to institute more severe measures," Celia confided to Arthur during one of his visits to the London home. A devoted family man, Arthur regretted that he was too preoccupied with his duties as steward of Stagsbridge to give sufficient time and attention to his wife and daughter while they were at the London residence.

"Managing a vast estate demands most of my time and energy," he complained. "A fellow such as Simon Buckford has two grown sons to aid him with Lammersley, but our Charles is still too young for me to begin educating him in the management of Stagsbridge which will be his one day. When you speak of 'other severe measures' with regard to Mary, to what exactly are you referring?"

"Well, I thought of sending her off to visit the von Rohrbachs in Germany," Celia replied.

"Now?"

"Why not? There are still months before the Season begins. Mary has plenty of time. I had her start her preparation classes with Lady Cargill early as a distraction to see if that could rouse her from her melancholy state."

Arthur contemplated his wife's words for a moment before responding. "Yes, that might bring around the desired change in Mary we've been hoping for, but I wonder how prudent a step that would be at this time. I'm concerned about Mary's safety with those dreadful Nazi's controlling the country."

"I think we needn't worry when she's with people of Kurt and Anne's station," Celia assured him.

Proceeding up the the Regent's Park home's wide staircase, which was hung with almost as many family portraits as the Stagsbridge manor house, to Mary's room, Celia knocked on the door.

"Mary...?" she called softly.

"Come in, Mother," Mary responded from inside.

Although it was mid-morning when Celia entered the room, Mary was still in her nightclothes, staring out the window at the falling rain in the London street outside..

With a disapproving frown, Celia said, "Why are you not dressed?"

"What's the point in dressing?" Mary responded, without turning around to look at her mother. "We're not venturing out in the rain."

"Yes, we are," Celia was quick to respond. Then noticing Mary's untouched breakfast tray, she added, "Your breakfast has been ignored, and after you insisted on having Polly bring it up to your room when you were perfectly capable of coming downstairs and joining me in the dining room.

"I'm not hungry."

Suppressing her rising exasperation, Celia said, "Get yourself dressed. Now."

"Where are we going?"

"Jamison will drive us to Mrs. Kazanjian's establishment. It's time you began the fittings for your various gowns."

"But the Season is months away," Mary replied. "Why do we have to go for a fitting today when it's raining?"

"Mrs. Kazanjian is very busy preparing gowns for other girls. The gowns for presentations at court are very elaborate and take months to make. Each gown requires a train of a minimum of three feet," Celia continued.

"Are train-bearers required?" Mary asked.

"Not necessarily."

"I'm very excited about the Season and my ball," Mary said. "But the elaborate nature of the preparations can be a bit tedious."

"Nonsense," Celia snapped.

Celia had not revealed to Mary that Alice and her daughter Jane would be at the dressmaker's for a fitting that afternoon. She hoped that Jane's cheerful presence would lift Mary out of her somewhat listless state.

Celia was not optimistic.

<hr />

Holding a black umbrella over their heads, Jamison sheltered Celia and Mary from the automobile to the door of Mrs. Kazanjian's establishment which was located in a commercial district of London. Jamison was forced jump to the curb to shield mother and daughter from a passing taxi which splashed a cascade of water from a curbside puddle.

"Londoners are so rude," Celia commented, shaking her head in disgust. "Especially the taxis."

The dressmaker, a dark complexioned, plump, middle-aged woman with a yellow measuring tape around her neck and straight pins clenched between her teeth, greeted Mary and Celia at the door.

"Come in, come in," she welcomed mother and daughter. "Your friend Lady Knightsgate and her daughter Jane are also here today in the drawing room."

For the first time in days Mary broke into a delighted smile. "Jane? Here?"

Hearing Mary's voice in the foyer, Jane rushed from the adjoining fitting room in her slip and embraced her.

"Mary! I can't believe it! I had no idea you were coming here today. What a lovely coincidence!"

"Yes, lovely indeed," Mary agreed.

Mrs. Kazanjian ushered Mary and Jane into the fitting room and ordered a maid to serve Celia and Alice tea.

While Mrs. Kazanjian was taking their measurements, the two girls chatted excitedly. Overhearing them, Celia was grateful and relieved that she had made a wise choice; Jane appeared to be lifting Mary out of her unhappy state.

"*Comment ca va, ma chere Marie?*" Jane asked, using the French they had learned from Mademoiselle Fouchet together in Paris.

"I've forgotten nearly all the French we learned last summer," Mary said.

"Shame on you, Mary," Jane reproached. "Mademoiselle Fouchet would be most unhappy to hear that."

"It's because of all that dreadful German that's been forced on me lately," Mary complained. "I much prefer Mademoiselle Fouchet to Fraulein Herzog."

"Yes, I remember her from dinner that evening on the 'Glorious Twelfth'," Jane said.

Mary sighed and reminded her. "Unfortunately, she was urged by Andrew to join us at the table, as you may recall."

"I do recall very well," Jane affirmed. "She rather captured Andrew's attention. I think your mother was a bit vexed with Andrew."

"So it seemed," Mary said.

Mrs. Kazanjian draped a bolt of blue satin over Mary. "This robin's egg blue goes perfectly with your beautiful blue eyes, don't you agree?"

"I suppose," Mary replied indifferently.

Mrs. Kazanjian, got on her knees to mark the hemline of Mary's gown. "Please, ladies, you must be still so that my measurements are correct," she cautioned.

"Sorry, Mrs. Kazanjian," Jane apologized but continued her conversation with Mary. "What a pity. I think you rather fancied him, if I'm not mistaken."

"I still do," Mary admitted hesitatingly. "Perhaps things will be better now that Fraulein Herzog has departed."

Surprised, Jane repeated, "'Departed'? Where to?"

"Back home to Germany," Mary replied. "She left rather unexpectedly with no explanation and no goodbyes to anyone."

"How odd," Jane commented.

"Yes, very odd indeed," Mary agreed.

When Celia and Mary returned home from Mrs. Kazanjian's, Jamison escorted them up the steps to the door, once again protecting the pair from the continuing rain with a large umbrella.

The maid, Polly, greeted them at the door and helped them out of their coats. "Lord Buckford is waiting in the drawing room," she announced.

Mary's heart began to pound at the news, "Lord Andrew Buckford?"

"Yes, ma'am," Polly confirmed.

Celia assumed that Andrew had come to demand an explanation for Ruth's dismissal, a confrontation she wished to avoid. "Would you please receive him, Mary? I have a slight headache and am going upstairs and retire to my room."

"Of course, Mother. I'll be happy to," Mary said. In a state of adolescent excitement, she was sure that Andrew had come to London to expressly to see her. With Ruth gone, had his interest in her been rekindled?

As she entered the drawing room, Andrew lay aside the leather briefcase in his lap and rose.

"Andrew! What a lovely surprise!" Mary said, resisting an impulse to offer more than her hand as a greeting.

Andrew smiled warmly. "It's good to see you, too, Mary. We've missed you at the Agricultural Council meetings."

"I've missed you as well," she responded. "Please, sit down. I'll ring for Polly to bring us some tea. It would be pleasant to have some nice hot tea after all that ghastly rain outside."

"Thank you, but I can't stay long."

"What a pity," Mary lamented.

"There's a rather serious matter I must discuss with you," he said.

"'Serious'?" she repeated, raising her eyebrows, hoping that whatever he wished to discuss had a romantic component.

Andrew drew a sheaf of official-looking papers from a manila envelope in his briefcase.

"As you know, Ruth has been forced to return to Germany," he began.

Disappointed at the mention of Ruth's name, Mary repeated with a puzzled frown, "'Forced'? Why do you say that?"

"The reasons behind her sudden and unexpected departure are not clear as yet and not important right now. She has arrived back in Germany and conditions there are deplorable. Ruth is desperate to return to Britain as soon as possible."

Thoroughly disheartened that this was the purpose of his visit, Mary said, "I don't understand what this has to do with me."

"It was mentioned the other day that you will be going to visit relatives in Germany – in Berlin, to be specific."

"Yes, possibly. Why?"

"I was hoping that if you go, you'd be willing to take these papers to Ruth. My father, as a member of parliament, has managed to arrange – with great difficulty, I might add – through his contacts in the upper echelons of government the proper documents to facilitate her return and legal residence in Britain."

Both shocked and deeply distressed by his request, Mary replied, "Me? Take papers to Fraulein Herzog? What is this all about, Andrew? I don't understand."

"Somehow Ruth managed to get a telegram off to me through a former and very loyal student of hers at the university where she was teaching before the Nazis dismissed her. The poor girl is absolutely desperate. Conditions for Germany's Jews are growing more dire by the day. Are you aware that Ruth is Jewish?"

"No, I wasn't. I never gave the matter much thought, although I did notice that she never attended chapel with the family and the rest of the household staff," Mary replied. "Why don't you simply post these papers to her?"

Andrew shook his head. "No, that's much too uncertain. She would never receive them. Her family home has been confiscated by the Nazis. She and her father are now forced to live in another area of the city designated for Jews where there is either no postal service or, at best, unreliable."

"Why don't you simply go to Berlin and deliver these papers to Fraulein Herzog yourself?" Mary suggested. She felt deeply resentful and thought it was inappropriate that he was asking her to undertake a task that he himself was apparently unwilling to do. "I'm sure she would prefer seeing you than me."

"I can't."

"Why not?"

"I am not eligible for a leave until my training is completed."

"What 'training'?"

"I've joined the RAF. I'm training to be a fighter pilot."

Surprised, Mary said, "I had no idea."

"Of course you didn't. I didn't tell anyone except Nicholas of my plans."

"What about your parents?"

"I didn't want to upset them. They don't consider war with Germany as inevitable, as I do," he explained. "Please, Mary, put aside whatever petty feelings of resentment or indignation you may have regarding my relationship with Ruth and say that you will do what I ask of you." Grasping Mary by the shoulders, his hazel eyes gazed into hers imploringly. "Do it for me, Mary. Please ..."

After deliberating a moment, Mary quietly answered, "All right. Give me the papers, Andrew."

Chapter Seven

After accompanying Philip and Alice Knightsgate to a performance of the Royal Opera at Covent Garden, Celia and Arthur, on one of his visits to London, conversed as they were getting out of the evening's formal attire and preparing for bed.

"I'm worried about Mary," Celia said as her husband stood behind her unfastening the glittering diamond necklace around her neck.

Arthur raised his eyebrows. "Why 'worried'?"

"Our daughter is not happy," his wife replied. "She's been moping about ever since we arrived in London. She has little interest or enthusiasm for anything. I offer her shopping jaunts to Harrods or Selfridges, evenings of theater at the West End or attending the cinema, even tea with close friends, but she wants none of it. Mrs. Kazanjian has designed some absolutely wonderful gowns for her to wear for the Season, but that has done nothing to raise her spirits."

"Well, Mary's a girl more interested in horses and country life than gowns or urban entertainments," Arthur said.

"Not only that, but we've been seeing Jane frequently here in London," Celia continued. "You know what a lively and vivacious young woman Jane is ..."

Smiling, Arthur nodded, "She is indeed – a delightfully amusing girl with that lovely red hair of hers."

"Mary has always been fond of Jane's company," Celia went on. "But not even her presence has not had the effect on Mary that I hoped it would." Celia paused a moment and considered. "The only bright moment for her was a visit from Andrew – albeit only a brief one, unfortunately."

"Well, the chap's gone off and joined the RAF to train as a fighter pilot," Arthur disclosed. "So I'm certain his time is limited these days."

Celia was startled. "How do you know that?

"Andrew confided to Nicholas that he was planning to join up, and Nicholas happened to mention that fact to me," Arthur responded. "I'm not sure he's informed our parents as of yet."

"I'm sure it will be a shock to Simon and Antonia when he does," Celia said.

"Not as much as you might think, my dear, given Andrew's view on the current state of affairs between our country and the Germans," Arthur replied as he raised the stiff collar of his starched white dress shirt and untied his black bow tie. "He's apparently been heeding the call of Mr. Churchill. The man has been advocating the build-up of the Royal Air Force since 1934. With the Germans behaving as they have been these days, it's an admirable step that Andrew has taken. Knowing that Mary won't be seeing Andrew nearly as often as in the past is undoubtedly a factor in our daughter's present state of mind. We both know how much she was looking forward to serving on the Agricultural Council with him and how fond she is of him."

"If only Andrew were as fond of her as she is of him," Celia lamented with a sigh.

"Perhaps in time he will be," Arthur replied.

"I do hope so," Celia said, adding, "Now that Fraulein Herzog has returned to Germany, Andrew may direct more of his attention to Mary."

"I must say that Fraulein Herzog left rather abruptly," Arthur commented as he removed his onyx cuff-links.

"She was anxious to return to her family," Celia lied. "They're Jewish, you know."

Arthur raised his eyebrows in surprise. "In that case, her return to Germany is even more curious. Hitler has made no secret of his contempt for the Jews. The Nazis have instituted an official policy of persecution of Jews for quite some time. They've even established some sort of detention camps for them." Arthur shook his head in dismay. "I wish I had known. I would have convinced her to remain in England."

"Why do they do such dreadful things?" Celia questioned as she stepped out of her evening gown, wondering for a moment if she had done the right thing. "Many British Jews have made wonderful contributions to our country – Mr. Disraeli, the English branch of the Rothschilds … "

"The Nazis claim they are leaders of the Communist opposition," Arthur said as he sat on the edge of the bed and removed his black patent leather shoes. "That's nonsense, of course. Totalitarian regimes always need a scapegoat. The Nazis chose the Jews. In doing so, it gave Hitler the right to seize Jewish property and assets to help finance his military ambitions."

"I really can't fathom the Nazis remaining in power much longer. Men such as Kurt von Rohrsbach and other decent Germans are surely not going to tolerate Hitler and his associates much longer. In her letters to me, Cousin Anne clearly despises Hitler and the Nazis and everything they stand for. She refers to them as 'gangsters' and 'thugs' and 'bullyboys'."

Arthur placed his hands on his wife's bare shoulders. "Darling, your cousin Anne is English at heart, even though she's married to Kurt."

"In her last letter, Anne wrote how much she misses Mary and suggested that I let her come to Berlin for a visit. I suspect she may be having difficulties with Karl-Heinrich. Anne believes that a visit from Mary will do him some good. She assures me that it is perfectly safe for Mary to visit at this time," Celia said as she sat before her dressing table mirror and began to remove her make-up. "It's a shame Anne never had a daughter."

"Perhaps, as has been suggested recently, a visit to Germany might just be the right thing for Mary at this time," Arthur mused. "A change of scene might raise her spirits."

"Yes, that may not be such a bad idea at all," Celia agreed. "In fact, it's a good one. Oddly enough, Mary herself suggested a trip to Germany the other day out of the blue. Can you imagine? I was stunned."

A small trunk occupied the center of Mary's spacious London bedroom. Jane, who was visiting for the day, sat on the bed chatting with Mary who was rather listlessly selecting clothes for her upcoming trip to Germany, transferring each garment to Polly who neatly folded it and placed it carefully in the trunk.

"I can't believe you're leaving," Jane said. "Especially now with the Season starting in a few months."

"I shan't be away long," Mary replied.

"You're going to miss most of Lady Cargill's classes."

"Mother can teach me what is required from her own experience as a debutante," Mary replied.

"But what about your fittings with Mrs. Kazanjian?"

With a dismissive wave of her hand, Mary said, "I can do those when I return."

"I can't help wondering why you are going now," Jane said. "Is it because Andrew has gone off and joined the RAF?"

"Mary was surprised. "Then you know, too?"

"Yes, one of Trevor's chums saw him in his uniform at a pub in Oxford. As you know, Mary, news such as that travels fast in our circle, and my brother can't keep secrets for the life of him. Are you sad because you will no longer be seeing him very often at Stagsbridge – or possibly not at all?"

"I'm going because I am very fond of Mother's cousin Anne," Mary responded. "I haven't seen her and her family for several years."

"Your cousin Anne has a son, does she not?"

"Yes. He's only slightly older than I," Mary responded. "His official name is Karl-Heinrich, but everyone calls him 'Heinzi'."

Jane's interest was piqued by the mention of Karl-Heinrich. "Is he an attractive chap?" she asked.

"I haven't seen him for several years – perhaps he's changed – but I would probably say 'no'," Mary answered. "When he was visiting us a few years ago, he asked Nicholas to instruct him in cricket and rugby. Nicholas labeled him a complete disaster and said that when they were playing croquet, he kept cheating by pushing the ball about with his foot when no one was watching."

Her face reflecting a degree of disappointment, Jane said, "He sounds a bit tiresome."

"Perhaps he's changed," Mary suggested as she passed Polly a sweater to fold. "In any case, I'll be finding out very soon."

The sun over the choppy English Channel burst through the heavy dark clouds long enough for its brilliant light to be reflected from Dover's celebrated white, chalky cliffs when Mary arrived at the ferry landing in the family MGWA 2.5 liter sports saloon driven by Jamison. Celia accompanied her daughter, grateful for the chance to talk to Mary alone before she departed for the continent.

"Lord Simon confided to your father that the Ministry of Defense fears that the Germans may attempt to establish a blockade around Britain if war between our two countries becomes a reality. In the event that things become more serious, Cousin Anne will see to it that you return before any sort of blockade is established. It would be frightful to have you stranded on the continent in the event of war, but everyone assures me that with Prime Minister Chamberlain's present negotiations with Chancellor Hitler, you'll be safe," Celia said.

"I'm sure I shall be," Mary replied.

At the pier, the sun once again became enshrouded in dark clouds as Jamison unloaded Mary's trunk. Before he had an opportunity to transfer it to a waiting porter, Celia ordered him to open it and take out Mary's raincoat.

"You'd better wear this," she advised as the chauffeur passed her the garment. "The sky looks very threatening."

Somewhat reluctantly Mary put the raincoat on over her flowered print silk dress.

Jamison locked the trunk, handed the key to Mary and then turned it over to the porter who hoisted it onto his back and carried it aboard the ferry.

As Mary and Celia ambled toward the boarding ramp, Celia, sensing that Mary seemed preoccupied and a little anxious, said, "I hope your visit with Cousin Anne and Graf Kurt will be a pleasant one."

"I'm sure it will be," Mary replied.

"Before you leave, I want you to know that I am aware how you feel about Andrew. He's a most charming young man – ideal for you, really, in so many ways. I'm certain that Fraulein Herzog was just a passing fancy – a most inappropriate one, to be sure. Now that she is back in Germany and Andrew is in the RAF. I'm sure he will soon forget her and turn his attention to you."

Feeling both dubious and wistful, Mary said, "I hope you're right, Mother," and started up the boarding ramp.

<hr>

Midway across the Channel, the ominous dark clouds released their pent-up rain. The violent downpour was accompanied by strong winds and rough seas. While the other passengers sought refuge in the interior of the ferry, Mary remained on deck.

One of the boat's crewmen in a yellow rain-slicker approached her. "You'd better go inside with the others, Miss," he advised.

Mary pulled the collar of her raincoat up and replied, "I'll be all right, thank you."

"Very well, Miss," the crewman muttered with a shrug and returned inside.

Alone in the now pounding rain, she reached into the pocket of her raincoat and extracted the official-looking papers which Andrew had entrusted her to deliver to Ruth in Berlin.

As the ocean grew increasingly turbulent, churning up high waves which crashed over the deck and tossed the ferryboat about, Mary, oblivious to the weather surrounding her, stared at the documents, holding them close to her body to protect them from the rain.

Clearly distraught by what these papers implied about Andrew's relationship with Ruth, her eyes began to well up with tears as her mind drifted to happier times, causing her to unconsciously expose the documents to the raging elements. Tears rolled down her cheeks and quickly united with drops of rain, causing the ink of the documents' all- important signatures to run and stain the now soggy paper.

Her nostalgic musings suddenly changed to angry disappointment, and Mary suddenly found herself considering a cruel decision.

Impulsively, she tore the papers to tiny shreds and let the wind scatter them, like errant snowflakes, over the churning, roiling sea.

Chapter Eight

After the ferry docked at Calais on the Normandy coast of France, Mary took a train to Paris where she called briefly on Mademoiselle Fouchet, her French tutor from the previous summer.

"And how is your friend Jane?" the older woman asked, choosing her heavily accented English instead of French; she was not sure how much Mary had retained from her prior study of the language.

"We're both busy preparing for the Season," Mary replied.

Mademoiselle Fouchet nodded. "Ah, yes, a busy time for young ladies such as yourself and Jane. But why are you now going to Germany?"

"To visit relatives."

"We here in France are quite worried about the Germans. In March was the *anschluss* – the takeover of Austria, uniting it with Germany – and now they have taken the Sudetenland from Czechoslovakia. Next they are preparing to invade Poland. *Mon Dieu!* What will be next? France?"

⁂

From Paris, Mary traveled by express train to Berlin where the von Rohrbachs had arranged to meet her. At the station, she was startled to see huge red banners bearing the emblematic Nazi swastika displayed everywhere.

After leaving the train, Mary headed for the baggage car to claim her trunk and secure a porter to help her with it. She observed grim-faced Gestapo agents patrolling the depot and suspiciously eyeing the arriving passengers. An oppressive and ominous atmosphere seemed to be pervasive

How different it is from railroad stations in Britain, Mary thought.

The steadily increasing militarization of Germany had resulted in a shortage of porters, but Mary, using the combination of her most dazzling smile she could muster and her limited German, eventually obtained a porter who followed her toward the exit gate on the other side of which a horde of individuals waited to greet new arrivals. Surveying the crowd, she spotted Kurt and Anne von Rohrsbach who stood out by virtue of their elegant appearances and aristocratic bearing. The pair was accompanied by a uniformed chauffeur.

"Mary! Hello!" Anne, a strikingly attractive, well-dressed, slender blonde woman in her late forties, called to her, waving her gloved hand excitedly from the opposite side of the fence.

Kurt, tall and distinguished-looking, in his early fifties with slicked back, graying blond hair was attired in an immaculately tailored, dark blue double-breasted suit. He joined his wife in waving and shouting, "Mary! Hello! We're over here waiting for you."

Mary, trailed by the porter with her trunk, passed through the gate and joined Kurt and Anne, each of whom embraced her in turn, kissing her on both cheeks.

"Welcome to Berlin," Anne said.

"We're so happy to see you," Kurt added.

"It's lovely to be here," Mary replied.

"How is your German?" Anne asked. "Your mother wrote me that you've been studying it with a private tutor."

"To be perfectly honest, my German is frightful," Mary confessed. "I promise not to inflict it on either of you."

Kurt turned to their chauffeur, whose name Mary learned was Willi, and instructed him to relieve the porter of Mary's trunk. Willi went immediately in search of a dolly to transport the trunk to the von Rohrsbach's Horch Type 930 V-8 automobile.

Flanking Mary on either side, Kurt and Anne escorted her through the station, followed by Willi wheeling the trunk. Near the exit to the street, a pair of officials wearing Nazi armbands at a Customs check point ordered them to halt in German.

"Don't worry. They only want to check our papers," Kurt reassured Mary. "Give me your passport. I'll take care of things."

Kurt handed the officials three documents: his own and Anne's *arbeits-bucher* and Mary's passport.

"Anne and I now have an *arbeitsbuch*," he explained. "It's an identity document which all Germans are required to carry under the present regime."

When the officials realized that Kurt and Anne were members of the aristocracy, their attitudes seemed to soften noticeably. However, when the Customs officer was presented with Mary's passport, he reacted to her British nationality by curling his lip in disdain and asked her in English: "What is the purpose of your visit to Germany, Miss?"

"I shall be visiting my relatives," Mary replied, indicating Kurt and Anne who were standing at her side.

With that, the official stamped her passport, curtly handed it back to her and shifted his attention to those next in line.

The three of them left the station followed by Willi, wheeling Mary's trunk.

Mary was ushered by Willi into the rear seat of the Horch sedan as soon as he had stowed her luggage in the rear of the car. Kurt and Anne sat on either side of her in the back seat.

As they drove through Berlin, Mary, who remembered very little of the city from her childhood, found it surprisingly lush for an urban capital with vast forests and sizable bodies of water. Historic sculptures and fountains were abundant, often standing before official buildings, mostly of neoclassical architecture, which graced the wide, often tree-lined avenues. The leaves of these trees were bright with early autumn colors

"Frederick the Great, like many Prussian rulers, loved sculpture. That's why you see so many statutes in Berlin," Kurt pointed out.

When Willi turned onto the Kurfurstendamm, Mary, having just arrived from Paris, was reminded of the Paris Champs Elysee.

The von Rohrsbach's residence was in an area of west central Berlin known as Charlottenberg-Wilmersdorf which not only contained the one time summer palace of Queen Charlotte but also the Deutsche Oper, Sovignyplatz and the Grunewald Park which lay at the western end of Kurfurstendamm. The park boasted a large lake called the Wannsee surrounded by an extensive forest.

"How is Heinzi?" Mary asked. "I'm eager to see him again. We used to have such fun when he came to Stagsbridge to visit. One day when I was teaching him to ride, he fell off his horse into fresh cow dung. He was embarrassed and furious with himself. I felt quite sorry for him."

"Our son is not much of a horseman, I'm afraid," Kurt said. "Nor did he master cricket and rugby, as I hoped he would. I played both when I was at Cambridge. Those sons of Lord Buckford struggled mightily to teach him those sports, but without much success."

"What are Andrew and Nicholas engaged in these days?" Anne asked.

"Andrew is in training to be an RAF fighter pilot, and Nicholas is starting a business," Mary replied.

As the director of a large bank, Kurt's interest was piqued. "Oh? What sort of business?"

"Selling scrap metal to Germany," Mary replied.

Kurt and Anne exchanged both surprised and somewhat disapproving glances, but refrained from commenting.

<hr>

The Charlottenberg-Wilmersdorf section of Berlin, Mary noted with some relief, was relatively free of the ubiquitous red Nazi banners with their ominous black swastikas. The von Rohrsbach's home was large with attractive landscaping.

Willi stopped the car beneath a portico covering the front entrance and allowed Mary, Kurt and Anne to get out.

"Willi will take your trunk up to your room," Kurt informed Mary as the chauffeur continued around to the rear of the house in the car.

A middle-aged woman in a maid's uniform with a crown of gray braids encircling her head opened the door and greeted them with a smile.

"This is our maid, Mathilde," Anne said, introducing her to Mary as they entered the marble-floored vestibule. "She and Willi are the only servants we have now. All the others have either joined the military or gone to work in the munitions and weapons factories."

"How do you do, Mathilde?" Mary said.

"*Angenehm, Fraulein,*" the maid replied in German with a slight curtsy.

"Mathilde will show you to your room and help you unpack your things," Anne said. "Dinner is at nine o'clock. I'm sure you must be tired and would like to rest a bit."

"Yes, a nap would be lovely," Mary replied, as she followed the maid toward the wide staircase which ascended to the second floor from the center of the vestibule. "By the way, is Heinzi at home? I'm eager to see him."

Anne and Kurt exchanged uneasy glances at the mention of their son's name.

"Heinzi isn't here right now," Anne said.

"Oh? Where is he?" Mary asked.

When Anne hesitated to answer, Kurt urged, "Go on, Anne, tell her."

"Heinzi has become very active in the group called Hitler's Youth," Anne said.

"Hitler *Jugend* in German," Kurt translated.

"At seventeen, he's now a squad leader," Anne continued.

"*Scharfuehrer,*" Kurt supplied.

"Today his group is conducting what's known as a 'control service'" Anne said.

"That's known as a *Streifendienst* in German," Kurt once again translated.

"What is it?" Mary asked.

"The Hitler Youth check on offenders such as store owners who fail to return the 'Heil Hitler!' salute," Anne explained. "Today they have targeted a Jewish grocery store owner. We'll talk more about Heinzi and his activities at dinner. You must go and have a rest now." Anne dismissed Mary with a wave of her hand, ending the conversation.

Although the table in the spacious and candle-lit dining room was elegantly laid with fine linen, crystal and china and graciously served by Mathilde, the meal was rather meager, food far less abundant than Mary recalled from her earlier visits to the von Rohrsbach home.

Anne seemed embarrassed by the nature of the fare as she said, "Food has become scarce and somewhat difficult to obtain lately."

"It's all going to feed the troops of Hitler's expanding army," Kurt remarked, a slightly bitter note in his voice.

"There's been some talk in England lately about the possibility of war between our two countries," Mary ventured, violating her mother's strict rule against discussing religion or politics.

Kurt raised his eyebrows as he ladled potato soup from the tureen Mathilde was holding. "'Possibility'?" he repeated. "Hitler's goal is to have all of Europe under Germany's domination, and he's determined to attain it at any cost. In my opinion he's nothing but a cunning, shrewd politician who tells the people what they want to hear: namely, that Germany will rise again, this time with greater glory to overcome the shame of our defeat in the Great War. He and his Nazi brown shirts are a symptom of these troubled times."

Mary turned from Kurt to his wife. "How do you feel, Anne?"

As far as I'm concerned Hitler is a vulgar, obscure nobody who happened to be in the right place at the right time with a superb gift for rabble-rousing," Anne replied.

"As with the British upper class, the German upper class suffers from mixed feelings about Hitler," Kurt said. "Some are relieved that he has stopped the Communists, who had become quite active and vowed to seize and re-distribute the lands of the aristocracy."

"So far the Nazis have allowed us to keep our property, and we're grateful for that, "Anne declared. "Although Hitler and his cohorts are not our sort at all."

"Germany's Jews have been most unfortunate. Many have had everything they own confiscated. They've been turned out of their homes and had all of their possessions seized, including their bank accounts," Kurt said. Pausing a moment, he added, "Of course, anti-Semitism in Europe is nothing new."

"A lovely Jewish family in our neighborhood – owners of one of Berlin's finest department stores – just simply disappeared one day. Nobody has any idea where they are. The Gestapo have taken over their home and are using it as a district headquarters," Anne related. "Some say the Jewish family fled to South America."

"It's more than likely that they were sent off to one of the forced labor camps such as Theresienstat," Kurt commented, shaking his head in dismay. "God only knows what happened to them after that."

Hearing that, Mary's thought momentarily of Ruth and felt a twinge of guilt.

Turning to Kurt, Anne decided to end the conversation by saying, "Let's not bore Mary with German politics – especially on her first night here."

<hr />

After dinner the three of them retired to the music room where Mathilde served them coffee and brandy. Kurt relaxed in his favorite leather easy-chair and lit his pipe while Anne went to the piano to play a Beethoven piano composition.

A little later, Mary's attention was distracted from the music by the sound of voices in the vestibule.

Anne stopped playing to listen and happily announced, "Heinzi is home. Last summer he marched with the Hitler Youth all the way to Nuremberg. It's a long distance from here, and the journey required several weeks. They were housed in private homes at night and given food by strangers along the way."

At that moment, Heinzi burst into the room. Tall and lanky with short, military-cut blond hair, he wore wrinkled dark brown short pants and knee socks, one of which had fallen down around his ankle. A Boy Scout-like neckerchief was around his neck.

Standing in the doorway, he clicked his heels together, extended his arm straight out and rendered the prescribed Nazi salute, shouting, "Heil Hitler!"

Mary noticed a bright red armband with a black swastika encircled the sleeve of his light brown shirt. She also noticed that there were blood stains on the shirt.

"You did not return my salute," he reprimanded his parents. "I could report you for that, you know."

Ignoring his threat, Anne patted the cushion on the piano bench beside her. "Come sit down, darling," she said. "You must be hungry. Shall I ask Mathilde to fix you a platter?"

"*Nein,* I ate a *Stulle* at the *Dienstelle* – lard on rye bread. Delicious!" Heinzi replied, licking his lips while his mother and father cringed.

"*Stulle* is a slang word for 'sandwich'," Anne explained.

"And the *Dienstelle* is the Hitler Youth headquarters," Kurt added.

Heinzi shifted his attention to Mary. At first, she assumed that he had been speaking English for her benefit, although she recalled that Celia had informed her before she left England that Anne complained in her letters to her that her German was still rudimentary. Thus, she concluded that his English might have been for his mother's benefit as well as hers.

"Well, I see we have a visitor from England," he said, his blue eyes bright. "Mary, how have you been?"

Afraid that he might try to kiss her on both cheeks, continental style, as his parents had done when she arrived at the train station, Mary extended her hand to him as a preventative measure.

Heinzi grasped it and raised it to his lips.

"I've been fine, Heinzi, thank you," she answered, pulling her hand away. His apparent Nazi transformation both puzzled and disturbed her. "It's been a long time."

"*Ja.* Years," he commented.

"It's good to see you again," Mary said, forcing a smile to mask the insincerity of her words. "I always enjoyed our times together as children."

"As did I also," Henzi replied. Then, addressing his parents, he said, "There was a bit of a scuffle at Herr Fiegenberg's grocery store today. His son intervened when we were disciplining his father. He said we were being too rough. Things got even rougher after that."

Mary assumed that the so-called 'roughness' probably explained the blood stains on his shirt.

"Herr Fiegenberg is an old man," Kurt reminded his son. "I hope you didn't injure him."

"We did what was necessary," Heinzi replied. "It doesn't matter because Feigenberg is a Jew and, therefore, sub-human."

Angered, Kurt responded, "That's a disgusting attitude."

Ignoring his father, Heinzi turned to Mary. "And now you must excuse me. I am in great need of a bath. I do, however, look forward to spending time with you."

Mary merely nodded, but made no verbal reply.

Anne rose from the piano bench. "I'll have Mathilde draw your bath."

"No need of that, *Mutti.* I can do it myself," Heinzi said. Then turning to Mary, he added, "We shall see one another in the morning, won't we?"

"I assume so," Mary replied.

"Splendid!" he declared and dashed out of the room.

Chapter Nine

Exhausted from her travels, Mary slept late in the great canopied bed in a guest room at the von Rohrsbach home. In the morning she was awakened by knocking on her bedroom door. At first she thought it was Mathilde until she heard Heinzi's voice in the hall outside.

"Get up, lazy. It's time for breakfast. I was awake hours ago, and I'm hungry. Can't you hear my stomach growling?" Heinzi teased, laughing.

Mary got out of bed and quickly dressed to accommodate Heinzi's hunger.

He was still waiting for her in the hall when she emerged from her room and wearing the Hitler Youth uniform again, complete with the traditional neckerchief knotted at his throat. This time the uniform was clean and freshly pressed, undoubtedly by Mathilde.

"Permit me to escort you to breakfast, Miss," he said, smiling and offering her his arm. The sleeve of his tan shirt was encircled by a red swastika arm-band.

Reluctantly, Mary accepted his invitation, and the two of them started down the carpeted hall toward the stairs.

In the dining room, Mary was surprised to find Anne and Kurt still at the breakfast table. Kurt, in a pin-striped, double-breasted gray wool business suit, was reading a copy of the newspaper *Die Zeitung*, and Anne, still in a silk dressing gown, was sipping coffee and gazing wistfully out the window at the last of the garden's summer flowers.

"Oh, dear! I hope you haven't been waiting for me," Mary said as Heinzi politely pulled out a chair to seat her at the table.

"It's perfectly all right, dear," Anne assured her with an affectionate pat on the arm as she placed her delicate china coffee cup on its saucer and rang the bell beside her plate to summon Mathilde from the kitchen. "We all know how tiring traveling can be."

"I have an exciting day planned for you," Heinzi said, his light blue eyes bright with anticipation. "The kind of day you won't experience in Britain."

"Oh, really?" Mary, not particularly enthused, replied. She was uncertain what he had in mind and whether she wanted to spend her first day in Berlin with him, especially when she had more urgent matters on her mind.

After gobbling his breakfast, Heinzi glanced at his watch and said, "You must excuse me, Mary. Unfortunately, I have to leave early to prepare for this afternoon's rally with my Hitler Youth group, but I shall return for you later when our work is completed. I think you will find this afternoon's rally interesting and perhaps enlightening."

Kurt scowled and wearily shook his head. "Good Lord, Heinzi, haven't we had enough of those damned rallies? They're nothing but Nazi propaganda."

Echoing her husband sentiment, but in a milder manner, Anne said, "Perhaps Mary would prefer to go shopping or visit one of our many fine museums rather than attend a political rally."

"I think Mary will find our rally far more interesting than those banal activities you suggest," Heinzi responded. "Especially since our Fuehrer will be speaking today."

"I doubt that the Fuehrer will have anything new to say and probably nothing that Mary would care to hear. Besides, traffic in the *Mitte* will be badly congested today around the Tiergarten," Kurt warned, referring to the central area of Berlin.

"What do you expect?" Heinzi said. "Huge crowds always turn out whenever our Fuehrer makes a public appearance."

***

Later that morning, pleading fatigue, Mary successfully persuaded Anne to go shopping without her. This, of course, obliged her to accept Heinzi's proposal that she attend the rally.

Remaining alone at the house alone, she leisurely bathed and dressed.

While soaking in the copper bathtub, she wrestled with the daunting prospect of calling on Ruth. There seemed to be no way she could possibly avoid contacting her former tutor since she had given Andrew her word she would in response to his pleading regarding Ruth's dire situation. She could think of no excuse that would be acceptable to him.

Mary was acutely aware of the challenging situation her impulsive nature had created. If she did not handle things in the right way, Andrew would surely terminate their friendship and be lost to her forever, something she did not want to happen. Not now. Not ever.

As she finished dressing, Heinzi rapped on her bedroom door for the second time that day.

"Mary! Are you ready?" he called through the door. "I have a taxi waiting outside to take us to this afternoon's rally."

Stepping out into the hall, she managed to muster a smile. "I am ready," she said, smoothing her tan cashmere sweater and plaid wool skirt.

"You look very nice," he said, looking her up and down. "Do you have your passport with you?"

"Why?"

"Everyone in Germany now is required to carry some form of identification with them at all times and present it on demand."

"Oh, yes. I remember from last night. I think I have it in my handbag."

"It's important that I see it."

As they descended the stairs, Mary opened her handbag and extracted her passport. As she did so, a slip of paper fell out and landed on the carpeted tread of one of the steps. Heinzi retrieved the piece of paper and glanced at it.

With a disapproving frown, he read aloud in a suspicious tone of voice, "'Ruth Herzog'? ... 'Rosenstrasse'? Who is this?"

"Ruth is my German tutor," she replied, snatching the piece of paper from him, irritated that he had had the gall to read it.

"Why do you have her address?"

"I am planning on visiting her while I'm here in Berlin."

"Do you realize that this address is in a Jewish relocation sector?"

Mary shrugged. "So what?"

"You must not go there."

"Why not?"

"There could be trouble with the Gestapo if you do -- not just for you, but also for me and my family."

As they left the house and got into the waiting taxi, Mary began to feel resentful of his dictating to her what she could and could not do, and it stirred a rebelliousness within her. Yet, at the same time and, in an odd way, he had partially solved her dilemma. Not only would she call on Ruth, she would do it today. How she was going to explain the missing papers, however, was another matter still to be resolved. After all, it was the rain that ruined them, she reasoned to herself.

The taxi slowly made its way along the wide, tree-lined avenue Unter den Linden upon arriving at the Tiergarten section near Berlin's *Mitte,* or central area. Mary observed that a large stage had been temporarily erected and hung with giant red swastika banners such as those she had seen at the train station when she arrived in Berlin. These banners were suspended from a line of massive columns at the rear of the stage, each column topped by a gigantic bowl which had been set ablaze creating an impressive series of flaming torches. Similar banners lined both sides of the Unter den Linden.

As they drew nearer, Mary noticed young men affixing posters to every available surface. These posters featured a yellow, six-pointed Star-of-David inside a circle with a slash mark across it.

"What are those posters they are putting up?" Mary asked.

"They're letting the Jews know they are not wanted," Heinzi replied.

"Why not?"

"Because they are enemies of the Third Reich."

"That's absurd," Mary scoffed. She found the notion of Jews as a threatening political force ridiculous.

"You are in Germany now, not Britain," Heinzi replied. "Things are different here. Things you cannot understand as an English woman."

"I understand perfectly well how offensive posters like those are. They're disgusting."

"You must also dispose of that address you have in your purse. If the Gestapo see it, they will misunderstand and possibly arrest you."

"Misunderstand what?"

Becoming irritated and impatient with her, Heinzi said, "The glorious future our Fuehrer has planned for us,is a future cleansed of Jews."

On the stage, Mary observed technicians swarming about setting up a row of microphones at the speakers' lectern on the raised dais as well as placing dozens of loudspeakers throughout the park, many of them in the trees.

Hordes of people were already streaming into the area before the stage when Heinzi ordered the taxi driver to stop at the edge of the crowd.

From the stage, a group of Hitler Youth members spotted him and signaled for Heinzi to come to the dais and help them with their work.

"Excuse me, Mary. They need me. It will be the duty of our Hitler Youth cadre to keep the masses in check," he said as he climbed out of the cab.

Uneasy at being suddenly alone amid a crowd of enthusiastic Nazi supporters, Mary asked, "But, Heinzi, what am I to do?"

"You will remain here. It's a good place to see and hear everything," he assured her.

Mary wasn't sure she wanted to see or hear any of it. "Please tell the taxi driver to stand by in case I become overwhelmed and feel a need to leave," she said.

Heinzi leaned into the window of the cab and spoke with the driver, a middle-aged man with a swarthy complexion and a gold earring in the lobe of one ear. He seemed to have difficulty understanding Heinzi's instructions.

Apprehensive, Mary asked, "What's the matter, Heinzi?"

"This man seems to be having trouble understanding German," Heinzi replied with a look of disgust. "He's one of those damned Gypsies. They're almost as bad as the Jews."

Eventually Heinzi managed to get his message across to the Gypsy cab driver and took off, waving goodbye to Mary as he threaded his way through the crowd to join a large contingent of his fellow Hitler Youth members.

With Heinzi gone, the taxi driver got out of his cab and crawled onto the hood to view the imminent spectacle and gestured for Mary to join him. At first, she was hesitant, then reasoning that it would be better than being jostled in the middle of a crowd, Mary accepted his invitation. For a girl who had spent a great deal of her life in the country around horses, climbing onto the hood of a car did not seem at all daunting.

Watching her, the Gypsy driver chuckled, displaying several of his gold-framed teeth.

Settling down next to him, Mary watched as the Hitler Youth volunteers unfurled an enormous portrait of Hitler as a backdrop. It completely dominated the stage, and the mostly working class crowd wildly cheered, shouting "Heil Hitler" repeatedly at the top of their lungs.

Just prior to the start of the parade, a caravan of limousines pulled up between the cordon of Hitler Youth guards and the stage to discharge Wehrmacht and SS officers. These stern. unsmiling men mounted the stage and took their assigned places on the dais. As they did so, loudspeakers announced their names and rank; propaganda minister Josef Goebbels was among the notables.

In an open Mercedes-Benz sedan, Hitler was the last to arrive. For propaganda purposes he made a point of shaking hands with some of the Hitler Youth guards when he got out. Mary noticed that he moved with surprising energy and confidence and, oddly, was not surrounded by a single personal bodyguard.

With the arrival of the Fuehrer, the parade commenced. Thousands of Hitler Youth marched smartly past the stage. Mary spotted Heinzi among them, looking smugly full of himself. The Hitler Youth formation was six young men deep and featured an astonishing two hundred drummers, all pounding away on their drums, and fifty flag bearers. The latter dipped their flags in respect to the dignitaries as they passed the Fuehrer and his staff on the dais.

The Hitler Youth contingent was followed by a Wehrmacht motorcycle squad roaring along on their deafeningly noisy bikes. They were trailed by thirty-six rows of Panzer tanks, also six deep, lumbering by. Next came a procession of all-terrain carriers.

Throughout this display of military might and the latest weapons of war, bands played the national anthem *Deutschland Uber Alles* as well as other military musical compositions.

A second unit of motorcycle troops ended the parade, and then Hitler rose to speak. The crowd cheered wildly as he approached the lectern.

Mary's meager German was insufficient to understand what Hitler was saying, delivered in a voice of an almost hysterical pitch which reverberated from the loudspeakers distributed throughout the Tiergarten. His words were frequently interrupted by cheers and thunderous applause from those in the audience.

Eventually bored with the blatant propaganda of the rally, Mary took the slip of paper with Ruth's address out of her handbag and passed it to the cab driver who had dozed off while lounging next to her on his cab's hood despite all the noisy activity around him..

He glanced at the paper, then glanced at her with a puzzled frown. *"Sie moesten nach Spander Vorstadt fahren?"* he asked. Observing Mary's puzzled expression, he switched to broken English. "You want go here? Yes?"

Anxious to leave the rally, her tone was almost pleading. "Yes," she affirmed. "Can you take me to the address on that piece of paper now?"

He frowned, but the anxious expression on her face made him reconsider. *"Ja, ja.,* I take you," he agreed.

He slid off the hood of his cab, then helped Mary down, and they both got back into the taxi.

"You speak English," Mary remarked.

"A little."

"Where did you learn?"

"I born in Romania but go to many countries. I am *Zigeuner* – Gypsy – *Rom,*" he responded, using the preferred term last. "My name is Radu."

"Have you been in England, Radu?"

"Yes, England," he nodded.

"What did you do there?"

"I sell horses."

"And now you're a cabbie in Germany."

"I have horses no more."

"What happened to them?"

"Nazis take away."

"For the cavalry?"

No. For food. Meat for soldiers."

Mary gasped, imagining her beautiful Blue Bonnet or Sable being cooked, carved up and consumed as meals for the military. "How awful!"

"Yes, very bad. They also take my *Rom* people and put them in camps. Make them work like slaves." he said. "Maybe someday they come and take me, too. For now, I drive taxi."

Because they were at the edge of the crowd, Radu was able to maneuver his taxi into the passing traffic.

Mary took a deep breath, knowing that she was on her way to what would probably prove to be a painful and challenging meeting with Ruth.

Chapter Ten

Mary realized that they were in a Jewish section of the city when they passed an impressive synagogue on Rykestrasse and an old Jewish cemetery on Grosse Hamburger Strasse; both of which had been defaced with anti-Jewish graffiti.

On Rosenstrasse, Radu stopped before a large, two story building that appeared to have been some sort of commercial establishment at one time but now appeared neglected.

The neighborhood contrasted sharply with the von Rohrsbach's Charlottenberg-Wilmersdorf area. Mary found it difficult to believe that an attractive, highly educated young woman such as Ruth, with a father who was a respected surgeon, would reside in such a poorly maintained building and suspected that it was not by choice.

As she prepared to get out of the cab, Mary said to Radu, "Wait for me here, will you please? I shan't be long."

Radu agreed, *"Ja, ja,* Miss."

Cautiously entering the dark, dingy central hall which was lined on both sides by a half dozen or so numbered doors, Mary had the impression from the configuration of the floor plan and the vague antiseptic smell that the building might have been some sort of convalescent home or auxiliary medical facility at one time.

Referring to the slip of paper bearing Ruth's address, she saw that *'Wohnung 6'* was a part of it and decided to knock on the door marked '6'. While waiting for someone inside to respond, she noticed that a tiny, cylindrical metal object bearing the Star-of-David was attached to the frame of the door. Inside, she heard a number of hushed but anxious voices; some of them seemed to be those of children.

Moments later, the door opened a crack and behind it, a thin, unshaven older man wearing a pair of wire-framed glasses held together by adhesive tape peered at her curiously, his dark eyes bore a cautious, haunted expression. He said nothing, waiting for Mary to speak first.

Once again, drawing on her limited German, she asked, "*Enschuldigen Sie, bitte, sprechen Sie Inglish?*"

"I do speak English," he replied. "What is it that you want?"

Looking over his shoulder, Mary observed an unusually dark, large room. All the window coverings were tightly closed. The only hint of furnishings in the room were mattresses with blankets strewn about the bare wooden floor. The walls were marred with rusty water stains indicating a possible leaking roof.

A pair of exceedingly thin, shabbily-dressed women looked apprehensive as they herded a group of small, undernourished children into an adjoining room and closed the door. For a moment, Mary thought that one of the women resembled Ruth, but the room was too dark for her to be certain.

"I'm looking for Fraulein Ruth Herzog, Is there anyone by that name here?" Mary asked.

Instantly on guard, the older man asked, "Who are you and what is your business with Fraulein Herzog?"

"I am Lady Mary Ashmore, and I wish to speak with her."

"Regarding what?"

"She was my German tutor in England."

"Ah, yes. Just a moment, please," he said and closed the door again.

While Mary stood waiting in the hall, a rat scurried past, eliciting a gasp from her.

A few minutes later, Ruth herself opened the door. She looked decidedly thinner and harried, not at all the attractive, confident brunette who had thoroughly captivated Andrew.

"Lady Mary!" she exclaimed "What are you doing here in Berlin?"

Why is she surprised? Mary wondered. *Had Andrew not told her about the papers and that I would be delivering them?*

"I'm visiting Mother's cousin and thought I would call on you while I was here in Berlin."

Obviously puzzled, Ruth asked, "How did you know where to find me? Where did you get this address?"

"Lord Andrew gave it to me when he heard that I was going to Germany. He wanted me to look in on you and see if you were all right," Mary lied, too ashamed after what she had done to reveal the original purpose of her trip.

Ruth gestured at the room behind her. "You can see how we are now forced to live."

In the bathroom, Mary could hear the children crying and the mothers trying to quiet them.

Mary had no desire to enter the apartment so she suggested, "I have a taxi waiting outside. Perhaps we could go somewhere and have tea?"

"Yes, I would like that," Ruth responded with a smile. "We rarely go out any longer because of the harassment and cruelty we are forced to suffer. Maybe if I am seen with someone such as yourself, it will be better."

Mary wondered if Ruth were referring to her blonde, obviiously Anglo-Saxon appearance.

<hr />

The two young women left the gloomy residence and got in Radu's taxi. He looked at Ruth curiously, as though he found it difficult to associate her with Mary.

"Tell the driver where we want to go," Mary said. "You know how poor my German is, although he does understand a little English."

"Yes, I remember what a struggle it was for you," Ruth remarked. Leaning forward from the backseat, Ruth relayed to Radu in German their desired destination. A brief discussion ensued which sounded to Mary more like an argument.

"What's the matter?" Mary asked.

"It seems he doesn't want to take us near to where I want to go. He says that a big rally just broke up in the area, and he doesn't want to get into the inevitable congestion there," Ruth explained.

Given the controversial political nature of the rally, Mary was reluctant to reveal to Ruth that she had just come from that same area.

"We'll go to another coffeehouse," Ruth said. "It's on Kurfurstendamm. I often spent time there during my happier student days."

Mary was also glad that they were not going back to the Tiergarten area because it would be very awkward if Hienzi spotted her with Ruth. He was already suspicious from the piece of paper with her address.

Settling back into the seat, Ruth said, "What a surprise to see you, Lady Mary."

"You left Stagsbridge so suddenly that I was unable to say goodbye to you properly," Mary replied.

"Yes, my departure from England was hasty and not of my choosing," Ruth said.

Mary thought she detected a note of angry resentment in her former tutor's tone.

"Conditions were bad when I initially left Germany, but now they're much worse," Ruth continued. "Everything has changed. When I arrived I discovered, much to my horror, that the Nazis had relocated my father from our beautiful home full of memories of my mother to this awful place. My father and I are forced to share it with strangers who are in worse circumstances than we are. Frau Weinstein has two small children and Frau Schaffner three. Their husbands were beaten and dragged away in the middle of the night to be deported to a labor camp before the women were relocated. My father has been very depressed. It makes no difference to then that he is a highly respected surgeon. They are forcing him to work in a munitions factory twelve hours a night. At first, they allowed him to continue his medical practice, but only permitted him to treat Jewish patients. Now, all that has changed. He can treat no one."

"I had no idea that things were so wretched for you," Mary said, appalled by the conditions under which her former tutor was now forced to live. Mary was beginning to feel sympathy for Ruth, even if she had usurped Andrew's affection.

"Andrew is my only hope," Ruth said.

"How so?" Mary asked, dreading the answer.

"He promised to use his father's influence, as a member of parliament, to obtain the proper documents so that I could escape to Britain, remain there permanently and immediately begin working to get my father out of Germany. Did Andrew mention anything to you about these papers before you left?"

"'Papers'? Not that I can recall," Mary replied, knowing she was lying and feeling deeply remorseful about it.

Ruth looked at her with suspicion in her dark eyes which made Mary squirm and avert her gaze. "Then he said nothing about papers when he gave you my address?"

"No. Nothing."

Ruth shook her head. "That's strange."

"Yes, quite," Mary agreed. "How did he get this present address of yours?"

"I managed to find a friend – a former student of mine at the university – who was willing to smuggle a letter to Andrew – for money, of course – so that he could get the necessary documents for me," Ruth explained. "I thought surely you would have them."

"Well, I don't," Mary said, avoiding Ruth's eyes once again.

Radu drove the two young women to the coffeehouse Ruth had suggested on Kurfurstendamm, and they got out.

"Please tell Radu to wait," Mary said. "He has to take us back later."

Ruth did as she requested.

The coffeehouse was bustling with activity and somewhat crowded and the atmosphere seemed cheerful. The fragrant smell of roasting coffee permeated the air and a rack of newspapers from all over Europe lined the walls. Although it was autumn and not yet very cold, a fire was burning in the stone fireplace. Mary noticed several young men in Hitler Youth uniforms chatting animatedly over mugs of coffee and assumed they had participated earlier in the day at the rally with Heinzi.

As Mary and Ruth were surveying the establishment for an empty table, the proprietor approached them with a scowl and pointed to a prominent sign in front of the cashier's cage which read: 'JUDEN UNERWUN-

SCHT'.

"What does it say?" Mary whispered to Ruth.

"It says: 'Jews not wanted'," Ruth answered.

Mary recalled the posters the Hitler Youth boys were putting up at the rally.

"The proprietor recognizes me from years of coming here as a student and knows I'm Jewish. I thought that by having you with me, he would accept me, but I was wrong. Jews are no longer allowed in this establishment, and he is unwilling to make an exception for me. So, come, let us leave."

The proprietor sneered contemptuously as Mary and Ruth left and climbed into the waiting taxi outside.

Feeling increasingly remorseful, Mary purchased some food for Ruth at a local store before she had Radu take Ruth back to her crowded living quarters. After dropping her off, they continued on to the von Rohrsbach home in the more upscale Charlottenburg-Wilmersdorf area. She was beginning to develop a deeper understanding of the precarious situation Ruth was facing. Feelings of sympathy were slowly replacing those of antipathy and resentment.

When Radu deposited her at the von Rohrsbach home, she asked how she could contact him again if she needed his taxi services, and he gave her a card with the name, address and phone number of a woman named Gisela Schmidt.

"You call her," he said. "She tell me, and I come for you."

"Is she your wife?"

"No, *freundin*," he answered. "You call. Yes?"

"I shall," Mary said and hopped out of the cab.

Mathilde silently met her at the door and took her coat. From the drawing room down the hall she could hear the agitated voices of Heinzi, Kurt and Anne engaged in an argument. Heinzi was shouting at his parents who were struggling to maintain a civil tone. Because they were speaking in rapid German, Mary had no clue as to what the apparent dispute was about.

Turning to the maid who was hanging her coat in the closet, she pointed to the drawing room and asked, "*Was sagen sie?*"

Mathilde merely smiled slightly and ignored her question, retreating quietly to the kitchen.

Mary proceeded to the drawing room. All three von Rohrsbachs fell suddenly silent when she entered. Kurt, seated in his customary leather armchair puffing on his pipe, reached for the daily newspaper, *Die Zeitung*, and pretended to read it. Anne was standing beside him, her hand on his shoulder. Heinzi, still in his Hitler Youth uniform, now badly wrinkled and sweat-stained, was pacing back and forth across the colorful Oriental rug on the floor in a state of great agitation.

Forcing a smile, Anne said, "Mary! Did you have a pleasant afternoon?"

Deciding to be straightforward about it, Mary replied, "I'm not sure I would call it 'pleasant'."

"Where did you go? What did you do? Tell us," Anne persisted.

Heinzi stopped pacing and flashed Mary an angry look. "I'll tell you what she did. She dared to leave the rally while the Fuehrer was speaking."

Unruffled, Mary said, "I could see no point in attending a noisy political rally in which I had absolutely no interest at all, so I paid a call to my German tutor."

Heinzi reached out and snatched the newspaper from his father. Furiously slapping the front page which featured the photograph of an adolescent boy, he said, "Jews, like that tutor of yours, will pay for this!"

Mary was completely baffled. "'Pay for' what? What on earth are you talking about, Heinzi?"

Hoping to stave off any controversial discussion, Kurt rose from his chair and reproached his son. "That is no way to speak to a guest in our home. We'll talk about the matter in the newspaper later."

"No!" Heinzi insisted. "We'll talk about it now. I think our little English cousin should wake up to what's going on in the world." Shoving the newspaper at Mary, he said, "This article describes the assassination of Ernst von Rath, a distinguished German political figure, by a Polish Jew, an illegal immigrant named Hershel Grynszpan."

"Herr von Rath was a Nazi," Kurt explained to Mary. "His assassin was a seventeen year old boy who was distraught because his parents had been deported back to Poland by the Nazis."

"Yes because they were Communists like thousands of other Polish Jews who are in this country illegally," Heinzi asserted. "Well, I will tell you one thing: the Jews will soon suffer severe retaliation for this crime."

"Yes, and Herr Goebbels will make the most of it. You can depend on that," Kurt added.

"Please, Heinzi – and you, too, Kurt," Anne pleaded. "We've had enough of this political ranting and raving for now. Let's talk about more pleasant subjects."

"Your mother is right," Kurt conceded. "We will say no more about it. Is that clear, Heinzi?"

"What is clear is that neither of my parents supports the Third Reich and are, therefore, traitors," Heinzi said, glaring at Kurt and Anne as he stomped toward the door, nearly colliding with Mathilde who was about to enter.

"*Telefon fuer Fraulein* Mary," the maid announced.

Mary was stunned. "For me? Who can it be? I hope nothing is wrong at Stagsbridge."

"The telephone is in my study," Kurt said. "Mathilde will show you where."

In the study, the maid passed Mary the phone.

"Hello. Lady Mary Ashmore here."

"Hello, Lady Mary," a cheerful, male voice said on the other end of the line. "Nicholas here."

Mary gasped in surprise. "Nicholas! Where are you?"

"I'm here in Berlin."

"What are you doing?"

"Shooting injured horses," he said, laughing.

"That's not at all funny," Mary reproached.

"Seriously, I'm here on business. Tell me, Mary, are you enjoying your sojourn to the German capital?"

Looking around first to be sure no one was listening, she said, "I'm not sure 'enjoying' is the proper word."

"What's the matter? Is that rotten sport of a cousin of yours -- Heinzi – boring you to death?"

"A little," she answered.

"Then I have the perfect solution," he announced in his customary jovial manner. "I'm having dinner with a very important German business associate and his wife this evening. I'd be pleased for you to join us if you can."

Mary would have preferred the invitation to have come from Andrew and not his brother, but on the other hand, it offered a respite from Heinzi and his political ranting.

"How kind of you to ask," Mary said.

"I promise you all the champagne you can drink and a seven course dinner at the Hotel Adlon. How does that sound?"

"Lovely," Mary replied.

"To be honest, Mary, I must admit that it would help my cause immensely if I arrived at the restaurant with a smashing blonde young lady on my arm this evening."

"That's very flattering, Nicholas."

"I'll come for you at eight o'clock tonight. Be ready," he said and rang off.

Chapter Eleven

Once again sharing a taxi, this time with Nicholas, elegant in his formal evening attire, his black hair slicked back in the current fashion, Mary returned to the '*Mitte*', or central Berlin, not far from where earlier in the day the Nazi political rally had been staged. This time, however, it was to be a much more pleasant occasion: dining at the Lorenz Adlon Esszimmer in the world-renown Adlon Hotel which offered *haute cuisine* and a view of the iconic Brandenburg Gate. Nicholas and Mary hosted Herr Reisner and his wife, a well-dressed, obviously affluent, middle-aged German couple.

For the occasion, Mary had opted for a sophisticated, 'glamorous' look reminiscent of the American film stars Jean Harlow and Carole Lombard in a floor-length, figure-clinging, off-white satin gown designed for her by Mrs. Kazanjian. A white ermine stole, borrowed from Anne, was draped over the back of her upholstered chair.

Gazing around the restaurant, Mary felt a bit uneasy with the number of high-ranking Nazi officers present.

"Most of the Nazi higher-ups prefer the Hotel Kaiserhof," Reisner commented, noticing her reaction. An important business magnate, Reisner spoke excellent English. "It's a few blocks south of here across from the Propaganda Ministry and Hitler's Chancellery on Wilhelmplatz, but my wife and I prefer the Adlon."

"We do indeed," Frau Reisner agreed as she waved to one of the wives of a Nazi officer at a nearby table.

Mary wondered if Reisner made that statement solely for the purpose of distancing himself from the Nazis for the benefit of his British companions.

Over the first course, a turtle soup with generous sherry, the talk quickly turned from casual to serious business.

"No one cares where the metal comes from – not the aircraft manufacturers, not the generals, not even the Fuehrer himself. I have them all in my pocket," Reisner boasted. "German air superiority is first and foremost for them."

Mary was well aware from the discussions of her father and his friends at Stagsbridge that if there were a war, the only way the Germans could take Britain was by air power. For that reason, Reisner's statement concerned her. The only comforting factor for her was the thought that Andrew would be a fighter pilot in the RAF. She was sure there would be many other British young men like him to defend her country if need be.

"I must ask you, Lord Buckford," Reisner continued, "As an obviously loyal Englishman, why are you selling British scrap metal to us Germans?"

"Yes, we're very curious," his wife added.

"As a so-called 'second son' I am obliged to make my way in the world on my own," Nicholas said. "My older brother Andrew will inherit the family estate."

Mary understood Nicholas' ambition. Many 'second sons' went off to Canada, South Africa, Australian or even America to seek their fortunes and many had been quite successful. Nicholas was doing it in Germany, although there were those who would disapprove of his business endeavors and severely criticize his lack of patriotism and loyalty.

At the mention of Andrew's name with regard to traditional British inheritance laws, Mary felt a twinge of nostalgia. As part of that tradition, her brother Charles would fall heir to Stagsbridge, and, therefore, it was incumbent upon her to make a suitable marriage. Andrew, of course, would be ideal.

How could he possibly prefer Ruth to me? she wondered.

"Enough of personal matters," Nicholas said as the waiter placed a plate of *sauerbraten* in front of him and refilled his wine glass. "You and I, Herr Reisner, must focus on how we will transport the scrap metal from Britain to Germany in the event of a North Sea naval blockade -- which I regret to say – is inevitable, given the direction in which relations seem to be proceeding between our two nations."

"I can arrange with the German high command for your ships to get through," Reisner replied. "Have no worries about that."

"That's comforting to know," Nicholas responded. "But then there's the question of land transportation of the metal once my ships are in German ports – getting it to where it's needed."

Reisner frowned and shook his head. "It is very difficult to obtain railway cars of any sort – even cattle cars -- these days. Most are being used for the deportation of Jews and others to labor camps."

Mary thought of Ruth and her physician father and wondered if they would have to suffer the humiliation of being shipped off to a labor camp in railroad cattle cars. She felt intuitively that it would be inevitable if things continued as they were. It was becoming increasingly clear to her that having destroyed the official papers Andrew intended for Ruth was a wicked thing to have done, and she was beginning to feel remorse for it. This trip to Berlin was opening her eyes.

Frowning, Nicholas asked, "Are you saying that's a problem, Herr Reisner?"

Reisner shook his head. "No, no," he said. "It's not a problem at all if one knows the right people in the Ministry of Transportation."

Frau Reisner reached across the table and affectionately patted her husband's hand. "My husband is very well connected."

"The price you are asking for the metal must, of course, be reasonable, Lord Buckford," Reisner said with a sly smile.

"What in your estimation is reasonable, sir?"

Reisner considered a moment. "Half the price you are asking."

"Perhaps not half, but I'm sure that something can be negotiated," Nicholas hinted. "The more metal purchased, the more reasonable the price."

Pleased with his response, Reisner signaled the waiter and ordered a bottle of champagne. "We must celebrate," he said.

***

At the conclusion of dinner, Nicholas suggested that they all go to a popular cabaret well-known for its show which featured female impersonators.

"No, no," Reisner said, wagging his index finger. "The Gestapo closed that club and arrested the performers, undoubtedly sending the poor fellows off to a labor camp."

"Men of that sort are disgusting," Frau Reisner said, curling her upper lip in revulsion. "I believe you call them 'poofters' in Britain. Is that not correct, Lord Buckford?"

"I wouldn't know," Nicholas answered. "Since the cabaret is closed, why don't we go dancing somewhere? The Nazis aren't against dancing yet, are they?"

"I'm afraid my wife and I are a bit tired," Reisner said. "I have a busy day tomorrow so, if you'll excuse us, I think we will return home."

Satisfied that a deal had probably been reached, the couple departed, leaving Nicholas and Mary alone in the elegantly appointed Adlon Hotel lobby.

"We can always go dancing by ourselves," Nicholas suggested.

"I don't fancy dancing tonight somehow," Mary replied.

"Come on, I want to celebrate," he urged.

Mary was not in a celebratory mood. "Celebrate what?" she snapped. "That you're selling metal to the Germans so they can build planes to bomb Britain?" She paused and took a deep breath. "It seems as though dark storm clouds are gathering over the world."

Nicholas grabbed her firmly by the shoulders. "Listen to me, Mary," he said, his voice unusually stern. "I am a businessman, and I intend to do business here in Germany as long as His Majesty's government permits it. You must understand that."

"Don't you understand that the Germans are going to use our metal to build airplanes that could not only bomb Britain, but might also shoot down your own brother who, at this very moment, is undergoing pilot training with the RAF?" Mary replied, troubled by his apparent lack of concern for Andrew and Britain.

"I can assure you that there is method in my madness," he said. "You must believe me."

"What are you talking about?"

Nicholas emitted a weary sigh. "I can't tell you any more than what I've already told you."

"You've told me nothing."

"And for good reason."

"And I wouldn't believe you, even if you did."

"Is that why you don't want to celebrate with me?"

"I'm not in the mood. I've had a difficult day. I was with my German tutor."

"That attractive brunette my brother is keen on?"

"Yes. Her living conditions are absolutely deplorable."

"I understand she's a Jew."

"She is," Mary affirmed. "And she's suffering terribly because of it."

"Well, there's nothing we can do about that," Nicholas said with a shrug of resignation as they stepped out of the hotel lobby.

An elderly doorman, opened the door for them.

"If you don't mind, Nicholas, I'd like to go back to the von Rohrbach's," she said.

"What?! And deprive me of your charming company when it's still early in the evening?" he replied, glancing at his wristwatch.

"I don't feel very charming tonight."

"On the contrary. I find you delightful – especially when you're annoyed with me."

Mary found herself wishing that the same compliment could have come from Andrew.

Nicholas was about to ask the doorman to hail a taxi for them, when Mary touched his sleeve and said, "You're right. It is early, and I would prefer to arrive at the von Rohrbach's after Heinzi is asleep. Let's take a walk. It's unusually warm for November, and my mood might improve with some fresh air," she added, clutching her ermine wrap about her shoulders.

"A walk is not exactly my idea of celebrating, but, hell, I'll be a good sport and give it a try," Nicholas conceded.

Mary and Nicholas strolled leisurely in the central area around the hotel, eventually trading Unter den Linden for some of the less prominent streets where there were fewer automobiles, less pedestrians and more shops with windows to peer into.

As they continued to walk, they encountered a sign prominently displayed on a lamppost which read: DESUTSCHE! BEHRT EUDY! KAUFT NICHT BEI JUDEN!

"I still don't know enough German to read it. What does it say?" Mary asked.

"'Germans! Defend yourselves! Do not buy from Jews'," Nicholas translated. "Signs such as these are all over Berlin."

A jewelry store a few doors away had a large yellow Star-of-David crudely painted on its door with the word 'JUDE' inscribed in its center.

Suddenly the stillness of the night was shattered by the loud, crashing sounds of breaking glass and the raucous shouting and yelling of male voices which frightened Mary. Nicholas pulled her close and cautioned her to remain calm.

Turning around, they observed a mob of rowdy young men at the far end of the street whose raucousness and aggressive energy indicated to Mary that they were undoubtedly members of the Hitler Youth she had observed earlier that day, although none of them were in uniform on this occasion. The younger men were soon joined by older and tougher-appearing males, also in civilian clothes. The fact that both groups were armed with clubs, rocks, axes, sledgehammers and flaming torches and moving closer alarmed Nicholas as well as Mary.

"The older ones are probably Storm Troopers and the younger ones Hitler Youth," Nicholas surmised as he put his arm protectively around Mary and pulled her close.

"But they're not wearing uniforms?" she pointed out.

"That's because Goebbels ordered them not to do so in his radio address today."

Mary was surprised. "How do you know?"

"I was in Reisner's car earlier today. He listened and translated it for me, but I wasn't listening carefully – just more Nazi propaganda, I thought – so I didn't realize it was tonight. If I had been more aware, I would never put you in harm's way."

"If they are Storm Troopers and Hitler Youth, why aren't they in uniform?"

"For propaganda purposes," Nicholas replied. "Goebbels wants it to look like a protest carried out by ordinary citizens. It's supposedly in retaliation for the assassination of von Rath by a Polish Jew."

"Yes. Heinzi was also going on about it today," Mary recalled.

The mob began smashing store windows and laughing as they shouted anti-Jewish slogans such as: *"Juden raus!"* and *"Auf nach Palastina!"*

Nicholas grew increasingly alarmed and pulled Mary into a concealed doorway from which they continued to watch in horror as the marauding hoodlums not only smashed the display windows of Jewish-owned stores, previously identified as such by official signs posted on the glass or graffiti Stars-of-David which Jewish owners were forced to paint on their doors, and looted merchandise.

Both were horrified by the destruction of property and chaos they were witnessing and Mary began to cry as she hovered next to Nicholas.

The tumult grew ever worse when the young marauders began to set fires with their torches, quickly transforming the street into a blazing inferno. Thick clouds of black smoke filled the air causing Mary to cough and choke.

Nicholas took a handkerchief from his pocket and passed it to her. "Cover your mouth and nose with this," he directed, and Mary did as he advised.

Throughout the city both police and fire sirens began to wail, and soon law enforcement vans, as well as a contingency of soldiers, appeared on the street.

Much to the amazement of Mary and Nicholas, the policemen and military men merely stood by watching the destruction and vandalism in silence. Some were even casually smoking cigarettes.

Stunned, Mary said, "Why aren't them doing something?"

Nicholas shook his head in dismay and replied, "Don't you see? They're part of this whole riot business. It's a propaganda ploy."

When fire trucks arrived, they were surrounded by the members of Hitler Youth who yelled, "Move on! Move on! A Jew owns that store" and "Let that Jew store burn!" or – even worse -- "Burn all Jews!"

Although Mary could not understand the shouted German epithets, she was sure that they were threatening to the firemen and prevented them from employing their equipment to extinguish the flames.

"This is intolerable!" she exclaimed.

When one courageous fireman attempted to drag a hose through the crowd of rioters to save a burning store, he was spat upon and viciously beaten with clubs and the fire hose slashed.

"Did you see that?" Mary gasped.

"Of course I did," Nicholas responded. "Shameful!"

After that, the firefighters remained on their trucks for safety and watched helplessly as flames consumed various structures, and columns of dense black smoke rose everywhere.

The police and soldiers continued to stand by and do nothing. Some even joined the mob in shouting for the firefighters to go away and let the targeted businesses burn.

Various proprietors, some of whom lived in apartments above their stores, appeared on the chaotic scene and attempted to defend their property. The Hitler Youth and Storm Troopers immediately set upon them, savagely beating them with their clubs. It made no difference to the attackers whether their victims were male or female. When a female owner of a women's clothing store attempted to save her establishment, she was thrown, screaming, to the ground and kicked viciously.

"I can't stand by and watch this brutality. I've got to jump in and do something," Nicholas said, stepping forward.

Frightened, Mary grabbed him by the arm and restrained him, pleading, "Don't leave me alone here, Nicholas!"

Instead of apprehending the woman's assailants, the police arrested the severely injured and bleeding woman and roughly shoved her into the police van while the Hitler Youth and Storm Trooper attackers stood around and laughed.

"It's too late to help her now," Nicholas said with resignation.

Mary tugged at Nicholas' sleeve and pleaded, "We've got to get out of here."

"The question is: where will we be safe?" he answered, glancing about. "Let me search around and try to find some way out of here."

Miraculously managing to escape the attention of the mob still at the opposite end of the long street, Nicholas' search for an escape route was hampered by darkness. Eventually, he managed to find a narrow service alley between two buildings which led to another similar street.

Taking Mary's hand, he guided her through the alley. At first, they did not realize that there was a synagogue on that street, but as they emerged from the alley, they saw three Hitler Youth members battering the ornately carved door of a Jewish temple with sledgehammers while other vandals smashed its beautiful stained glass windows.

In reaction to the assault on the house of worship, the synagogue's resident Rabbi, an elderly, gray-bearded gentleman, appeared from his home behind the temple, hoping to stop the desecration. The Rabbi was horrified to see that not only had the magnificent doors been reduced to splinters, but that the vandals had dashed inside and returned with books, a large menorah and other sacred objects which they threw into a pile and set ablaze with their torches. One of the vandals shouted in triumph as he tossed a scrolled Torah into the flames and gleefully watched it burn.

Horrified, the Rabbi shouted at them to stop but was ignored until he attempted to throw a bucket of water on the fire. At that point, the vandals began beating him with their clubs.

Hearing the ruckus and her husband's cries for help, the Rabbi's wife arrived on the scene in her nightgown. Screaming, she grabbed at the back of one of the hoodlum's shirts and tried to pull him away in an effort to thwart their attack on her husband.

Another Hitler Youth grabbed her, roughly threw the elderly woman down onto the street and ripped off her nightgown. Then, unbuttoning his pants, he prepared to rape her.

Shocked and outraged by this action, Mary, disregarding her own safety and her previous pleading, shoved Nicholas forward. "Help her!" she urged.

While Mary hid from the mob behind a thick cluster of shrubbery, Nicholas instantly dashed to the woman's aid.

Frozen with fear, Mary watched as he grabbed the would-be rapist and landed a powerful blow to his jaw which sent him reeling onto the stone steps of the synagogue.

Quickly surrounded by a group of Hitler Youth and Storm Troopers, Nicholas utilized his boxing skills to hold them off long enough for the woman in her tattered nightgown to scramble to her feet, grab her injured husband and drag him to the safety of their home.

From behind the shrubbery Mary realized that Nicholas was far outnumbered and bound to lose the fight against the Nazi hoodlums. Racing to his aid, she began wildly pummeling and kicking his assailants and shrieking, "Monsters! Disgusting monsters! All of you!"

At first they were amused and laughed mockingly at her efforts, but as she grew increasingly combative, a pair of Hitler Youth grabbed her arms in an attempt to restrain her.

Suddenly a shrill whistle sounded and a familiar voice shouted a stern order in German which resulted in the pair releasing her and the others abandoning their attack on Nicholas.

Whirling around to learn the source of the whistle and the command, Mary was stunned.

"Heinzi!" she gasped, then broke into sobs.

Chapter Twelve

A lone in her room at the von Rohrsbach home, Mary had changed into traveling clothes and was packing her trunk. Although the house was a considerable distance from the scene of the previous night's riots, black smoke from the many fires – some still burning -- filled the outside air and drifted into the house, causing her to cough.

Hearing a knock on the bedroom door, Mary was certain from the gentle nature of the knocking that it was not Heinzi, whom she had not seen since he brought her home during the early hours of the morning and presumably returned to his Hitler Youth unit to continue the rampage.

"Come in," she called out.

Anne entered and, obviously distressed, started at once to apologize. "I can't bear to have you leave without telling you how sorry Kurt and I are for the dreadful things that happened last night. It was disgraceful, terrible for everyone. Riots occurred, not just in Berlin but all over Germany – and Austria as well. We are deeply ashamed that our son participated in the melee. How can I ever apologize for what you and Lord Buckford suffered?"

"What Nicholas and I experienced last night was the most frightening and the most appalling episode of my life," Mary replied, folding one of the many articles of clothing she was packing. "He and I have decided to return to England as soon as possible,"

"How is Lord Buckford?"

"He's doing well despite his injuries. The deep gash in his scalp from one of the hoodlum's club required a great number of sutures," Mary said. "The scene at the hospital was chaotic, of course. So many people were viciously attacked and seriously injured in the riots. Nicholas was given priority because he was a foreigner, probably to save this country embarrassment. Heinzi offered to wait at the hospital until the doctors had finished treating him and take him back to his hotel, but Nicholas refused. He wants nothing more to do with your son."

"And you, Mary? What are your feelings toward my son?"

Mary stopped her packing for a moment and contemplated Anne's question. "Quite frankly, my feelings are rather confused at this time," she said. "Heinzi did commandeer a motorcycle with a side-car from one of the Storm Troopers in which he transported Nicholas and myself to the hospital. I must say it was quite a ride – a bit crowded with both Nicholas and myself crammed into that little side-car and the cold night air rushing past us. Afterward, Heinzi brought me back here in it, as you know. At the hospital, Nicholas assured me that he was quite capable of returning to his hotel on his own."

"I'm pleased that my son had your welfare at heart in spite of the distressing activities of that despicable Hitler Youth group he insists on being a part of," Anne commented, with a sigh of despair.

"If Heinzi hadn't appropriated that motorcycle and rushed Nicholas to the hospital, he might have bled to death from his head wound." Mary paused for a moment and then with a shudder added, "I dread to think what would have happened to me if Heinzi hadn't come along when he did."

Anne went over to the bed and examined Mary's white satin gown. It was now ragged, filthy and stained with blood. She shook her head sadly.

"I had to rip a piece from it to use as a bandage for Nicholas' head wound," Mary said. "I'm afraid it's ruined."

"The important thing is that you and Nicholas are safe," Anne said.

"Actually I think those cohorts of Heinzi's who set upon Nicholas got the worst of it before one of them struck him on the head from behind," Mary mused.

"Neither Kurt nor I can comprehend Heinzi's devotion to that awful Hitler Youth organization," Anne said. "As a boy he was never like they are. In fact, he was more often the victim at school rather than the perpetrator. This change in him greatly distresses his father and myself, as you've probably noticed during your brief stay here."

"Yes, I have noticed."

Anne continued to vent her frustration. "We seem to have lost all control of him. Since he began associating with those Hitler Youth hooligans, he's lost his sense of decency. Those damnable Nazis have robbed us of our son."

Moved by Anne's utter despair and helplessness with regard to her son, Mary put her arm around the older woman to try and console her.

On the verge of tears, Anne said, "Well, I'd better go downstairs and let you attend to your packing," and left the room.

Later in the day, as Mary was on the staircase going downstairs for lunch with Anne, she nearly collided with Heinzi. He was still wearing his Hitler Youth uniform which was now in a state similar to the gown Mary had worn the previous evening: torn, dirty and blood-stained. Startled by this unexpected encounter, she lowered her eyes to avoid contact with his and tried to side-step away from him.

Heinzi grabbed her by the arm. "Where are you going?" he demanded.

Forced to look at him, Mary noticed that his eyes were red and blood-shot and his breath smelled of stale beer.

"Downstairs," she answered. "To have lunch with your mother."

"I heard you're leaving."

"I am."

Heinzi sneered. "Running away, are you?"

"No." Her blue eyes blazing with anger, she snapped, "I'm not at all frightened by you and your bully-boy friends, but I am disgusted. The things you and your cohorts did last night were appalling. You're all nothing but horrible, stupid, ignorant monsters! Now let go of my arm."

"What you fail to realize, dear little English cousin Mary, is that one day soon the Third Reich will triumphantly rule the entire world. Nothing will stand in our way – not even your beloved Britain," he declared, his speech slurred.

"You and your bully-boys are vile beasts," Mary declared. "All of you should be arrested and jailed for the havoc you created last night. The inaction of the police was outrageous and disgraceful."

"Our police understand that enemies of the Third Reich must be eliminated," Heinzi shot back.

"Your police are corrupt cowards."

Swaying from side to side, Heinzi grinned as he reached out and attempted to caress Mary's cheek, moving his face close to hers.

She shoved him away and glared at him in disgust.

"What's the matter, Mary? Don't you like me anymore?" he cajoled.

"I can never forgive you for your participation in the events which transpired last night, even if you were decent enough to commandeer that motorcycle in order to take Nicholas to the hospital and bring me back here." Mary paused for a moment in her tirade and, with a calmer tone, added, "Nevertheless, whatever friendship we may have enjoyed in the past is now destroyed. Gone forever."

Chapter Thirteen

Once again back at Stagsbridge, Mary watched the return of the fox hunters in their bright red jackets followed by a pack of yelping and excited hounds from her bedroom window. Nostalgically, she recalled the hunts in which she had participated with her beloved Blue Bonnet. An unusual winter-like storm had left patches of snow scattered about on the limbs of the leafless trees and on the fields. Although the calendar decreed that it was still fall, the air had a wintry chill. Still recovering from her traumatic trip to Germany, Mary had no desire to join the hunters, especially not without Blue Bonnet.

Among the hunters she could make out her mother, father and sister Lucy. Charles was still considered too young to take part in a fox hunt and, much to his dislike, was forced to remain in the house with Mary and the servants. Celia had seen no reason to remain in London while Mary was in Germany and preparations for her debut were temporarily suspended.

On this occasion none of the Buckfords were included among the hunters. Simon was busy with the activities of parliament, and Antonia was not a dedicated horsewoman as the Ashmore women were. Andrew was in pilot training with the RAF, and Nicholas was still recovering from the head wound he had suffered in Berlin.

Jane Knightsgate and her parents were present for the hunt, and this time they were accompanied by Jane's older brother Trevor, briefly home from Oxford especially for this hunt. Also included were those residents of the county who were sufficiently affluent to own horses, such as the Dangerfields, the Davises and the Lymes.

At the conclusion of the hunt, the fox hunters eventually gathered in the area of the stable block where they were attended by the Ashmore grooms and stable-boys who aided them to dismount and took charge of their horses. Footmen circulated among them with trays of brandy and mulled wine.

Much to Mary's great surprise, she observed Nicholas, astride his favorite black stallion and wearing country tweeds rather than the traditional foxhunting outfit, a short distance away, crossing a vast meadow en route to Stagsbridge. She found it odd that he was leading a riderless chestnut mare but gave it little thought, assuming it was a brood mare he was considering breeding with one of the Ashmore stallions.

When Nicholas reached Stagsbridge, the hunters parted to allow him to reach Arthur and Celia. To whom he tipped his cap in greeting. Although it had been several weeks since he had been attacked by the Hitler Youth in Berlin, Mary could see from her window that his head still bandaged.

"Good morning, Lady Ashmore, Lord Ashmore," he said as he dismounted, retaining the reins of both horses.

"Hello there, Nicholas," Arthur responded, signaling a footman to offer the young man a drink from his tray.

Smiling, Celia responded, "It's good to see you up and about, Nicholas."

"It's good to be up and about," Nicholas replied.

Lucy, who had been chatting with Jane and Trevor, immediately left them and hurried to her parents' side to greet him.

"Hello, Nicholas," she said with a delighted smile.

"Well, Lady Lucy," Nicholas said. "I see you're becoming quite the horsewoman, like your sister Mary. I saw you hurtling over fences and hedgerows as I was riding over from Lammersley."

"How did I do?" Lucy asked anxiously.

"Splendidly," Nicholas complimented her.

Lucy responded to his compliment with another delighted smile. "I hope someday to be as accomplished a rider as my sister, perhaps even better."

Nicholas chuckled. "Well, keep at it," he encouraged.

"I know that my husband has already expressed his gratitude to you for looking after Mary during those awful riots in Berlin. I dread to think what might have happened to her if you had not been present to protect her," Celia said.

"I think it might be more correctly said that it was Mary who protected me," Nicholas replied.

"Come now, my boy, you're being modest," Arthur chided.

"If you want to know the truth, sir, it was actually that boorish Heinzi who saved us both – no offense to you."

"No offense taken. That young chap is causing his parents a great deal of distress by associating himself with those Nazis." Arthur said..

"More than simply 'associating'," Nicholas corrected. "Heinzi has actually become a member of the Hitler Youth and a staunch one."

"How dreadful! Poor Anne," Celia said, sadly shaking her head. "In her recent letters, Anne mentioned that Karl-Heinrich – 'Heinzi', as you call him – has become quite difficult."

"He sounds perfectly awful," Lucy remarked.

"I think the only reason Heinzi came to our aid is because he's a bit keen on Mary," Nicholas speculated.

"Well, I can assure you of one thing: Mary will most definitely not be returning to Germany," Arthur declared. "At least not as long as the Nazis are in power."

Nicholas surveyed the gathering of hunters. "Speaking of Mary, where is she?" he asked. "I don't see her. In the past, I've never known her to miss a fox hunt."

"Mary's been staying in her room most of the time since she's returned," Lucy piped up.

"She's still quite shaken by what happened in Berlin and needs time to recover," Celia explained.

"I'm not at all surprised," Nicholas said. "Mary suffered an experience no one should have to experience."

"After the awful things that happened, will you be returning to Germany, Nicholas?" Lucy asked anxiously.

"Unfortunately, I must," he replied. "I still have business obligations there."

Arthur frowned, indicating that he did not approve of Nicholas engaging in business dealings with the Germans. "The *London Times* reported that ninety people were killed during the riots there and thirty-three others were arrested," he said, adding, "And those arrested were the victims and not the perpetrators."

"Yes, most of them were Jewish," Mary heard Nicholas explain. "The police did nothing to try and stop the hooligans." Then realizing that the conversation had taken too serious a turn for something as festive as a fox hunt, he decided to switch topics. Gesturing toward the chestnut mare whose reins he was still holding, he asked, "Do you think I might possibly have a word with Mary?"

For the first time since she had been observing the scene beneath her window, Mary felt a desire to join the group.

"I don't think Mary is keen on talking to anyone," Lucy said. "She barely spoke to Jane, and Jane is her best friend."

"I think it would be good for Mary to talk to Nicholas," Celia said and summoned Dunsmuir who was busy supervising the footmen and the staff from the Ashmore stable.

"Yes, my lady?" the butler asked.

"Please inform Lady Mary that Lord Nicholas would like a word with her?"

"Certainly, ma'am," Dunsmuir said and proceeded into the house.

Arthur and Celia invited the hunters to join them in the Hunt Room of the manor house, and all accepted, although Lucy moved inside with the others only when ordered to do so by her parents. It was obvious that she would have preferred to remain outside with Nicholas and the two horses.

A few minutes later, Nicholas broke into a broad smile as Mary emerged through the front door.

"You're looking well," he said.

"Thank you. You are also looking quite well," she replied. "How are your injuries coming along?'

"Quite nicely, actually."

"I'm so glad," she said, captivated by the chestnut mare whose reins he was holding. "What a beautiful horse! She reminds me a little of Blue Bonnet. Is she yours?"

"No," he replied, adding, "But she can be yours, if you will accept her."

Mary was puzzled. "Mine? What on earth are you talking about?"

"I'm giving her to you as a gift to make up for what happened to Blue Bonnet," he said.

"You can't be serious?"

"I am."

Mary reached out and began to stroke the horse. "I love her!"

Pleased by Mary's reaction, he said, "I must admit that she is a fine filly."

"She is indeed!"

"Then, you'll accept her?"

"Don't be foolish," Mary laughed – the first time since returning from Berlin. "Of course I will!" She rushed up to Nicholas and threw her arms around him, giving him a hug which nearly knocked him off his feet.

Nicholas grinned and signaled a stable-boy to come and find a stall for the horse in the Ashmore stables. His black stallion whinnied as the mare was led away.

"You must go inside and join the others, even if you didn't take part in the hunt," Mary urged. "I'll have one of the stableboys take care of your horse."

"No, thank you. I have business at home to which I must attend."

"Is your business with Herr Reisner?" Mary asked.

"As a matter of fact it is," he answered.

"How can you continue to do business with the Germans after what we experienced?" Mary's tone was reproachful.

Nicholas shrugged. "Business is business and, besides, Herr Reisner is no Nazi. He just follows the money – so to speak," he replied, placing his booted foot in the stallion's stirrup. Throwing his other leg across the horse's back, he eased himself into the saddle. Turning the stallion in the direction of Lammersley, he waved goodbye to Mary and rode off.

~

Feeling exhilarated by the gift of such a beautiful horse and remembering what Radu had told her about the Nazis slaughtering horses to provide food for their troops, Mary vowed to herself, *Only over my dead body will any horse of mine be eaten.* She decided to join her parents and their guests.

The walls of the Stagsbridge Hunt Room were decorated with ribbons, photographs and trophies, some of which had been awarded to Mary for her riding skills. Footmen circulated about the room with trays of hors d'oeuvres and drinks, and a cheerful fire was burning in the large stone fireplace.

Mary gravitated toward the younger group which included Jane, Trevor and Lucy.

"How were Lady Cargill's classes during my absence?" she asked Jane.

"As always, they were a terrible bore," Jane replied, rolling her eyes. "You know, the usual drills: how to properly curtsy without falling flat on your face or a discussion of topics suitable for dinner table conversation."

"I hear there is a girl from South Africa who's here in England to do the Season this year with you and Jane," Trevor said to Mary. "It's rumored around London that she's simply loaded with diamonds at every occasion."

"I wouldn't know," Mary replied. "I've been away."

"My brother is referring to Darlene van der Voordt," Jane said. "She's one of those dreadful girls from the colonies who are so ostentatious with their jewelry and their gowns."

"And their motorcars, as well," Trevor added.

"Some even bring a houseful of servants with them," Jane continued.

"How vulgar," Lucy remarked.

"Darlene's been quite popular with the chaps at Oxford," Trevor said.

"Well, bully for her," Lucy quipped.

Jane turned to Lucy. "Just think, my dear, next year you will be reveling in the Season as your sister and I are currently."

"That is, if there is a Season next year, " Trevor remarked.

"What do you mean?" Lucy asked.

"I'm talking about the possibility war," Trevor answered.

"Oh, Mr. Chamberlain will keep us out of it," Jane said.

"I'm not so sure," Mary said, recalling her afternoon at the Tiergarten rally.

A few moments later, the unexpected appearance of Andrew, impressive in his RAF uniform, startled everyone. Glancing around the room, he headed straight for Mary without stopping to acknowledge Arthur and Celia or any of the other guests, a social *faux pas* he ordinarily would not have done.

Jane, Lucy and Trevor greeted Andrew to which he responded with only a cursory nod of his head, immediately focusing his attention on Mary.

"I must speak to you alone," he said, his expression intense. "Privately."

"All right," she agreed, struggling to control the excitement she felt at his presence. She realized that the attraction he held for her had not dimmed in the slightest in spite of all she had recently experienced.

Scanning the room, she decided that the most private place for them was outside on the terrace, and they left the Hunt Room through a pair of French doors..

Outside, he began, "First of all, I must know how Ruth is. I'm desperate for news of her." His voice was filled with urgency "Those Nazis must be making her life an absolute hell."

The intensity of his questioning rendered Mary uneasy, reminding her that she was obliged to confess to him what she had done. "There's something I must tell you – something very difficult."

Andrew frowned. "What?"

Mary hesitated. "I don't quite know how to tell you."

Filled with anxiety, Andrew reached out and, taking hold of both her arms, shook her. "What is it?" he demanded. "Tell me!"

Mary stammered, "I...I never gave the papers to Ruth."

Andrew's hazel eyes blazed with anger. "You what?!"

"I lost the papers when I was aboard the ferry crossing the Channel."

Andrew shook her again, even harder this time. "You 'lost' the papers?! I don't understand. How is that possible?"

Lowering her eyes to avoid his furious gaze, she confessed, "I tore them up aboard the ferry and threw the pieces into the sea."

Andrew stared at her in disbelief. "How could you do such a despicable thing?"

"I suppose I did it out of ... "

"Out of what?"

"Jealousy," Mary blurted.

Andrew's fair complexion turned crimson with anger. "'Jealousy'?" he repeated, stunned.

"I was jealous of Ruth and your affection for her," Mary said, starting to break down. "It all seems so petty now that I've witnessed the oppressive conditions under which Ruth is currently forced to live. I'm appalled by what I did and deeply ashamed." On the verge of tears, she continued, "It was monstrous, absolutely wicked of me. For days I've been dreading the moment when I would have to tell you. I wish there were some way in which I could make amends – something I could do to change things. Anything. You must believe me when I say that I am truly sorry."

As the emotions of both Andrew and Mary escalated, their voices, but not their actual words, rose and were audible on the other side of the French doors. Those who heard them grew curious and concerned about the nature of their encounter, especially Celia and Arthur.

"You're 'sorry'?!" Andrew exploded. "Do you even have – in that childish, addled brain of yours -- the slightest inkling of the danger Ruth is in if she remains in Germany? The Nazis are transporting hundreds of Jews to their so-called labor camps every day where they'll undoubtedly perish. Ruth has no idea when they will come for her and her father. It could be any day now." He shook his head in disgust. "My God, Mary, how could you do such a thing?"

Now weeping, Mary, unable to respond, hung her head.

With a final look of scorn, Andrew stormed off the terrace and back inside to the Hunt Room, once more ignoring Lord and Lady Ashmore and their guests as he headed straight for the door.

Those present regarded the normally calm and courteous young man curiously, never having witnessed Andrew in such an agitated state before. Although they did not know what was behind the heated exchange on the terrace, its confrontational nature had not escaped their attention.

After a momentary silence, an undertone of shocked chatter filled the room. The guests were equally stunned and appalled by Andrew's behavior and treatment of Mary.

Mary, stricken with shame and guilt, fled from the terrace to the familiar refuge of her bedroom.

Chapter Fourteen

During the days that followed, Arthur urged Celia to try to elicit from Mary what had transpired between her and Andrew that once again had resulted in her confining herself to her room for much of the day, usually going out only to exercise her new horse.

"I've never seen Andrew so angry before," Arthur remarked. "That's not at all like him. He's always been even tempered in the past. Andrew and Mary have always gotten on very well."

"I suppose that German tutor we hired may have had something to do with it," Celia said.

Arthur was puzzled. "What do you mean?"

"It seems that Andrew was seriously smitten with the young woman."

Arthur raised his eyebrows in surprise. "Really?"

"Oh, yes," Celia assured her husband. "Antonia was quite disturbed by the situation."

"Well, the girl is gone now – back to Germany, I understand – so that's that as far as Andrew is concerned," he said, swiping his hands together.

"So it would seem," Celia said, her tone uncertain.

Later that day, Celia charged into Mary's room, followed by one of the maids struggling under an armload of dresses designed and sewn by Mrs. Kazanjian for her debutante Season. She directed the maid to spread the garments out on the bed and then leave the room.

"I want you to try them on," she said.

"I really don't feel up to it, Mother," Mary replied, without so much as a glance at the clothes. She was at the window, gazing wistfully at the vast Stagsbridge acreage and the small river which separated it from Lammersley.

"You'll do it now," Celia ordered, her voice stern. "The Season will be upon us before you know it. You've got to prepare a suitable wardrobe for the many social engagements it's going to entail."

Reluctantly, Mary tried on one dress after another without enthusiasm under the scrutiny of Celia's critical eye. How her daughters were attired was of crucial importance to her.

Attempting to sound as casual as possible as Mary modeled one of the dresses, Celia asked, "What happened between you and Andrew out on the Hunt Room terrace? You and he have always gotten on so well in the past."

"Nothing, Mother," Mary answered. She was still too disturbed by the confrontation with Andrew to discuss the matter. "It was just a misunderstanding."

"Well, I hope it's resolved before the Season begins. You'll need him as an escort for the various balls and social engagements. You know how much your father and I have always admired him, and he looks splendid in his uniform. I do hope that his RAF duties don't interfere too much with your activities.." Celia circled around Mary inspecting the dress from every angle. "Of course, there's always Nicholas. He did give you that lovely new mare which was very kind of him." Celia knew that any mention of the new horse would raise Mary's spirits and hoped that it would make her daughter open up more.

"Yes, it was," Mary agreed.

"Have you named her yet?"

"One of the stable-boys suggested the name 'Sable' because of her beautiful burnished shade of brown," Mary replied. "I think I'm going to call her that."

"Speaking of Nicholas, I wish we could find out why he is spending so much time lately in Suffolk lately. I had hoped to learn the answer from Antonia, but she insists that she hasn't a clue. I don't believe her, of course. I suspect that Nicholas may be involved with an unsuitable young lady that she's not comfortable talking about."

"It's possible," Mary said, slipping out of the dress and moving on to the next one laid out on the bed. "I have no idea."

"And all this fund-raising Nicholas has been doing for some business venture he's engaged in. I must say, he has been rather secretive about it. It has required numerous trips to Germany recently on his part. What has he disclosed about it to you?"

"Very little," Mary replied, buttoning the front of a silk floral print frock. "Just that he's selling scrap metal to the Germans so they can enlarge their air force."

"Not a very admirable enterprise for him to be engaged in, given the tense nature of relations between Britain and Germany at this time," Celia said, squinting to appraise the garment. "Turn around so I can see how that dress looks from the back."

As she spun around, Mary commented, "I doubt that Nicholas is very concerned about being 'admirable'."

Later that day, astride Sable, Mary headed for Lammersley, jumping several fences en route to test the horse's ability to hurdle, and was pleased that the mare executed the jumps well.

At the sprawling estate, she turned the horse over to one of the Lammersley grooms and proceeded into the manor house to visit Antonia and learned from the butler that she was confined to bed. The butler sent a footman with Mary's calling card to his mistress. The footman returned in a few minutes, saying that Lady Buckford would receive Mary in her rooms.

Antonia was resting against a pile of pillows in a huge canopied bed. She appeared pale, her face and hands puffy as if slightly swollen, and she seemed to be experiencing some degree of difficulty breathing. Her nightstand was crowded with a profusion of medications, and a uniformed nurse sat in a chair at her bedside knitting.

"Good afternoon, Lady Antonia," Mary said. "How are you feeling?"

Antonia mustered a wan smile. "How nice of you to visit, Mary. I'm feeling a bit better."

"That's good," Mary said. "I rode my new horse that Nicholas gave me over here today."

"Oh? How do you like her?"

"I like her very much. She's a splendid jumper. I'm grateful to Nicholas for such a fine gift."

Antonia sighed. "Nicholas is in Suffolk again today. He hardly spends any time at all at Lammersley any more – always off to Suffolk or London or the continent. I see very little of my sons these days. Nicholas traveling about all the time and Andrew with the RAF. Lord Simon is frightfully busy at parliament with all that saber-rattling on the part of Germany. I find myself feeling a bit lonely at times."

"I'm sure you'll be up and about quite soon, Lady Antonia."

Addressing the nurse, Antonia said, "Would you leave Lady Mary and myself alone for a few minutes?"

The nurse gathered her knitting together and prepared to depart from the room.

"Don't you be staying too long, Miss," the nurse cautioned, wagging her finger at Mary. "You mustn't tire her ladyship too much."

When she was gone, Antonia remarked, "What a tiresome woman, although I suppose she means well."

"One would hope," Mary said, wondering why the older woman had asked the nurse to leave.

"I must tell you, I had a terrible shock," Antonia said with a shudder.

Mary was puzzled. "What sort of a shock?"

"Severe enough to confine me to bed," the older woman answered. "Andrew telephoned me from the British embassy in Berlin. He went there straightaway after he left you the day of your parents' fox hunt."

Attempting to sound as casual as possible, Mary asked, "What was Andrew doing in Berlin?"

"He's arranging to be married."

Stunned, Mary gasped. "'Married'?"

"Yes, to that young German woman Fraulein Herzog who was your tutor," Antonia replied. "It seems that Nicholas has a German acquaintance with connections in high places who is going to help Andrew accomplish this."

Incredulous, Mary repeated, "Andrew?! Marrying Ruth?!"

Antonia reached over the side of the bed and clasped Mary's hand. "I know what a blow this must be for you, my dear. You've always been so fond of Andrew."

Mary felt free to admit, "Yes, I have."

"Nothing would have pleased me more than to have welcomed you to Lammersley as Andrew's bride. Your mother and I have always favored a match between you and my elder son. I would never have imagined this unfortunate turn of events in my wildest dreams."

"Nor I," Mary murmured.

Leaving Lady Antonia, Mary, sobbing, spurred Sable into a gallop down Lammersley's entrance road.

Married! How could he? she kept repeating to herself.

As horse and rider reached the end of the road they nearly collided with the turquoise Delahaye 135 MS driven by Nicholas, a long plaid woolen scarf around his neck for warmth in the open car. He was forced to slam on the breaks and blast the horn.

"What the hell are you doing?" he shouted at her.

Not wanting to reveal to Nicholas that she had been crying, Mary wiped her tears on the sleeve of her jacket and hoped that he wouldn't notice her reddened eyes and nose. She halted her horse at the side of the open automobile.

"I suppose you've heard the news about my brother?" he asked.

"I have," she replied.

"Well, what do you think?"

"I can't believe it – Andrew actually marrying Ruth?"

"Poor Mother has taken to her bed over it," he remarked. "It was quite a shock for the old girl."

"And for me as well," Mary said. "I just visited with your mother. She said you helped Andrew arrange for the wedding."

"I did," he admitted. "I enlisted Herr Reisner's help."

"How could you do this to your mother and your family?" Mary demanded.

"Don't you mean, how could I do this to you?" Nicholas countered.

Mary declined to respond.

"I did it for Andrew," Nicholas continued. "For the first time in his life my brother has acted according to his own desires and ignored stuffy British conventions. Frankly, I'm proud of him. I applaud his marrying a woman of the Jewish faith. After all, they are a people of extraordinary accomplishments in every field of human endeavor. You've got to give them credit. I would be the last to stand in Andrew's way."

Mary sniffled, and Nicholas extracted a handkerchief from the pocket of his jacket and passed it to her from the car.

"Stop crying, Mary," he snapped. "You're no fool. You know damned well how much he cared for Ruth. Despite the differences of nationality and religion, they have quite a bit in common as well."

"I knew that Andrew was fond of Ruth and that he wanted to help her escape from Germany, but I never expected him to marry her," Mary said.

With a wry smile, Nicholas responded, "You hoped he would marry you."

Hesitating a moment, Mary confessed, "Yes, I did."

"Well, it's not going to happen now," Nicholas called to her callously as he resumed his drive toward the Lammersley manor house.

Chapter Fifteen

At Nicholas' urgent request, Herman Reisner was able to smuggle a message to Ruth letting her know that he was Nicholas' business associate and asked her to meet him at a certain outdoor stall selling potatoes and cabbage at Hackesche Markt in central Berlin. He knew that her predominately Jewish neighborhood was under Gestapo surveillance, and it would be too risky for someone in his position to go to her apartment in his recognizable Grosser Mercedes 770. The car was similar to one of Hitler's own personal models and, indeed, had been a gift from the Fuhrer.

To appear inconspicuous, Reisner traded his impeccably tailored suits for a shabby overcoat over old clothes for his encounter with Ruth.

Nervous, she eventually appeared at the potato and cabbage stand carrying a potted poinsettia as he had specified so that he would be able to recognize her since they had never met. All communications between them had been through one of Ruth's former – and very loyal – university students whose name had been given to him by Andrew.

As planned, he started the conversation with her by admiring the red-leafed plant and asking politely if she had recently visited Austria. She answered, as arranged, that she had just come from Salzburg. Following that opening, several other identifying code words were exchanged after which both Reisner and Ruth relaxed.

"Walk with me to my car," he said to her quietly. "It's parked in a nearby alley with very little foot traffic or cars. I will open the trunk and you will get in quickly."

Ruth glanced at him dubiously.

"Don't worry," he assured her. "It's sufficiently roomy and you'll only be in there a short time."

Still uneasy, Ruth asked, "Where are we going?"

"To the British Embassy. There, you and Lord Ashmore will be married as planned. He's flying in today from England in a small private plane and landing at a small airfield outside Berlin which I frequently use for my business. I had my wife purchase a very nice dress for you to wear at your wedding. It's already at the embassy. She guessed what size you might require from Andrew's description of you. You can change there prior to the ceremony." Pointing to the poinsettia, he added with a chuckle, "You already have your bridal bouquet."

Checking out the alley in both directions to be sure no one was lurking in the area, Reisner unlocked the trunk and motioned for Ruth to get in.

Although apprehensive and somewhat hesitant at first, she did as he directed, and Reisner closed the trunk.

His car and person were well-known to the guards at the British embassy, and, thus, Reisner was waved into the building's interior garage where, once it was parked, it would be safely concealed. Opening the trunk, he let Ruth out and then escorted her to the ambassador's private office where Andrew, in civilian clothes, was already waiting.

Seeing him, Ruth flew into his welcoming arms.

"Andrew! *Ach, mein* Andrew! I can't believe you're here – that this is really happening! It's like a *wunder!*" she cried, lapsing into German, which she rarely did, in her excitement. "A miracle!" Tears of joy began to well up in her dark eyes.

"I can't either," he said, struggling not to join his bride-to-be in tears. "I've been dreaming of this day."

Folding her into his embrace, he noticed how much thinner and frail she had become, but said nothing.

Through his father's connections as a member of parliament, Andrew had arranged for the ambassador himself to perform the ceremony.

In a small apartment reserved for the embassy's V.I.P. Guests, the ambassador's secretary helped Ruth change into her wedding dress, added a few touches of make-up to her face and styled her hair.

The ceremony got underway almost immediately and concluded with Andrew slipping a gold ring on his bride's finger and she a similar ring – also supplied by the groom – on his, as the ambassador declared them man and wife.

Afterward, the same secretary had also prepared a small, quiet reception for the newlyweds in the office which included not only the bride and groom and Reisner, but most of the embassy staff as well, some of whom were acquainted with M.P. Buckford and his wife. Little did they suspect that Lady Antonia would not share their joy at such a wedding.

Taking Andrew and Ruth aside, the ambassador advised, "It would be prudent for you to wait until the early hours of the morning when it's still dark before you set out to the airfield for your flight back to England. Security is more lax during that period. In the meantime, there is the small apartment which we reserve for certain VIP guests. My secretary tells me that you are already acquainted with it, are you not, Ruth? – or should I now address you as Lady Buckford?"

"I am," Ruth said.

Andrew and Ruth exchanged happy smiles.

"That's most kind of you, sir," Andrew said.

"I must, however, warn you that this marriage is in violation of the laws recently enacted at Nuremberg which forbids the union of a Christian with a Jew. The punishment is severe. Once the two of you leave this embassy you will be on German soil and subject to arrest by the Gestapo," the ambassador warned them. "I have performed this ceremony in defiance of German law to facilitate your bride's entrance into Britain."

As Andrew and Ruth proceeded toward the embassy apartment, Andrew addressed Reisner, "I flew here in a two-seater plane in which Ruth and I will fly back to Britain. You've been more than kind to us so far, but I feel it's an imposition to ask you to get out of bed in the middle of the night to drive us to the airfield, but even more importantly, as a high-ranking German citizen, you'll also be taking yet another enormous risk for us."

"Your brother has taken many risks for me in the past, albeit not of the same kind, but risks nevertheless. In addition, he has been providing me with the raw material from which German aircraft are manufactured. That connection with him has rewarded me enormously, including many special privileges. On the other hand, the Nazis need me and my connections," Reisner answered. "Therefore, I am willing to help you in any way I can."

In the bedroom of the embassy apartment, Ruth turned down the silk sheets of the double bed.

"I must ask you to turn out the light before I undress, she said quietly. She was still wearing the borrowed bridal gown.

Baffled, Andrew asked, "Why?"

"There has been very little food for us lately, and I am now very thin. My ribs are quite visible. My body has changed greatly since I returned to Germany. I am not the same as you may remember."

"My God, Ruth, I don't care," Andrew said as he once more gathered her into his arms.

Relieved, Ruth smiled again and allowed him to carefully remove the wedding dress.

Naked, she slipped between the sheets into bed, pulling them up to her chin, and waited while Andrew removed his own clothing.

"I feel sorry I have no lovely negligee for my wedding night," she said.

Now also naked, he prepared to crawl into bed beside her. "And I have no pajamas," he said with a laugh. "But, hell, both negligee and pajamas would be discarded in a moment anyway."

"Do you think so?"

"Absolutely," he answered as he reached for her and drew her close, pressing his eager body against her equally eager body, preparing for their first love-making.

"I've dreamed of this moment for a long time, dearest," Andrew whispered, planting a string of kisses along her neck.

"Ja, ich auch," Ruth answered softly – and unexpectedly – in German.

"What?" Andrew asked, surprised.

"Me, too," she replied, then lapsing into German again, added, *"Ich liebe dich, Andreas."*

This time he did not need a translation. "I love you, too, Ruth. I always will no matter what happens. I promise."

⁂

As planned, Reisner returned to the embassy for Andrew and Ruth in the middle of the night.

"You'll have to lie on the floor of the car on the drive to the airfield. You'll be covered with a blanket, of course, so you will not be cold. Near the airfield, however, you will have to return to the trunk temporarily as before. At the guard shack, the guards on duty will search the interior of the car before they allow us to proceed inside, so it's necessary," the German businessman explained.

Grateful to escape, Ruth agreed. "I understand."

Worried, Andrew asked, "What if they search the trunk?"

"They never have in previous trips," Reisner assured him."I seriously doubt that they would this time."

A host of emotions overwhelmed Ruth – the joy of leaving Germany with the love of her life, the fear of getting caught, the fear of what leaving her father behind may mean and the terrifying dread that she may never see him again.

Turning to Andrew, she pleaded, "Promise me that we will do everything in our power to bring my father to England."

"There is nothing I won't do for you, Ruth," he replied without hesitation.

⁂

A high fence topped by barbed wire surrounded the airfield on the outskirts of Berlin. As Reisner's Grosser-Mercedes 770 approached the guard station at the entrance, an armed sentry stepped outside and stood before the automobile, forcing it to stop. The youthful guard demanded to see Reisner's and Andrew's official documents which they readily produced. He sneered as he examined Andrew's passport and contemptuously muttered, "English." After sweeping his bright flashlight around the interior of the vehicle, he ordered Reisner to open the trunk.

In German, Reisner informed him that he could not comply because he had lost the key to it.

The young sentry summoned his superior from the guard shack and relayed Reisner's excuse for refusing to open the trunk of the automobile.

Continuing in German, the superior demanded, "What is the meaning of your refusal to obey orders?"

"Do you not know who I am?" Reisner questioned indignantly. "I have made many trips to this facility."

The superior stared closely at Reisner. Suddenly recognizing him, he apologized. "Sorry, Herr Reisner."

"Apology accepted," Reisner replied.

"But who is this other gentleman with you?" the superior persisted.

"This gentleman happens to be a major supplier of metal to the Third Reich," Reisner said. "We have just had an important meeting which lasted late into the night and now he must return to Britain."

The officer raised his eyebrows. "He is a British subject?"

"He is," Reisner affirmed. Then turning to Andrew said, "Show the officer your passport, Lord Buckford."

Andrew did as requested.

The superior merely glanced at it and handed it back almost immediately. Reisner's influence became suddenly apparent to Andrew, and he was grateful that they had become friends and not just business acquaintances.

As the superior waved them on, Andrew could hear him chastising the young sentry for hassling one of the Third Reich's most important supporters.

Reisner drove through the gate, across the vast air field with its network of runways and ended up at Andrew's plane.

As he climbed out of the car, Andrew informed Reisner, "I am required to inspect the plane before take-off – international aviation rules. It won't take long." Then, looking around and seeing no one in the early morning darkness, he added, "Do you reckon that it would be safe to let Ruth out now?"

"No, we can't take that chance until you finish your inspection, but I will open the trunk a little so she can get some fresh air."

While Andrew climbed about the plane to perform the routine inspection, Reisner got out of the car, unlocked the trunk and raised the lid a few inches so that Ruth could take a deep breath.

"*Vielen dank,*" she whispered.

Quickly completing the inspection, Andrew eased into the cockpit, strapped himself in the pilot's seat and started the plane's single engine.

Just as Reisner was about to help Ruth out of the trunk, a vehicle with a pair of Gestapo agents suddenly drove up in the darkness at top speed and screeched to a halt beside Andrew's plane. A beefy Gestapo agent with a clipboard in hand jumped out while a second agent remained in the vehicle. Reisner shoved Ruth's head down and quickly closed and locked the lid of the trunk. He was worried that they might have seen him at the rear of the automobile talking with Ruth through a pair of binoculars specially adapted for night vision..

The Gestapo agent glanced at his clipboard and then addressed Andrew, seated in the cockpit of the plane, in English.

"You are Captain Buckford, are you not?"

"I am," Andrew responded, struggling to maintain his calm while his heart was pounding.

"Were there any problems in your inspection, Captain?"

"No, officer, all seems to be in order."

"You have been cleared for take-off and your fifteen minute window is about to expire. As a member of the British military, I suggest that you depart at once in order to avoid an incident," the agent said.

Hoping that, if they could stall for time, the Gestapo would leave and allow him to safely transfer Ruth aboard the plane, Reisner spoke up in German.

"Captain Ashmore has some doubt about the plane's engine, but being proud of the British aircraft, he is reluctant to mention it to you," he said.

Surprised by such a statement, the Gestapo agent scowled and remarked, "*Wirklich?*"

"Yes, really," Reisner assured him. "Perhaps it might be wise for Captain Buckford to make a second inspection of this plane to be sure it can make it safely back to Britain."

Unlike the earlier encounter at the sentry post, the Gestapo agent eyed Reisner suspiciously. "Is this your car, sir?" he asked, continuing his questioning in English, obviously for Andrew's benefit.

"It is," Reisner affirmed. "A gift from the Fuhrer."

Undeterred, the Gestapo agent ordered, "Open the trunk."

"I can't. I have lost the key," Reisner said.

The agent turned to his subordinate, still seated in their vehicle, and ordered in German: "Get a crowbar."

Feigning outrage, Reisner said, "You're not going to pry my trunk open and damage this fine automobile, which I just pointed out, was given to me by the Fuhrer himself in recognition of the extraordinary service I have performed for the Third Reich. He would not be pleased if word reached him that it was damaged."

The Gestapo agent's subordinate whispered something to him, and he consulted his clipboard, then asked, "Are you Herr Reisner of the Air Ministry?"

"I am," Reisner replied proudly.

The agent addressed Andrew in the cockpit. "You are fortunate to have such a friend as Herr Reisner, Captain," he said.

"I'm well aware of that, sir," Andrew replied.

Then, looking at his watch, the Gestapo agent announced, "You have exactly three minutes remaining."

Reisner urged, "I must advise you, Captain Buckford, to take advantage of this rare opportunity. It is not easy to get permission for a foreign aircraft to depart from German air space these days. I shall take care of any unfinished business we have."

Desperate not to return to Britain without his new bride, Andrew protested, "But the inspection will only require a few minutes."

"You will leave at once or you will be arrested," the Gestapo agent threatened.

Knowing if he resisted further that the consequences could possibly result in death for Ruth, Andrew realized that he had no other alternative except to comply with the agent's order. With tremendous regret, he closed up the plane and taxied down the runway.

When Andrew's single engine plane was airborne, the Gestapo agents remained and watched, leaving Reisner no alternative except to leave the airfield at once. He agonized over what Ruth in the trunk might possibly be feeling.

As soon as he felt he had driven a safe distance from the airfield and was in a deserted rural area, Reisner stopped the car, got out and released a sobbing and badly shaken Ruth from the car's trunk.

Chapter Sixteen

A few days after Mary's visit to Antonia, Celia announced that she and Mary would be returning to their London residence so that Mary could continue with her preparation for the approaching Season.

Once again, Mary found herself at Madame Filipescu's salon surrounded by a dozen or so prospective debutantes, most accompanied by their mothers. When the girls' instruction was about to begin, the mothers withdrew to another room where Madame Filipescu's maid served them tea. Mary was pleased that Jane was still in the group. Although it was early afternoon, the girls were required to wear gowns and high-heeled shoes for the practice.

"I will instruct you young ladies in the management of your trains, but that will come later after you have properly mastered the curtsy. I will notify you when to bring your trains with you," Madame Filipescu, a portly woman in her sixties with a prominent continental accent, said. An unsubstantiated rumor was circulating about in London that she was once a rival of Magda Lupescu for the affection of a former Romanian ruler. Her sessions were accompanied on the piano by a sleekly handsome young man named Sergei whose relationship with Madame Filipescu was also the source of speculation.

Madame Filipescu clapped her hands to get the chattering girls' attention. "Line up, please, ladies," she said as Sergei played a march on the piano.

As Mary lined up with the other girls, she felt that after all she had recently experienced, these classes seemed frivolous and irrelevant, especially with potential war on the horizon.

"You have all heard that a graceful curtsy is difficult to accomplish," the Romanian woman continued. "I'm sure you have been told about disasters which have occurred – girls who took a nasty and embarrassing fall before Their Majesties. I promise you that this will not happen to young ladies who have been prepared by Madame Filipescu." With that, she moved to the front of the room and seated herself in a throne-like armchair on a raised dais. "You will pretend that I am Their Majesties. One by one, you will come forward and curtsy before me. Listen carefully to the tempo of the music that Sergei is playing and gauge yourselves accordingly so that your movements are stately and graceful and never rushed or awkward," she cautioned. "All right, begin!"

One by one, the girls filed forward and curtsied before Madame Filipescu. Jane preceded Mary and executed a somewhat wobbly curtsy.

"Go to the end of the line, Lady Jane, and do it again," Madame Filipescu ordered.

"Oh, damn!" Jane swore under her breath, and she and Mary quietly chuckled.

As Mary was about to approach Madame Filipescu, she glanced for a moment at the doorway of the salon and was shocked to see Andrew hovering there in his RAF uniform. As their eyes met, he motioned for Mary to come to him.

Abruptly whirling about, Mary left the line of girls and hurried across the room to Andrew, wobbling in her unaccustomed high heels.

Madame Filipescu jumped to her feet. "Lady Mary, come back here at once! What do you think you are doing?"

Mary ignored her and joined Andrew in the hall.

"Andrew! What a surprise! I never expected to see you here. You look so dashing in your uniform," she gushed, delighted that he had come to London presumably to see her, although somewhat anxious because of the nature of their last parting. This unexpected appearance of his made her doubt that the rumor that he had secretly married on a whirlwind flight to Berlin were true. The rumor had started when one of Trevor Knightsgate's friends saw Andrew in a London pub wearing a shiny, new wedding ring and questioned him about it.

"I must speak to you privately," he said quietly, looking around for a suitably secluded space. "Where can we go? Your mother and other ladies are having tea in the drawing room down the hall."

"Then let's go outside," Mary said, suddenly feeling faint from the excitement of Andrew's visit which prompted a sudden desire for fresh air.

"But you have no coat and the fabric of that gown is thin," he reminded her.

"It doesn't matter," Mary said.

Together they exited the house and stood talking on the steps. The wind was chilly, and Mary began to shiver, but Andrew was so intense about what he had to say that he failed to notice.

"I don't have much time," he said. "I go on active duty tomorrow morning at six at Duxford. I'm on my way there now. I suppose you've already heard from your friends that Ruth and I were married?"

Hearing the rumor confirmed directly from him, Mary's hope that Andrew was still single was dashed in a heart-breaking rush. "Yes, I heard something to that effect," she said, struggling to sound casual and indifferent.

"Poor Ruth is trapped in Berlin," he said shaking his head sorrowfully. "I devised what I thought was a fool-proof plan to get her out of Germany, but it failed miserably."

"I'm sorry to hear that," Mary said, rubbing her bare arms to keep warm.

"Ruth is absolutely distraught. The Nazis have recently begun deporting some of her Jewish neighbors to their so-called 'work camps'."

Mary shuddered. "How awful..."

"It may be only a few days before Ruth and her father are also shipped off to a labor camp. I can't let that happen," he declared. "I must get her out of Germany as soon as possible, but my commanding officer won't grant me leave to do so right now, especially after he got wind of my initial failure."

"Tell him what you just told me."

Andrew shook his head. "I can't do that. He'd never approve my going to Germany right now for any reason. My pilot's training is at a crucial stage. The country needs me here. Besides, he was furious about my last unauthorized trip to Germany, saying that I could have been captured and held there as a political prisoner indefinitely, resulting in Britain's losing a future pilot." Extracting an envelope from an inside pocket of his uniform, he removed a British passport. Mary wondered whose it could be.

"This passport was issued in the name of Maria Leonetti Hopkins, an Italian-born, naturalized British subject," he said as he passed it to Mary for her inspection.

Mary noted that it bore Ruth's photograph and included a host of required stamps, seals and visas.

Puzzled, she looked at Andrew. "I don't understand..." she said, continuing to shiver from the cold.

"It's a forgery," Andrew said "Ruth will simply be Mrs. Hopkins who has been on holiday in Italy and is now returning to her home in Britain by way of Germany. I need someone to deliver this bogus passport to her as soon as possible. As I've already told you, it's impossible for me to do it right now because of my military commitment, and time is of the essence. Besides, Nicholas' friend Herr Reisner has advised me that I would now be under official surveillance by the Gestapo if I should return to Germany because of the circumstances of my last visit."

"What about Nicholas? He travels to Germany frequently with his scrap metal business," Mary suggested, desperately hoping at this point that Andrew was not, as she suspected, going to ask her to get involved in another escape plan for Ruth.

"I haven't been able to reach my brother. No one seems to know where he is. My guess is that Nicholas is probably off on one of his wild schemes – God only knows where and for how long. Time is crucial. I can't wait for him," Andrew said, his hazel eyes gazing at Mary with a beseeching look. "Would you do it, Mary? Would you deliver this passport to Ruth? Because of your family connection, you are able to come and go easily and safely between England and Germany. I realize that you are very young for the task I am asking you to perform, but the fact of your youth makes it far more unlikely that you would arouse suspicion."

"The Season is starting soon," Mary said, her shivering becoming more intense.

"Is the Season really that important to you? More than someone's life?"

"My parents would never allow me to go. They've been looking forward to my presentation at Court since I was born. Jane's ball is coming up soon, as are the balls of all the other girls. I'm expected to attend all of them and my own – the most important ball of all – as well."

"Mary, I'm begging you. It's a matter of life and death."

Her teeth chattering, she said, "I can't, Andrew."

"So you're refusing? Is that it?"

"Why me, Andrew? Why can't you just pay someone to deliver the documents?"

"They're far too important and sensitive to trust with a hired courier."

Becoming increasingly anxious, she finally summoned the courage to voice the one issue both of them had been avoiding: "How can you trust me after the terrible thing I did?"

He contemplated her question a moment before responding: "I trust you because I believe that you deserve an opportunity to redeem yourself."

Chapter Seventeen

At the end of the week Arthur traded his duties as lord and steward of rural Stagsbridge for the Ashmore residence in urban London in preparation for the Caledonia Ball, an annual event to which he and Celia looked forward every year.

Because Mary's Season was rapidly approaching, her parents viewed this Scottish ball as a preview of things to come, and she agreed, somewhat reluctantly, to attend this traditional ball with them. Although her enthusiasm for social events had cooled markedly after Andrew's disturbing visit and request at Madame Filipescu's.

On the evening of the ball, Polly was in Mary's room helping her to dress.

"If you don't mind me saying so, my lady, you don't seem very keen on going to the ball tonight," the maid said.

"I'm not," Mary admitted as Polly fastened the back of her off-white ball gown trimmed in lace, one of many gowns recently created for her Season by Mrs. Kazanjian at Celia's urging.

As Mary appraised her appearance before the full-length mirror, Polly remarked, "My goodness, how lovely you look! You're sure to turn the head of every gentleman at the ball tonight."

There was only one gentleman whose head Mary wished to turn but, now that he was married, it was out of the question.

A knock at the door interrupted Mary and Polly.

"May your father and I come in?" Celia called through the door.

Mary nodded her approval to Polly who admitted them.

Both parents were elegantly attired in formal wear with a distinctly

Scottish flair, Celia in a royal blue satin gown with a tartan sash and Arthur sporting a kilt in a matching tartan, a sporran and Scottish dancing shoes which laced up over the mandated knee socks. Celia was holding a large white box which she presented to Mary.

"This box contains a sash which Polly will pin over your gown," she said, extracting a long, narrow piece of plaid fabric from it. "This was your Scottish grandmother's tartan. I'm sure she would only be too happy to pass it on to her favorite granddaughter if she were alive." Celia, proud of her Scottish ancestry, kissed Mary's cheek as she presented the box to her.

"One cannot attend the Caledonia Ball without the proper tartan," Arthur commented.

When Polly finished attaching the tartan sash, Celia circled her daughter, carefully appraising her appearance.

Clasping her hands together in delight, she acclaimed, "You look absolutely lovely, darling."

"Smashing, I'd say," Arthur added. "Lucky the chaps who will be dancing with you tonight."

"Thank you, Mother, Father."

"Alice Knightsgate telephoned me earlier today to inform me that Jane's brother Trevor will be attending the ball tonight, together with Jane and her parents, of course," Celia related. "Trevor will be motoring down from Oxford with some of his friends. Alice said that Trevor is looking forward to seeing you at the ball and hopes you'll save at least one dance for him."

Mary was not excited about dancing with Trevor whom she considered shallow and immature and a much more suitable prospect for Lucy.

"It won't be long now until it's your own ball your mother and I will be attending," Arthur reminded her.

Seated on a bench adjacent to one of the two parallel runways at the Duxford RAF fighter station and wearing his leather flight jacket, helmet and other essential flying gear, Andrew hunkered down silently to conceal himself in the shadows.

A light fog was rising from the River Cam which flowed through this ancient village in Cambridgeshire where the RAF had decided to locate this fighter station. He fervently hoped that the fog would not get any heavier and interfere with what he had planned.

Deep in thought, he reviewed each step of his plan of action over and over. Any slip-up, any mistake, any miscalculation in his hazardous scheme could prove disastrous.

Nervously, he twirled the newly acquired gold wedding band around his finger as he waited for the sentry patrolling the perimeter of the air base to finish has rounds and leave the area.

His eye was steadily on the nearby single-seater Hawker Hurricane on the runway. At first he had contemplated utilizing a Supermarine Spitfire, which had surpassed the older plane, for his daring, unauthorized flight, but later changed his mind, deciding that the penalties incurred from his rash plan to rescue Ruth might be less severe if he appropriated a plane of lesser esteem. Initially he had even considered using a Bristol F-2 fighter which he felt confident piloting. A remnant of the First World War, it was still in use at the RAF flight training school, but he ultimately selected the more modern aircraft, fully aware that his contemplated flight had staggering risks, not only for his own military career, but politically for his country as well. Relations between Britain and Germany were becoming increasingly uncertain every day. He did not want to be the spark that erupted into out-and-out warfare, although there were many who now believed war to be inevitable. Nevertheless, he felt that whatever the consequences of his daring mission to rescue Ruth might be, it was worth the risk. After all, she was his wife now, and it was his duty to save her from Nazi Jewish persecution by bringing her to Britain. Although she had automatic British citizenship as his wife, German law forbade Jews, whom the Nazis used as slave labor, to leave the country.

As soon as the sentry's footsteps receded farther and farther into the distance so that eventually they were no longer audible, he grabbed his gear and made a dash in the fog-bound night for his unauthorized flight in what would be a stolen fighter plane.

⁓

The Caledonia Ball, a swirl of bagpipes, kilts and colorful tartans, proved to be a more enjoyable occasion for her parents than for Mary. She did her best to hide her feelings of indifference as she danced and forced herself to chat with her dance partners which included Trevor Knightsgate and his Oxford chums, but her heart was elsewhere. The entire purpose of her attending the ball was not only to please her parents, but also to distract herself from thinking about Andrew and his request. At this point she felt it was important not allow him to become an obsession. He was married now and no longer eligible, and that was that.

⁓

Relying on his instruments as he flew over the North Sea in the foggy darkness inside the Hawker Hurricane, Andrew was stunned when a pair of German Messerschmitt BF110 night fighter planes came out of nowhere and began firing at him.

The bastards must have picked me up on that damnable new radar business that my brother Nicholas has been going on about to me, Andrew thought as he prepared himself for a dogfight.

Rolling his plane, then pulling up steeply, then nose-diving again while continuously firing, he managed to down one of the twin engine heavy fighters, but caught the fire of the other German plane and realized that he was also going down.

Blowing out the cockpit window, he ejected himself from his aircraft and descended in a parachute.

The surviving German plane swooped toward him, and its pilot lined him up in its sights, firing at Andrew as he parachuted down.

Forced to cut the parachute, he plummeted quickly out of the German pilot's aim, then opened his second chute and began floating down.

Unrelenting, the German pilot approached again, guns blazing. Desperate, Andrew grabbed the flare-gun attached to his belt and aimed it squarely at the diving German fighter plane. He fired the flare at the pilot in an attempt to temporarily blind him. This move proved successful, preventing the Messerschmitt from pulling out of the steep dive in time and, in his own continued descent, Andrew observed the German fighter plane crash spectacularly into the ocean below him.

As he landed in the frigid sea with its gigantic, roiling waves, Andrew could see his own Hawker Hurricane plane burning as it, like the German planes, sank in the distance.

Chapter Eighteen

In the library of the Ashmore London residence on a rainy morning after the Caledonia Ball, Mary obediently sat down with her mother and began formulating plans for her own upcoming ball, although her enthusiasm for the event was lacking with Andrew out of the picture. It now seemed inevitable that Trevor Knightsgate would be her escort. He was certainly what her parents would consider 'suitable', but, as far as Mary was concerned, this callow Oxford undergraduate was a far cry from Andrew.

"I don't want the guest list for the ball dominated by the friends of your father's and mine," Celia declared. "I want you to have your fair share of friends at the ball as well."

"I don't really have that many friends, Mother," Mary replied.

Celia sighed and nodded in agreement. "Perhaps it would have been better if your father and I had chosen a boarding school for you, as we have for Lucy and Charles, instead of relegating your education to governesses and private tutors.

Well, if it weren't for my private tutor, I might have had Andrew as my escort for this all-important ball, Mary thought to herself but said nothing.

"I think it's perfectly acceptable to invite our country friends from Surrey such as the Lymes and the Dangerfields and the Davises," Celia said as she looked at the guest list in front of her on the desk, pen in hand, ready to cross off names to which Mary or she might object. "It's really not that inconvenient for them to come to London for an event as important as your ball."

"They're fine, Mother."

"Sadly, Nicholas will probably be the only one of the Buckfords able to attend. If he does, I do hope he'll be on good behavior. Antonia is still not feeling well, and Simon can't dance with that artificial leg of his, although he does manage to walk quite well with it," Celia paused for a moment and raised her pen as if debating whether or not to cross off a name. "What about Andrew?"

"What about him?"

"Shall we invite him? I doubt if he'll be able to attend with his RAF commitment and a wife trapped in Germany. I still can't fathom why such a young man with his excellent prospects made such an odd choice of a wife for himself," Celia said. "But then, many things in life defy explanation."

Outside on the street, beyond the windows of the library, the sound of a car's screeching brakes shattered the relative quiet of the Regents Park neighborhood.

"What on earth was that?" Celia gasped.

Mary got up and went to the window where she observed Nicholas hop out of his car and, without an umbrella, dash for the door in the pouring rain.

Turning to her mother, Mary said, "It's Nicholas."

Celia looked up from the list in surprise. "Nicholas? Here? I wonder what he's up to now?"

"I'm sure we'll find out in a moment," Mary said.

She could hear Dunsmuir's footsteps hurrying to the door in response to the banging of the heavy brass knocker outside. A few moments later, she heard Nicholas' voice as he and the butler exchanged words in the vestibule.

Bursting into the library before Dunsmuir had an opportunity to properly announce him, Nicholas stood in the doorway, his raven-wing black hair, which only partially covered the recent stitches in his scalp, sopping wet from the rain.

Observing that he appeared upset and distraught and not his characteristic jaunty, devil-may-care self, Mary rose to her feet and asked, "Nicholas, what's wrong?"

Struggling to maintain his composure, he blurted, "It's Andrew..."

Suddenly anxious, Mary responded, "What about Andrew? Is something wrong?"

"He's dead."

Mary turned immediately pale and grasped the back of a chair for support, fearing she was about to faint.

"'Dead'!?" Mary echoed.

At that point, Celia also jumped to her feet. "How did it happen?"

"It seems he was in a plane he appropriated without official permission and was flying over the North Sea in a dense fog. His plane apparently went down shortly after take-off," Nicholas answered as best he could. "No one is sure what exactly happened. Some of his fellow RAF pilots suspect that German fighter planes may have somehow intercepted him and shot him down. The German Foreign Office is, of course, officially denying it. The RAF has managed to locate pieces of wreckage of the plane which they had discovered missing shortly after Andrew took off on his unauthorized flight. They still haven't located his body as yet."

"Your parents must be devastated," Celia said. "I must go back to Stagsbridge at once to be with them. What a horrible tragedy!"

"Why did Andrew do such a foolish thing?" Mary asked, although she suspected that she knew exactly why.

"I assume my brother was on his way to Berlin. He was desperate to get Ruth out of Germany and was determined not to let anything stand in his way – not the Nazis, not the RAF, not anything or anybody," Nicholas declared.

Celia pulled out a chair. "Do sit down, Nicholas," she urged. "I'll ring for Polly to bring us some tea. We know how upset you must be. It's much too tragic to even contemplate."

Nicholas remained standing. "It's even a worse tragedy than you think," he said.

"Whatever do you mean?" Celia asked.

"How could it be?" Mary said, tears flooding her blue eyes.

"Ruth had informed him through a loyal former student of hers that she was expecting their first child," he revealed. "That added to his determination to get her to England so that his child could be born here."

Stunned, Mary repeated, "A child? I had no idea..."

Chapter Nineteen

Deeply shaken by the news of his brother's plane crash and his presumed death, Nicholas sped along narrow, twisting Ferry Road in his Delahaye, skirting the Alderton Marshes, to Bawdsey Manor. As he reached the mouth of the River Deben, he could see the imposing nineteenth century red brick baronial mansion. This former private estate, presently the site of top secret radar research, had been acquired by the British Air Ministry. Accordingly, the grounds were fenced and rigidly guarded by RAF airmen, so rigidly, in fact, that Nicholas was obliged to submit his identity documentation to the guard in the sentry post at the gated entrance each time he visited the installation.

"Good afternoon, Lord Buckford," the sentry said, rendering a salute. "Dr. Watson-Watt is expecting you."

Originally a meteorologist and now an esteemed scientist, Robert Watson-Watt, a descendant of James Watt, inventor of the steam engine, was the superintendent of Britain's Chain Home radar station, the nation's first, and the name by which Bawdsey was now known. At present, the majority of his work was carried out in a laboratory, converted from the estate's former stables which still retained a faint equine odor. This odor inspired Nicholas' alibi of breeding polo ponies for his frequent, but covert, trips to the former Bawdsey Manor.

Nicholas parked, then hopped out of his car and entered the laboratory where he was greeted by Watson-Watt himself. Surrounded by all manner of technical equipment, which he customarily referred to as 'my gadgets', the middle-aged physicist-engineer said in his quiet voice with its thick Scottish burr as the two men shook hands, "Good to see you, Lord Buckford."

Watson-Watt was an unassuming man who wore glasses with thick, round lenses, clipped his own shaggy hair and was always attired in a long, gray laboratory coat.

"Likewise, sir," Nicholas replied. Watson-Watt's accent always brought back nostalgic memories of his university days at Edinburgh.

"I've got a surprise for you today," the scientist said with an impish grin. "Come along and I'll show you."

Watson-Watt led Nicholas outside to an area about two hundred yards northeast of the manor house. They passed several windowless structures with reinforced concrete walls and blast-proof roofs surrounded by earthen mounds. Nicholas surmised that these structures were recently constructed by the British Ministry of Defence and housed top secret activities.

As they reached a cliff overlooking the North Sea, Watson-Watt stopped and pointed to a pair of towers thrusting into the gray, overcast English sky.

"Well, my boy, there they are," he said, beaming with pride. "That smaller wooden one, approximately two hundred and forty feet high, is the receiver, and its higher companion, three hundred and sixty feet high, is the transmitter. You are looking at the first radar installation in the British Isles. The plan is for it to be followed by a protective ring of about fifty additional radar stations guarding the perimeter of the country."

Nicholas stood and gazed at the towers in awe. "And to think that they were paid for with German money is rather amusing," he said with a laugh. "Now the German's Luftwaffe planes, constructed with British scrap metal, will – ironically – never be able to safely reach our shores without our knowing it, thanks to you and your fellow scientists, Dr. Watson-Watt."

"And thanks to you as well, Lord Buckford," Watson-Watt said. "Your efforts and powers of persuasion made the implementation of my scientific theories possible."

"As I understand the concept of radar, radio waves from these towers will bounce off approaching enemy aircraft and count their numbers as well. Is that correct?" Nichols asked.

Watson-Watt nodded. "Correct, sir."

"As soon as enemy planes are visible on the radar screens, our Spitfire and Hurricane fighter planes will be in the air to meet them?" Nicholas questioned.

"Correct again," the research scientist said. "Radar will be the eyes of the RAF Fighter Command. Without it, the Germans would gain the upper hand. Their Luftwaffe has two thousand, six hundred planes to the RAF's measly six hundred and forty. With our recent research, we've been able to extend the range of radar approximately one hundred miles which will give our fighter planes more time to intercept German aircraft and prevent them from bombing Britain into defeat."

Impressed, Nicholas remarked, "Listening to you, sir, it sounds as if radar might well turn the tide in our favor in the event of all-out war."

"Prime Minister Baldwin has been informed of our recent progress here, and I'm told that he's quite enthusiastic," Watson-Watt said.

"As well he should be," Nicholas agreed.

"We owe our latest developments to the late Heinrich Hertz, who, ironically, was a German Jew," Watson-Watt said. "And we both know how the Nazis treat Jews these days."

Nicholas agreed. "How advanced was his research before he died?"

"Reasonably far. Then his daughter Johanna carried on his work until conditions for Jews in Germany forced her to flee, even though Johanna is only half Jewish. Her mother was a Christian, but to the Nazis a single drop of Jewish blood is anathema."

"Just think, sir," Nicholas replied. "If the Nazis hadn't made Hertz's daughter feel threatened by their anti-Jewish policies, they might have been the beneficiaries of his radar research instead of us. Foolish buggers."

Watson-Watt chuckled. "I suppose so."

"Where is Hertz's daughter now?"

"There are rumors in the scientific community that she's hidden away in Scotland," Watson-Watt replied.

"She would be a fine person with whom to collaborate," Nicholas said excitedly.

Watson-Watt grinned coyly. "Yes, she would, wouldn't she?" Then with an ironic chuckle, he continued, "In the beginning, the War Ministry dismissed me and my colleagues as a 'bunch of weathermen' who knew nothing," he said. "They denied us the funds we needed to complete our work. If it weren't for your money-raising efforts, Lord Buckford, these towers you see before you would still be on the drawing board. Once we were able to successfully demonstrate the effectiveness of radar at Daventry in Nottinghampshire, the War ministry was then willing to support our work."

"I'm glad I am able to help," Nicholas said modestly.

Chapter Twenty

After first going out to the Stagsbridge stable to say goodbye to Sable, Mary returned to her room to ostensibly select her wardrobe for the week-end house party at Thurstonbury Hall, the Knightsbridges' estate in Kent. Still grieving over Andrew, Mary expressed little joy in the various outfits her mother had had Mrs. Kazanjian design and execute for this event which heralded the imminent approach of the Season. She had still not recovered from the service honoring Andrew in the Lammersley chapel the previous week conducted by Vicar Stouthammer. Although some of the wreckage from the plane had been recovered from the North Sea, his body still had not been found.

"You don't think there's a chance that Andrew might have survived?" Mary asked Nicholas after the service.

"Realistically, how long can one survive in the icy waters of the North Sea, even with a life-jacket?" he responded with a sigh of heart-broken resignation. "I saw pieces of the wreckage of the plane. It's extremely doubtful that he could have survived."

❦

Celia studied the half dozen or so dresses laid out on Mary's bed. "You know, Mary, I'm glad you agreed to go to Jane's house party this week-end. I was afraid you would decline her invitation. I know how much Andrew's death and the memorial service has grieved you. Getting away from Stagsbridge and Lammersley – if only for a week-end – and being with other young people will do you good. I'm quite sure Lady Alice will seat Trevor next to you at dinner Saturday evening."

"Trevor and his Oxford chums are boring," Mary complained. "All they talk of is sports or what branch of the military they favor."

"Well, dear, there is all this talk of war." Celia selected a blue silk crepe dress. "You should wear this blue number for that dinner. It will bring out the lovely blue eyes you inherited from my Scottish mother." Without waiting for Mary's approval or disapproval, she passed the garment to Polly, who was standing by. "Pack this," she instructed the maid.

"Yes, ma'am," Polly replied and began to carefully fold the dress.

"Pearls with a slightly silver cast would complement that dress nicely," Celia speculated. "I have a lovely pearl necklace that belonged to your grandmother. Let me go to my room and get it for you. Polly can continue packing until I return."

Mary went to the window and gazed sadly across the meadows and forest to Lammersley on the other side of the river.

"It's hard to believe that Lord Andrew is gone forever," Mary lamented.

"It is, Miss," Polly agreed.

When Celia returned, she not only brought with her the pearl necklace but other items of jewelry as well that she deemed appropriate for the house party. She also had a manila envelope with Mary's name written on it.

"If you don't think the pearls are right, I brought some other pieces you might try," Celia said.

Mary's attention, however, was focused on the envelope in her mother's hand.

"What's in that envelope, Mother?"

"Probably nothing of value," Celia said with an indifferent shrug. "I was visiting with Antonia when we returned from London just before the service dedicated by Vicar Stouthammer to prayers for Andrew, and she gave it to me to pass along to you when she saw that it had your name written on it."

Recognizing Andrew's handwriting, Mary assumed it merely contained papers pertaining to the activities of the Agricultural Council of which she and Andrew were members.

Celia passed her the envelope.

As she unsealed it and peered inside, she was startled to realize that it contained the forged passport that Andrew had obtained in order to smuggle Ruth out of Germany and into Britain.

Observing her daughter's somewhat stunned reaction to the envelope's contents, Celia asked, "What's in it?"

"Nothing much. Just a booklet on how meetings of the Agricultural Council are to be conducted," Mary lied, knowing that such a counterfeit document could be seized by the authorities if discovered. Mary was not ready to let that happen, at least not yet. "Where did Antonia get it?"

"One of Andrew's pilot friends found it in his locker at the Duxford air base and passed it along to Antonia with his other belongings. Since it had your name on it, she thought it only right and proper to see that you got it," Celia replied.

The passport conjured up memories for Mary of the last meeting she had with Andrew. The hurt expressed in his hazel eyes when she refused to take this same bogus document to Ruth in Berlin brought tears to her eyes.

"Thank Antonia for me, will you, Mother?" Mary said, dabbing at her eyes with a handkerchief.

The family chauffeur Jamison drove Mary to Thurstonbury Hall. When she arrived at the sprawling Kent estate, Jane, trailed by several of the Knightsgate family servants, dashed out of the baronial mansion to greet her guest.

"Mary! How lovely to see you! I'm so glad you decided to join us," Jane said, embracing her. "I was so afraid you wouldn't want to so soon after what happened to Andrew. How are you? And how are Lord and Lady Buckford? Almost as an afterthought, she added, "And Nicholas?"

"We're all grieving," Mary answered. "As one would expect."

"Yes, of course," Jane said, nodding her understanding. "It's so sad, so very sad. We shall all miss Andrew terribly. Of course, there's still Nicholas to carry on the Buckford line at Lammersley now. Mother insisted that I invite him for the week-end, but he declined. I'm not at all surprised nor disappointed. Rumors abound in London that he may be involved with a woman in Suffolk – of all places – and spending a lot of his time there. He says he's developing a new breed of polo horses by crossing Scottish ponies with Argentine horses, but nobody believes that. Of course, one has to admit that he is terribly attractive in a *'roue'* kind of way, as Mademoiselle Fouchet would probably characterize him," Jane said with a laugh.

As Jane was about to escort Mary into the house, trailed by the Knights-gate servants with Mary's luggage, Jamison asked as he was closing the car's trunk, "Will there be anything else, my lady?"

"No. You may go, Jamison," Mary said.

As Mary and Jane entered the Thurstonbury Hall vestibule, Jane gushed, "Oh, I have an absolutely marvelous week-end planned. It's going to be such fun. Croquet on the lawn today until all the guests arrive, hope-fully by tea time. Dinner Saturday night will be followed by dancing in our ballroom. The servants have been waxing the floor all week. It's positively gleaming. I hope no one falls." Jane laughed as she guided Mary toward the grand staircase leading to the second floor.

Mary abruptly stopped and grasped Jane's arm. The servants who were following with Mary's luggage were also compelled to stop. "It's rather silly for my things to be carried upstairs," she said.

Jane looked at her, puzzled. "Whatever are you talking about?"

Lowering her voice to a near whisper, Mary confided, "I shan't be staying."

"What?!" Jane exclaimed.

"I'll explain later when we're alone," Mary said, casting a glance at the servants.

Eager to hear more, Jane dismissed the servants, instructing them to merely leave Mary's luggage in the vestibule for the time being, and ushered her friend into the library, closing the door behind them.

"Now tell me what is going on, Mary," Jane demanded.

"I must leave soon," Mary said.

"Oh, Mary, you mustn't leave!" Jane said. "Trevor and some of his chums from Oxford will be so disappointed. They're coming especially to spend the week-end with you. They will never forgive me if you leave."

"I can't tell you how dreadfully sorry I am, Jane," Mary apologized. "Please forgive me. Right now, there is something I must do that requires my leaving here as soon as possible."

Thoroughly baffled, Jane asked, "What is it? What is this thing you feel so compelled to do?"

"It's something for Andrew."

"But Andrew is no longer with us."

"All the more reason for me to do what I have to do," Mary insisted.

"Why can't you tell me what it is?"

"I'll tell you afterward," Mary promised. "As soon as Jamison is well on his way back to Stagsbridge, I plan to leave here and go to London."

"What's in London?"

"I'll take the boat-train to Calais in London and from there another train to Berlin."

Astonished, Jane said, "Good Lord, Mary, you're not going back to Berlin after the awful things that happened to you there the last time, are you?"

"I have no choice. I must."

"How long will you be gone? And what about the Season? And your ball?" Jane asked.

"I hope to complete my mission and return as quickly as possible – hopefully before the Season starts."

"And if you don't?"

Mary shrugged indifferently. "What I hope to accomplish is of far greater consequence and more important to me than the things you mentioned."

"Have you told your family about this 'mission' of yours?"

"I've told no one. I'll telephone my parents from here, if I may..?"

"Yes, of course you can." Jane said.

"I'll tell them that I've decided to spend the entire week here with you and your family."

Increasingly anxious, Jane asked, "And if they call and ask to speak to you, what am I to say?"

"You're to lie and tell them I'm not in at the moment, that I've gone walking or riding with Trevor. Tell them anything except that I've gone off to Berlin."

"I must ask you, Mary, if I may, how are you funding all this intricate travel of yours without the knowledge of your parent?"

"I contacted the trustee of my grandmother's estate in Scotland and requested a confidential advance on my inheritance," Mary replied.

"But can you trust him not to inform your parents?"

I think he will under the circumstance," Mary said, then grinning, she added, "You see, I told him I was going to the Continent for an 'operation'."

"Oh, dear!" Jane gasped.

"I didn't specify what sort of operation. I'm sure he assumed surgical."

Jane chuckled. "He probably thought you were pregnant."

"That was my goal. I certainly hope that my secret is safe with him. The important thing is that he released sufficient funds to me, and if my parents find out, it will already be too late to stop me," Mary replied. "As a friend, just do what I'm asking of you this one time. You must trust me, Jane, when I say that it's literally a matter of life and death."

⌘

While Jane distracted her parents, servants and guests, Mary telephoned Arthur and Celia and informed them what she had confided to Jane earlier.

After that, she called the von Rohrsbachs in Berlin to alert them of her impending arrival, and they agreed to meet her, as they had before.

She then called for a taxi to take her to London and miraculously managed to get away from Thurstonbury Hall without anyone noticing, thanks to Jane's cooperation in distracting the other guests for her.

Arriving at Victoria Station, Mary bought a ticket for a first class compartment on the London to Paris express and carefully guarded the bogus passport for Ruth during the ferry crossing from Dover to Calais.

God love Jane! she thought as she rested on the rail of the ferry as it traversed the Channel.

⌘

Jane had a difficult time concentrating on the game of croquet she and her brother Trevor and the group of prospective debutantes and young university men were playing on the vast green lawn spread out before Thurstonbury Hall. She was deeply concerned about Mary and this mysterious trip of hers to Berlin – of all places – especially at a time when relations between Britain and Germany were strained almost to the breaking point.

Jane was about to tap the big wooden ball through a crucial wicket when the sound of an approaching auto horn caught her attention. Moments later Nicholas roared up to the lawn in his Delahaye, stopped and beckoned to Jane.

Jane excused herself from the game temporarily and, with her wooden mallet over her shoulder, crossed the grass to Nicholas.

"What a lovely surprise!" she exclaimed. "I never expected to see you here after you declined my invitation."

Nicholas anxiously surveyed the other croquet players. Looking confused, he asked, "Where's Mary Ashmore? Her parents said she's here."

"Mary is at the house," Jane lied, as required by her promise to her friend. "The poor girl has a wretched headache."

"I must speak to her," Nicholas insisted. "It's urgent."

"She specifically asked not to be disturbed."

"In that case, then, I'm afraid I'm going to have to disturb her," he said.

"You can't."

"Try and stop me," he challenged, racing his engine, about to continue on to the manor house.

"Stop!" Jane cried out. "Mary is not here."

"Then, damn it, where is she? She phoned her parents and told them that she was staying the week with you. My mother gave her something belonging to my brother which I must get back as soon as possible."

"That's not feasible."

Angered by Jane's resistance, Nichols grabbed her by the wrist, risking getting clubbed with the mallet in her other hand. "No more nonsense out of you, Jane. Where is she?"

Jane stammered nervously. "I...I can't tell you."

"Why not?"

"Because I gave her my word."

"Well, you're going to have to break it right now," he said, squeezing her wrist hard. "I must know."

"All right, I'll tell you," Jane capitulated. "She's on her way to Berlin."

"Berlin!" he exclaimed. "Why?"

"There was some unfinished business there she felt she simply had to finish," Jane said, adding, "For Andrew."

Nicholas released his hold on Jane and slapped his forehead. "Oh, my God!" he said. "The girl is mad, I tell you. Sometimes I think I'm going mad myself. Did she mention where she was going to stay in Berlin?

"No, but she rang up her cousins in that city before she left, so I think one may safely assume that's where she plans to stay."

"Thank you, Jane," he said.

Then making a U-turn, he sped away from Thurstonbury Hall, leaving Jane behind, worried about having betrayed Mary's confidence as she crossed the lawn to rejoin her friends at croquet.

Chapter Twenty-one

Mary arrived at her former French tutor's flat, which overlooked the booksellers' stalls on the banks of the Seine, exhausted from her somewhat frantic day.

"I'm always happy to see you, Mary," Mademoiselle Fouchet said, kissing both her cheeks lightly in a typically French greeting. "I did not expect to see you so soon again."

"This trip was unexpected," Mary replied.

With a look of concern, Mademoiselle Fouchet asked, "Is there trouble with your family in Berlin?"

"No, nothing like that," Mary said, removing her coat.

"Then why would you go there when there is now so much turmoil in Germany?" the French tutor asked as she took Mary's coat and hung it in a closet in the small apartment.

Wishing to keep the true purpose of her return visit to Germany secret for the present, Mary merely answered, "I'm really not free to discuss it at this time. I hope you don't mind."

"Of course not. Why would I?" Mademoiselle Fouchet said with a typically Gallic shrug. "Would you like some tea or would a glass of wine suit you better at this moment? You seem perhaps a little stressed, no?"

"Yes, I am -- a little," Mary conceded, hoping that wine would relax her. "A glass of wine would be lovely, thanks."

The French woman filled two glasses from a decanter, lit a cigarette and, settling into a nearby sofa, said, "Perhaps you do not know, but the trains from Paris to Berlin and other German cities do not run often now. The schedule is quite irregular. There are only two trains a week, but sometimes none at all. One must go to the station early every morning and inquire if a train is going on that day. No one in France goes to Germany any longer," she informed Mary, adding with an ironic laugh, "In fact, we are becoming afraid that the Germans will be coming here soon – and not as friends or tourists."

Beginning the next morning, as Mademoiselle Fouchet, had advised, Mary went to the Gare du Nord train station daily. On the third day, she learned that a train would be going to Berlin later that same day and instantly purchased a first class ticket.

<hr />

Arriving in the German capital, Mary was immediately struck by how much the Nazi presence in that city had escalated since her previous visit. The number of bright red banners with their central black swastikas now dominated the entire station, and the number of Gestapo vigilantly patrolling the corridors and scrutinizing the passengers, both arriving and departing, with their formidable shepherd dogs had markedly increased.

Feeling uneasy in this virtual sea of Nazi symbolism, Mary strove not to appear nervous when it was her turn to pass through Customs. A stern-looking Gestapo officer studied her passport at length while another searched through her single suitcase and ordered her to empty the contents of her handbag on the counter. Anticipating this degree of scrutiny from her prior visit, Mary had concealed the bogus passport for Ruth, still in its manila envelope, in a secret compartment beneath the bottom of her jewelry box within her suitcase.

"What is the purpose of your visit, Miss?" the English-speaking Gestapo officer asked.

"I will be visiting relatives – my cousin Graefin von Rohrsbach and her husband, Graf von Rohrsbach," she answered confidently, hoping the aristocratic names would favorably impress the inspectors.

The Gestapo officer frowned, narrowing his eyes suspiciously. "I see from the stamp in your passport that this is your second visit to Berlin in a short period of time," he said.

"I happen to be very fond of my cousin and her husband," she explained, quickly adding as an after-thought, "And their son, Karl-Heinrich von Rohrsbach as well. Perhaps you know him? He's a staunch member of the Hitler Youth."

Unimpressed, the Gestapo officer shook his shaved head, which reflected the lights above him, and muttered, "No, I don't."

"I also greatly admire your beautiful German capital and the wonderful things the Nazi party has done for the country," she nervously chattered on. "I am also eager to absorb German culture…"

With a contemptuous sneer, the Gestapo officer cut her off, stamped her passport and motioned for her to move along.

Mary felt greatly relieved at having passed through Customs without incident and the passport still safely hidden inside the little jewel box in her suitcase as she searched about for a telephone where she could call Kurt and Anne to let them know she was now in Berlin and to ask them to come and meet her, although she was well aware of the dangerous challenge that lay ahead of her.

Surprisingly, Kurt arrived alone, driving the familiar Horch type 930 V-8 which had been driven by his chauffeur Willi in the past.

"I have to do my own driving now. Willi is in the army," Kurt explained as Mary climbed into the front seat beside him. He seemed resigned to the loss of his driver. "I can't tell you what a surprise it is to see you here again so soon – considering the rather disturbing circumstances under which you departed. Anne will be delighted. She's engaged in war work at home now. That's why she didn't come with me to meet you."

"I behaved quite rudely when I left, and one of the reasons I have returned is to apologize in person to you and Graefin Anne."

"We've already forgiven you, Mary," he said with an affectionate laugh. "Surely, that's not your only reason for returning?"

Mary sighed. "To be quite frank, I've been worried about my former, tutor Fraulein Herzog," she said, refraining from telling him that she had secretly married Lord Andrew Buckford and was expecting his child. Although she felt she could trust Kurt, she did not want to put Ruth and her unborn infant in even greater danger if somehow word of the forbidden marriage was accidentally leaked, and Heinzi learned of it.

"As you will quickly discover, things have grown considerably worse for the Jews since you were last here. Regretfully, there's really very little you can do for your tutor now. She might have already been sent off to one of the labor camps or – God forbid – even killed," he warned.

⁓

Mary quickly learned that Kurt was right; things in Berlin had changed in a short period of time. Mary decided that it would be wise to evaluate the situation before trying to contact Ruth. As a result, she spent her first few days at the von Rohrsbach home chatting with Anne, who was occupied most of the day with the task of preparing bandages to be used in military medical facilities. She had taken on this duty solely to avoid trouble with the Nazis, should Heinzi ever make good on his threat to denounce his parents for their lack of support of the Third Reich.

"No more frivolous shopping, card playing, luncheons and afternoon teas with friends," she commented regretfuly. "But at least it's better than going to a munitions plant to work every day. Thank goodness my husband still has influence among some of the Nazi higher-ups because of his vital banking connections." She expertly folded a bandage, indicating to Mary that she had become quite adept at the procedure. "I suppose Heinzi's devotion to Hitler Youth helps as well, although it's not something that his father and I are at all pleased with."

Since Mary's arrival there had been no sign of Heinzi. "Where has he been?" she asked.

"He's been gone for a few days," Anne replied, her tone reluctant, as if what she was about to disclose was uncomfortable for her. "He volunteered as a guard aboard a train transporting Jews to the work camp at Thereseinstadt."

Hearing this, Mary desperately hoped that neither Ruth nor her father were aboard that train. If they had been, her trip would be in vain.

"I must ask you, Mary," Anne said, looking up for a moment from her bandages. "Did you inform your parents that you were coming here before you left? We were quite surprised to get a call from you at the station, especially when I hadn't heard a word from them regarding this visit. In the past, they have always informed me by either letter or telephone to let me know of your visits."

Mary's heart suddenly beat faster as she tried to fabricate an answer which would satisfy Anne. She disliked lying, although sometimes – especially lately – she had found it necessary.

"Both my parents are badly shaken up over the tragic death of Lord Andrew Buckford in a plane crash," Mary said.

Anne was shocked. "Nicholas' brother...dead...in a plane crash?"

"Yes," Mary nodded.

"Oh, how dreadful!" Anne gasped. "You were quite fond of him, were you not?"

"Quite," Mary answered with a catch in her throat.

Several days after her arrival, Mary, still battling travel fatigue, went to bed early one evening. Shortly before midnight, she was awakened by a loud racket from the street outside the von Rohrsbach residence.

Crowds of people seemed to be shouting and cheering, various vehicle and motorcycle engines roaring, the rumbling of what sounded like the Panzer tanks she had heard at the Tiergarten rally, the clanking of big anti-aircraft guns, the clomping of horses' hooves, all accompanied by the thunderous stomp of thousands of marching boots.

Alarmed and curious, Mary jumped out of bed and dashed to the window. Although it was dark outside, she could see that a military parade was passing by, an almost endless procession of row after row of jubilant soldiers who were preceded by officers on horseback and followed by trucks, tanks, big anti-aircraft guns and other military hardware. A phalanx of Hitler Youth, each carrying a huge Nazi banner, followed the regular army troops. Although it was too dark for Mary to ascertain if Heinzi was among that group, she had no doubt that he was.

Cheering throngs of men and women, many in their night clothes, lined the street or hung out of the windows of their homes singing, shouting and waving Nazi flags. Young girls showered the marching soldiers with flowers.

Mary had never seen a similar display on such a scale before. The coronation of George VI, a few years earlier in London, paled by comparison. She found it simultaneously impressive and frightening.

⁂

The next morning Mary shared the dining room breakfast table with Kurt and Anne, all of them feeling sleep-deprived after the tumultuous commotion of the previous night. As Mathilde served them, the normally energetic and cheerful maid also seemed unusually weary. Being older, she had loyally remained part of the von Rohrsbach household staff instead of joining the military or gravitating to more lucrative jobs in the munitions and weapons factories as some of the younger servants had done.

"I suppose all that noise last night wakened you, Mary?" Anne inquired.

"It did," Mary replied.

"Nazis thrive on parades. They're like children in that respect," Kurt remarked as he speared a slice of ham from the tray Mathilde proffered and slid it onto his plate next to a pair of fried eggs. "Heinzi participated in it, you know. He's still upstairs sleeping."

Eager to change what was for her an uncomfortable trend in the morning conversation, Anne turned to Mary and, raising her teacup to her lips, said, "I spoke to your mother. It's been very difficult getting through to England on the telephone, but last night I was finally successful."

Mary tensed, dreading to hear what her mother might have said and what consequences their conversation might have on her plans. "Really?" was her only comment as she cracked the soft-boiled egg Mathilde set before her.

"She was astounded to learn that you were here with us," Anne went on. "She had no idea. Poor Cousin Celia thought you were with your friend Jane in Kent. She was a bit concerned about your being here in Germany with us and not telling her about your plans. In any event, she wants you to return home at once so that you can continue with preparations for the Season."

Kurt surprised Mary by coming to her defense. "I don't blame Mary for leaving. All that Season and debutante business is a lot of nonsense."

Undeterred, Anne continued, "Nevertheless, I promised Cousin Celia

158

that I would send you home as soon as possible, even though we shall miss your company."

"It could be days before there's another train to Paris," Kurt speculated.

"That's good. It will enable Mary to stay longer," Anne said, looking pleased. "Not having a daughter of my own, you bring much joy to my life." Reaching across the table and affectionately patting Mary's hand, she added, "Especially these days."

At that moment, Heinzi burst into the dining room, nearly colliding with Mathilde who was balancing a tray with bowls of porridge and a pitcher of milk. He was dressed in a clean, freshly pressed Hitler Youth uniform.

"Well, did everyone participate in the victory celebration in the streets last night?" he asked facetiously, looking from each of his parents and then to Mary. With a contemptuous sneer, he added, "No, of course you didn't."

He then circled the table and leaned against the back of Mary's chair, placing his hands on her shoulders, his breath emitting the sour odor of stale beer.

"And you, my little English rose," he said, pressing his lips into Mary's ash blonde hair. "Did the parade of the victorious army of the Third Reich disturb your sleep?"

"I heard nothing at all," Mary lied. "Apparently I slept through the whole business."

"This is such a glorious time for the Third Reich!" he went on excitedly, his enthusiasm not in the least dampened by Mary's indifference. "We began by triumphantly uniting Austria and Germany with the *anschluss*. Soon we will free the captive German people in the City of Danzig from Polish domination. Eventually we will take Poland itself. Then will come the liberation of the German populace in Sudetenland from the Czechs. The German army is the most powerful in the history of mankind. No one dares to challenge us, not even Stalin's Russia, which is considering a treaty with us," Heinzi ranted.

"That treaty will probably not be worth the paper it's written on," Kurt remarked.

"Heinzi, dear, please sit down and let Mathilde serve you," Anne urged. "Surely you must be hungry?"

Ignoring his mother, Heinzi continued on, now directing his remarks at Mary. "Your Prime Minister Chamberlain is pursuing his policy of peace at any cost. He will meet with our Fuehrer in Munich to formulate an accord to promote peace between our two nations."

"Also worthless," Kurt muttered.

Using a sterner tone, Anne said, "No more political rants, please, Heinzi. Sit down and have your breakfast."

"Why? Are you afraid that my rants are going to upset our little English cousin?"

Kurt slapped the newspaper which lay still folded beside his plate. "That's enough!"

Heinzi reluctantly took his place at the table, shoveled Mathilde's tray of remaining sausages onto his plate and attacked them hungrily. With his mouth full he ordered the maid to bring him a half dozen fried eggs.

<hr />

Later that morning, Kurt left for his office, dropping off Mary and Anne who had decided to go walking at the forested Grunewald Park. The two women took some stale bread with them to feed the peacocks which wandered about the lawns.

<hr />

Heinzi, alone in the house except for Mathilde, who was busy in the kitchen, sneaked upstairs to Mary's room. Suspicious that the motivation for her unexpected visit to Berlin might have concerned her Jewish tutor, he decided to search her belongings for evidence to support his suspicions.

He hurriedly sorted through the contents of Mary's suitcase, tossing her garments carelessly about after checking the pockets, lining and folds of each item for something to substantiate his hunch.

Finding the small jewel box beneath the clothes, he seized it and dumped out its contents, suspecting that it had a false bottom, common to many jewel boxes. Carefully removing the velvet lining, he discovered the manila envelope with Mary's name scrawled across it.

"Was ist das?" he said to himself.

Opening the unsealed envelope, he was surprised to discover a passport inside. Slipping the passport out, he opened it and was puzzled by the name 'Maria Leonetti Hopkins' and an identifying photograph of an attractive young brunette woman on one of its pages.

"Wer ist diese Frau?" he asked himself.

Knowing how indispensable a passport was for traveling from one country to another, he quickly surmised that the document was a crucial part of an escape plan devised by Mary to rescue her Jewish tutor.

"That little English traitor!" he said aloud.

His first impulse was to destroy the passport, but after considering the situation a few moments, he came up with what he reckoned would be a better plan and put everything back – passport, jewel box, clothes, every-thing – into the suitcase exactly as he had found them.

Chapter Twenty-two

Mary and Anne returned from their excursion to Grunwald Park by the S-Bahn, although Anne was not in favor of taking public transportation. Kurt had offered to drive them home from the vast wooded park with its lake-like Wannsee, but Mary protested, saying she wanted to learn how to get around Berlin on her own using the municipal transport system since taxis were becoming scarce.

Mary went to her room to change for dinner, and, opening her suitcase to select clothes for the evening, she sensed from the wrinkled state and careless folding of her clothes that someone had been into her personal belongings in her absence. Quickly checking to be sure the passport for Ruth was not missing, Mary was relieved to find it still in its hiding place beneath the false bottom of the jewel box.

Since, to the best of her knowledge, Mathilde and Heinzi were the only individuals in the house during her absence, Mary concluded that one of them had been responsible. She was fairly certain that Mathilde, an elderly and trusted servant, was not the guilty party which meant that Heinzi must have been the one who violated her privacy. Was it because of curiosity or some weird fetish – her lingerie seemed especially disordered – or were his motivations more sinister? She considered confronting him on the issue, but since she had no concrete evidence, and he would probably deny it anyway, she dismissed the notion, at least for the present.

At dinner that evening, Heinzi was once again absent. Mary had learned that it was no longer necessary to speculate where he might be. Everyone in the household knew that he was undoubtedly participating in an activity of the Hitler Youth organization which was usually harassing Jews in some manner or occasionally trying to disrupt a Catholic Mass.

"By the way, Mary," Kurt said as he began to slice the pork roast which Mathilde set before him, "I got word at my office this afternoon that there is a train leaving for Paris tomorrow."

"Oh, really?" Mary replied. "I must look into it."

"Kurt and I are sorry to see you leave so soon, but I do understand your mother's concern, Anne said. "The Season is so terribly important in the life of a young lady, such as yourself. It is, after all, where many girls encounter their future husbands."

"Yes, I suppose it is," Mary answered.

The prospect of an imminent departure made it clear that she had to contact Ruth as soon as possible so that they could formulate a plan for her escape. Mary was determined that this time it would be successful – for Andrew's sake and also that of his unborn child.

⚬⌁⌁⚬

The following day, Mary informed Anne and Kurt that she would be off to the railroad station to learn more about a possible train to Paris. Kurt had offered to drive her to the train station later in the day, but Mary said she didn't want to trouble him and would arrange for a taxi. Heinzi, she learned, had still not returned from a Hitler Youth camping excursion to the Alps so she was unable to confront him about rummaging through her suitcase.

Knowing that other cab drivers would be reluctant – or even unwilling – to take her to the Spandaner Vorstadt, a section of Berlin in which the Jews were relocated and confined prior to transport to the labor camps, she decided to contact Radu

She had kept the phone number of Gisela Schmidt, which he had given her on her last visit to Berlin, and had it in her purse.

While Anne and Mathilde were busy preparing bandages in the drawing room and Kurt was at his office, Mary crept secretly into the library and phoned Gisela, who spoke passable English, and promptly put Radu himself on the phone. Mary was pleased that he instantly remembered her and assured her that he would be happy to accommodate her request.

"I come for you maybe in one hour, *Ja?*" he said.

"That's fine," Mary said, sighing in relief, knowing that at least Step One was accomplished.

"*Aber erst moechte ich ins Hackescher Markt fahren, bitte,*" she said to Radu as she climbed into his battered cab, once again struggling with German and wishing she had applied herself more diligently when Ruth tutoring her.

"*Sehr gut, Fraulein,*" Radu replied, then switching to English said, "But why do you want to go to the market first?"

"I must buy food for a friend and also for a trip we may take," she answered.

Radu nodded, his gold earring jiggling, indicating that he understood.

It was already late afternoon when Mary climbed out of the taxi at the dilapidated former convalescent home with her suitcase and a bag of food she had purchased.

"Will you wait here for me? I may be a while," Mary asked. "I'll pay you well."

Although uneasy about the prospect of remaining in the area, he agreed. "I wait for you," he said, pulling a *Gitane* cigarette out of his pocket and lighting it.

In the musty hall full of rat droppings and spider webs, she went to the door of Ruth's quarters and knocked several times, each time louder than before, but received no response. In contrast to her previous visit, all was silent behind the door, no children's voices, no sound of adults quieting them -- nothing --which gave Mary an eerie feeling of foreboding. Was she too late? Had Ruth already been deported to a labor camp as Kurt had speculated?

Bracing herself, she decided to try the knob. Much to her great surprise, she found the door unlocked and, with a certain degree of trepidation, proceeded inside the dark, dingy living quarters. Its lack of furnishings had not changed. The sole item of décor was a brass menorah, empty of candles, which still graced the mantle over the fireplace. The door to the bathroom was closed.

"*Hallo! Ist jemand hier im haus?*" Mary called out in German to see if anyone might respond, her voice reverberating in the nearly empty room.

Then, louder in English, she called out again, "Ruth! Are you here?"

When the bathroom door opened a crack, and Mary saw a single dark eye peering out at her, she gasped.

"Ruth?" she repeated, and the door opened wider revealing her former tutor.

Appearing thin and haggard with a haunted look in her dark eyes, Ruth came slowly forward.

"Ruth, are you all right?" Mary asked anxiously, reaching out to her.

With a wan smile, Ruth allowed Mary to embrace her and said, "Thank God, it's you, Lady Mary. When I heard someone come in just now, I was afraid it was the Gestapo coming for me, so I tried to hide under the bathtub which sits on four iron legs. As you probably know, the escape Andrew and his German friend Herr Reisner so carefully planned failed, and I was forced to return here. Everyone is gone now: my father, the children, their mothers, everyone. The Gestapo came for them – ironically -- the night of my attempted escape. They were taken away without their valuables – jewelry, gold, foreign currency – which they had hidden here. I have been very frightened alone and unable to lock the door. The Gestapo removed all the locks in the building. Every sound I hear strikes terror in my heart. Now, I can go out only in the middle of the night to salvage discarded food from garbage cans. I have to eat. I have to live ....for the baby, Andrew's baby." She placed her hands over her swollen abdomen which was disproportionately prominent because of weight loss.

"I brought you some food," Mary said, setting her suitcase down and opening the bag she was carrying in her other hand. She offered her a loaf of rye bread and a small chunk of cheese. "Eat something first and then we've got to get out of here. I don't want you fainting from hunger along the way. We have a lot ahead of us."

Ruth looked at her hopefully. "You have a plan?"

"I do," Mary affirmed.

Ruth managed a smile. "I have been very worried – more about the baby than about myself. I even thought about leaving the child at a church or on the steps of a Gentile home so it could survive – that's if I live long enough to give birth."

Mary tore off the end of the loaf of rye bread and passed it to her. Then, taking a nail file from her handbag, she cut a piece of cheese. "Here, Ruth. Make yourself a sandwich," she said. Then reaching into the shopping bag again, she produced a small bottle of milk. "Drink this – all of it – for the baby."

Ruth looked at Mary in astonishment. "I cannot believe that a girl whom I always considered spoiled and pampered and inconsiderate would display such a generous spirit," she said. "Why are you doing all this for me? It's very dangerous, even for you to come here. The Gestapo could arrest you."

Wanting to respond, *I'm doing this for Andrew, not you,* Mary held her tongue and instead said, "Hurry and finish. We've got to get moving. I have a taxi waiting outside. There's not a lot of time to accomplish what we must."

"But it's growing dark," Ruth reminded her. "Night comes early in this part of Germany at this time of the year."

"What we must do, is best done in the dark," Mary answered.

"You haven't mentioned Andrew," Ruth said. "Is my husband all right?"

Mary was hesitant about telling her of Andrew's probable demise, feeling her emotional reaction to it might impede the planned escape. Instead she evaded the question, electing to inform her at a less critical time.

"Andrew obtained a false passport for you," she informed her. "From now on you will be 'Maria Leonetti Hopkins', a naturalized British subject, born in Italy."

Deeply moved, Ruth smiled and said, "I knew Andrew would save me."

"For the present, *I* am the one saving you," Mary said, emphasizing the 'I'.

Chapter Twenty-three

Picking up the phone on his office desk, Herman Reisner answered, "Reisner *hier.*"

Outside, beyond his window, a giant magnet on the end of a crane was hoisting a pile of scrap metal from a train's former coal car and transferring it to a waiting truck.

"This is Lord Buckford. I'm telephoning from England. I'm afraid I have some rather bad news for you, Herr Reisner," Nicholas said from inside one of the bunker-like buildings at the now functioning radar center at Bawdsey.

Concerned, Riesner frowned and asked, "Bad news? What is it?"

"Your company has received the last shipment of British scrap metal," Nicholas informed him. "His Majesty's government has just prohibited all future trade with Germany."

"I'm not surprised," Reisner said with a resigned sigh. "I was expecting this. War between our two nations is imminent, I'm sure, despite Mr. Chamberlain's attempts to appease Hitler."

Glancing out the window as he was speaking, Reisner was startled to see a Nazi SS car approaching his office.

"I'd better ring off now, Lord Buckford," Reisner said, his voice suddenly quavering. "Something has come up while we were talking to which I must attend."

"Since I doubt that we will be speaking again soon, I just want to say, Herr Reisner, that I respect you as a gentleman of great integrity in a country whose leadership seems to have lost all sense of honor and decency,"

Nicholas said.

"I've enjoyed our relationship, Lord Buckford, and I respect you as well," Reisner said, adding a farewell in German, *"Lieb wohl, mein freund."*

As Reisner hung up the phone, the SS car screeched to a halt and a pair of SS men jumped out, their guns drawn. Moments later, they burst through his office door.

The scrap metal business magnate calmly remained seated behind his desk.

"Herr Reisner, you are under arrest for acts of treason against the Third Reich," the larger and more formidable of the two SS men announced, glaring contemptuously at Reisner before grabbing him by the arm and roughly yanking him out of his office chair. His smaller cohort took Reisner's other arm and jammed a revolver in his back.

"Schwein!" he muttered. *"Schmutziges schwein!"*

Together, the two SS officers hustled him out the door and into their vehicle.

Chapter Twenty-four

Outside, darkness was beginning to envelope the city as Mary sorted through the clothes in her suitcase, appraising each garment with a critical eye.

"We have to dress you properly," she said to Ruth.

Puzzled, Ruth asked, "What are you talking about?"

"We must be certain that you appear as British as possible," Mary answered, selecting a tartan plaid skirt and a gray Shetland sweater. Passing them to Ruth. "Quickly, put them on. We have much to do before catching that train to Paris tonight."

Ruth did as her former student directed and, when she was dressed in Mary's former clothes, she asked, "How do I look?"

"You look convincingly British," Mary said, then after pondering a moment, added, "Have you a coat?"

"I do," Ruth responded hesitatingly, "But I can't wear it. The yellow Star-of-David will get us arrested immediately."

Unexpectedly, Mary's face lit up. "Perfect!" she said. "Go and get the coat. Also get your German passport stamped '*Jude*' and your *arbeitsbuch* and any other identification documents you have."

Baffled, Ruth asked, "Why?"

"There's no time for questions now. Please, just hurry!"

Although bewildered by Mary's requests, Ruth went into the adjoining room and returned with not only the coat and documents but a velvet dressing gown lined with satin as well.

"What are you doing with that dressing gown?" Mary demanded.

"I sewed my valuables – mostly my late mother's jewelry – inside the lining," Ruth said, holding up the garment.

Mary could hear the clink of jewelry inside the lining. "You're going to require a suitcase for it. There's no room in mine for a bulky item like that dressing gown, even with the sweater and skirt I gave you no longer packed."

"I have a suitcase, but it's a rather old one."

"Good. Go and get it," Mary said. "It will look less suspicious if we both have luggage with us when we board the train."

Ruth folded up the dressing gown and put it in her small, battered suitcase. When she started to put the coat in the suitcase as well, Mary stopped her.

"No, not yet," she ordered sternly. "First, you must stuff all your personal identity papers inside the pockets of that coat. When you finish doing that, you can put it in the suitcase with your dressing gown. Then we can leave."

Fearing that the main entrance of the former convalescent facility was under Gestapo surveillance, Ruth insisted they leave through a basement exit.

Ruth grabbed a box of matches, once used to light the menorah, from the mantel. "The basement is dark," she said

The two young women dashed down the rickety wooden stairs to the pitch black, foul-smelling basement, each carrying her suitcase.

"I can't see a thing," Mary said, gasping as a rat ran over her foot.

Ruth lit a match, illuminating the dank basement, causing the rats to scurry in all directions.

"Is that better?" Ruth asked, heading toward the exit.

"Not really," Mary muttered, brushing a cobweb from her face as she followed Ruth out a badly weathered wooden door which opened into a dark alley dotted with puddles of stagnant rain water.

"Are we going to the railway station?" Ruth asked.

"Not yet. First we have to go to the Grunwald Park."

Ruth was stunned. "Why Grunwald?"

"I don't have time to go into that now. I'll tell you when we arrive there," Mary answered.

"But it's quite far," Ruth protested.

"I have a taxi waiting for us in front of the building. You stay right here in the alley. I shall go and tell the driver. We will pick you up here in the alley."

"No," Ruth said. "I can't go in a taxi. I don't trust the drivers. They will report us to the Gestapo – me as an escaping Jew and you as my facilitator."

"You can trust this driver. I managed to contact the driver who drove us before," Mary assured her. "The Gestapo hate Gypsies almost as much as they hate Jews."

With considerable misgivings, Radu helped the two young women out of his cab at Grunwald Park, whose paths and by-ways through the dense forest around the Wannsee lake Mary had explored earlier with Anne as her guide and mapped out an escape plan in her head. She had realized early on that her mission would require precise planning. She was willing to undertake the dangerous challenge for Andrew – anything for Andrew.

"You hide here?" Radu asked, directing his question at Ruth.

"No," Mary responded for Ruth.

"Good place to hide. Many *Rom* – Gypsies -- hiding here," Radu said, gesturing toward the forest. "Maybe they help you if you need. *Rom* good people. They give you food if you need. A Gypsy can survive anywhere. We know how from many years on the road, many countries."

"That's good to know," Mary said. "Thank you."

Radu got back in his cab. "*Viel gluck!* Good luck!" he hollered as he drove away, disappearing into the night.

Gazing at the tall pines and other trees surrounding them in the darkness, Ruth looked at Mary suspiciously and said, "Why did we come here? This is not a safe place. The Gestapo patrol this park all the time looking for Jews who might be trying to hide among these trees."

"You've got to trust me, Ruth. It's essential to our escape plan."

"I can no longer trust anyone," Ruth said ruefully.

"You trusted Andrew, didn't you?"

"Yes, of course."

"He is responsible for everything I am now doing," Mary declared. "You must understand that and believe it."

Trailing Mary somewhat reluctantly, Ruth followed her along a network of trails through the urban forest until they arrived at the shore of the lake known to Berliners as the Wannsee. A wooden pier for small boats extended out across the water beneath which a flock of ducks were sleeping. With the approach of the two young women, the aquatic birds quacked noisily and scattered, flapping their wings and splashing water about as they fled.

"Go to the end of the pier and drop that coat with the yellow star and all your identity papers into the water," Mary directed. "I'll wait for you here."

This part of Mary's plan suddenly dawned on Ruth. "Ah, I am now starting to understand. You want it to appear as if I've committed suicide, don't you?"

"Exactly," Mary confirmed.

"As so many of my people have already done, rather than be imprisoned in one of the Nazi's labor camps," Ruth said.

As Ruth started toward the pier with the coat, a Gestapo officer riding a motorcycle suddenly roared out of the shadowy forest. The two young women instantly dove into a pile of fallen leaves and pine needles behind a nearby fallen tree.

They watched in fear as the Gestapo officer got off his motorcycle and began searching the area with a flashlight. At one point he came so close that they could hear the footsteps of his shiny black boots crushing the dead leaves and snapping twigs from fallen branches around them.

The beam of his flashlight grazed their heads, forcing them down even lower into the leaves and pine needles, their hearts pounding.

Eventually, apparently satisfied that no one was lurking around, the Gestapo officer climbed back on his motorcycle and rode away with an even louder roar.

Mary and Ruth rose to their feet and brushed themselves off, both still shaking and breathing hard from the close call.

"I think it would be safe now for me to get rid of the coat," Ruth said, starting toward the pier once again. "I don't think the Gestapo will be back for a while."

Mary waited silently in the shadow of a giant pine tree while Ruth walked to the end of the wooden pier. She listened anxiously for the sound of the coat splashing as it hit the water.

Reaching the end of the pier, Ruth released the coat with the yellow star, its pockets stuffed with her identity documents, and watched as it slowly sank. The yellow star glimmered in the dark waters of the lake, slowly fading from sight.

"There! It's done," she muttered to herself aloud. "Ruth Herzog is gone, committed suicide by drowning herself in the Berlin Wannsee, as so many like her have already done."

Returning to Mary, Ruth asked, "Now what is next?"

"We go to the Wannsee S-Bahn station and ride to the Gleisdreieck terminal where the U-Bahn crosses rails with the S-Bahn and from which the long distance steam trains for Paris depart," Mary replied. "You and I are going to be on that Paris train."

Ruth began to visibly shake. "I can't go to that Gleisdreieck Station."

Mary was stunned. "Why not?"

"Because many of the Nazi deportations of Jews occur there," Ruth answered. "And, besides, I have no papers."

"You will have," Mary reassured her without taking the time to explain further.

⚉ ⚉

Both young women were thoroughly exhausted by the time they reached the Grunwald S-Bahn station. Ruth regarded the facility with considerable trepidation. To reassure her, Mary opened her suitcase in the shadows outside the station and took the bogus passport out of the secret compartment in the jewel box.

"From now on you are Maria Leonetti Hopkins, a naturalized British subject born in Italy," she said as she handed the quasi-official document to Ruth. "Try and act the part."

"That's what it will be – acting," Ruth said, accepting the bogus identity.

"Now, are you ready to board the S-Bahn to the Gleisdreieck Station?"

Ruth shook her head. "No. I am afraid to be seen on the S-Bahn. The Gestapo ride it even at this hour of night when there are very few passengers."

"Why are you afraid?" Mary challenged. "You have your new identity papers."

"How do I know the Gestapo will believe them? Many agents have been to our relocation place. They will recognize me."

Becoming exasperated, Mary said, "Then how do you propose we get there? It's much too far to walk with suitcases…"

"I know a way, but it still will require walking," Ruth informed her. "But not nearly as much as walking on the streets – and it's much safer."

Mary was confused. "What are you talking about?"

"Come. I'll show you," Ruth said, taking her by the hand.

Ruth led Mary through the dense forest to the entrance of a tunnel totally concealed by a tangled mass of briers, vines and weeds.

Ruth furiously tore the vegetation away so that they could enter. "This is an old, abandoned U-Bahn tunnel that is no longer used," she said. "It leads underground directly to the Gleisdreieck Station."

Mary was incredulous. "How do you know that?"

"A group of Jews I knew hid here for a while."

"What happened to them?"

"The Gestapo dogs eventually picked up their scent, and they were arrested and sent off to one of the labor camps," Ruth explained, her voice breaking. "The SS use it now to hide precious works of art they have stolen from museums and Jewish homes. They store them in this tunnel until they can secretly sell them for huge amounts of money to buyers in other European countries or America."

Mary frowned. "Is it safe then?"

"We'll soon find out," Ruth said, starting into the tunnel. "I doubt that the SS men are going to come for their art works at night."

"Do they store such valuable treasures without someone to guard them?"

"I've gotten word that there is not enough manpower for that," Ruth replied. "But they depend on the fact that most people are too frightened of the SS to try and steal anything."

Mary looked dubious. "Then we're taking a chance?"

"We have no choice," Ruth responded.

Mary followed her and felt tracks beneath her feet, but could see nothing. "Do you have any matches left? I can't see in this blackness."

"Yes, but I'm saving them for emergencies," Ruth advised. "Just follow the tracks."

"How can I follow them when I can't see them?" Mary complained.

"Then just follow me," Ruth answered.

It seemed to Mary as though they had walked for hours, stumbling along the former U-Bahn tracks, often encountering sections covered by ankle-deep water. Unlike Mary, Ruth seemed undisturbed by spider webs or rats as large as cats or even bats suspended on the roof of the tunnel.

Eventually the abandoned tunnel connected with another tunnel which was currently in use.

"Fortunately, very few trains operate at night," Ruth said. "Be sure to stay in the middle of the tracks and away from the rail which conducts the electric current."

"Oh, lovely!" Mary groaned.

Minutes after Ruth finished speaking, a U-Bahn train whooshed past them with a loud roar, pinning them against the wall and blasting them with gusts of fetid air.

＊＊＊

It felt like a miracle when the two young women finally emerged from the end of the tunnel and entered the train station with relatively few mishaps, despite the numerous hazards and often wading through ankle-deep water. The two vigorously brushed dead leaves, pine needles and dirt from their clothes.

Although they were nervous and paranoid about being suspect when buying their tickets, both Mary and Ruth were ecstatic that they were able to book passage aboard the Paris-bound train. Because they carried British passports, they were given priority and a first class compartment. Very few German citizens were permitted to leave the country at the time and then only under the most dire circumstances.

As soon as permission to board their train was announced, Mary and Ruth, who had been hiding in toilet stalls in the women's restroom to escape the vigilant eyes of the Gestapo who relentlessly patrolled the corridors and platforms of the station, sought the sanctuary of an empty compartment.

Once inside, they stowed their suitcases in the overhead racks, pulled the shades and prepared to take their seats on opposite benches in the compartment.

"My shoes are soaked and my feet are very wet," Mary complained.

"There are worse things than wet feet," Ruth responded. "Your shoes will dry with time. Remove them until they do."

"What? And ride a train to Paris with my shoes off? I don't think that would be fitting. We're probably going to have to share this compartment with others. "

"Das macht nichts, Ruth muttered in German, "I'm concerned about more important matters."

"Such as?" Mary asked.

"Getting my jewelry through Customs at the border," Ruth responded.

"None of the Customs officials will be able to see it sewed in the lining of that dressing gown of yours."

"No, but they could possibly feel it," Ruth countered. "Or hear it jingling about."

"Why are you thinking of this now?"

"I was too concerned with other things earlier," Ruth answered. "I must get rid of it. These items are not worth our getting caught over. The only two things I can't leave behind are my mother's wedding band and my own wedding band from Andrew."

Yes. Andrew, Mary thought to herself.

Ruth retrieved her suitcase from the overhead rack and placed it on the seat. Then she knelt on the floor of the compartment, removed the dressing gown from the valise and carefully opened a few stitches in its inner lining. Mary heard a soft, jingling sound as Ruth began to shake out the enclosed jewelry. She found the two rings and put them aside, but as she viewed the other heirlooms, which could be the only mementos she would ever have of her family, she reconsidered. With a heavy heart and more trepidation, she returned the jewelry inside the lining, expertly pulling and tying the thread tightly to seal the seam shut.

"Stop fretting. We'll soon be in France," Mary assured her. "France is different from Germany. There are no Gestapo or SS there."

"Not yet," Ruth replied.

At that moment, the door of the compartment slid open and a middle-aged couple entered speaking German. It startled the girls.

"Damn!" Mary swore under her breath. "I was so hoping we would have this compartment to ourselves."

"*Guten abend,*" the middle-aged, buxom woman and her slight husband each greeted Mary and Ruth.

In an attempt to remind Ruth not to say a word in German, Mary quickly answered, "I'm sorry but my friend and I don't speak German. We're English."

Remaining silent and relieved by Mary's swift thinking, Ruth smiled at the new arrivals.

"No matter," the woman said. "My husband and I speak English. Permit me to introduce ourselves. I am Helga Busch and this is my husband Franz."

Good evening, ladies," Franz Busch said, removing his hat in deference to Mary and Ruth.

Studying Ruth, Helga remarked, "You do not look English."

"I was born in Italy," Ruth answered.

Franz's face lighted up. "Ah, then you are Italian, *Signorina?*"

"*Signora,*" Ruth corrected him, mustering the best Italian accent she could. "My husband is British."

"How interesting," Helga commented.

Ruth got up and moved to Mary's seat. It was obvious that she did not want to share a seat with either of the Germans.

Mary felt that the German couple seemed to be studying her and Ruth with more than casual interest and concluded that sharing the compartment with this pair to Paris would be psychologically uncomfortable.

Perhaps even dangerous.

Chapter Twenty-five

After dinner, Mathilde served Anne and Kurt coffee in the library. Anne was once again preparing bandages, and Kurt smoking his pipe and reading the day's newspaper.

"Well, I wonder if Mary managed to get aboard the train to Paris this evening," Anne mused as she lay her bandages aside and lifted a steaming cup from Mathilde's tray. "She hasn't telephoned us."

"Yes, it would be good to know, but telephoning from one country to another is not easy these days," Kurt reminded his wife, lowering the newspaper to add a generous splash of cognac to his coffee. A bottle sat on the end table next to his chair. "Tonight's Paris train will probably be the last one for a few days with all the rail lines now being used to supply the military and transport Jews to labor camps. I'm sure we'll get word from Mary, or her parents, when she arrives back in England."

"I do hope so," Anne said.

As Mathilde was leaving, Anne asked, "Has Heinzi returned yet? We missed him at dinner tonight."

"Yes, a few minutes ago," the maid replied. "He's in the kitchen. I'm re-heating dinner for him."

At that moment, Heinzi strolled into the room, still in his Hitler youth uniform, and nearly collided with Mathilde as she was leaving. He snatched the bottle of cognac from the end table beside his father and, raising it to his mouth, took a generous swig.

Kurt scowled.

Anne indicated the nearby china cabinet. "There are brandy glasses in the cabinet, Heinzi," she said, her tone reproachful.

"I don't need a glass," he sneered, taking a second swig from the bottle.

"Get a glass, damn it," Kurt ordered sternly, but Heinzi ignored him and defiantly took a third swig from the bottle.

"You're drinking too much these days," Anne remarked.

"So what?" Heinzi shot back.

"It's not good for you, dear."

"Neither is living in this house with the two of you," Heinzi complained.

Anne and Kurt exchanged troubled glances.

"That's enough, Heinzi," Kurt snapped with as much authority as he could muster.

Changing the subject, Heinzi asked, "Any word from Mary?"

"Not so far," Anne replied. "Your father and I are just wondering if she got on the train to Paris all right."

"If she did, she's going to be in trouble at the border," Heinzi remarked, startling his parents.

"Why do you say that?" Kurt demanded to know.

"Because she's probably trying to smuggle that Jewish friend of hers out of the country," Heinzi answered.

Kurt scowled again. "How do you know?"

"I found a counterfeit passport hidden in her luggage. It was issued in the name of Maria Lionetti Hopkins. Why else would Mary have such a passport in her possession?"

Anne gasped. "You rummaged through Mary's personal luggage?"

"It was my duty," Heinzi replied.

Kurt was incensed. "What the hell do you mean that it was your 'duty'?"

"I had to find out if my parents were harboring an enemy of the Third Reich in their home. That counterfeit passport gave me my answer," Heinzi said as he paused to take yet another gulp of cognac. "Well, it won't do that Jew friend of hers any good. I intend to see to it that Maria Leonetti Hopkins won't be crossing any borders."

Kurt slammed his cup down on the end-table, splashing coffee on its surface and threw his newspaper aside. "You'll do nothing of the sort!" he declared, jumping to his feet.

"Oh, no?" Heinzi challenged. "Just you wait and see. Mary Ashmore is a meddling Jew-lover. She and that Jew friend of hers will get what they deserve."

"What a shameful way to talk," Anne said.

Sneering in defiance, Heinzi crossed the room and grabbed the telephone.

"Who are you calling?" Kurt demanded.

"Gestapo headquarters," Heinzi replied and gave the operator a number.

"Put that damned phone down!" Kurt ordered. "Put it down this minute!"

Ignoring his father, Heinzi calmly said to the Gestapo officer at the other end of the line, "I wish to inform you that there is a young English woman who is aiding a Jewish female by the name of Ruth Herzog to escape."

Shocked and alarmed by Heinzi's actions, Kurt sprang across the room and tried to wrest the phone from his son's hands just as he was starting to give a description of Mary and knocked over a lamp.

"Stop it! Both of you!" Anne cried out, tossing her bandages aside, and preparing to intervene.

Enraged, Kurt raised his fist and landed a fierce blow squarely on Heinzi's jaw, knocking him to the floor. The cognac bottle he was still holding and the telephone went flying. The bottle struck the china cabinet, smashing its glass front.

"Stop!" Anne cried.

Standing over his son, who was massaging his jaw and bleeding from the corner of his mouth, Kurt, breathing hard, said with disgust, "What kind of monster have you become? Do you realize the danger you have put those young women in with your phone call to the Gestapo? Your conduct is a disgrace. You have become a detestable human being without a trace of decency or honor."

"I serve the Third Reich," Heinzi declared, dabbing at his bleeding mouth with his Hitler Youth neckerchief. Raising his arm in a Nazi salute, he shouted, "Heil Hitler!"

It was nearly midnight when the Paris Express pulled out of the station. The German couple sharing the compartment with Mary and Ruth fell asleep almost immediately. The wife, Helga, rested her head on her husband Franz's bony shoulder and snored loudly.

Despite their earlier escapades, Mary and Ruth were wide awake on the opposite seat. Although exhausted, they were too wary and anxious to sleep.

"I won't be able to sleep until we are safely in France," Mary remarked.

"It will be England and Andrew for me," Ruth said.

Shortly after dawn, the train was still traveling through the rural German countryside when a porter rapped on the compartment door to announce that breakfast was available in the dining car.

His notification awakened the sleeping Helga who yawned and shook Franz to wake him. Glancing at Mary and Ruth, she asked, "Shall we have breakfast together?"

"I'm not hungry," Ruth snapped.

"I'm going to remain here with my friend," Mary informed the couple.

"As you wish," Helga said, sounding peeved. She and Franz straightened their clothing, combed their hair and left the compartment.

When they were gone, Mary asked, "Why do you not want to go to the dining car for breakfast?

Ruth shook her head. "Not with that pair," she said. "I don't trust them. Didn't you see the way they kept staring at us? I think they are spies."

Mary decided not to attempt to argue the point with her former tutor. After the harsh living conditions and unrelenting persecution Ruth had suffered in Berlin, Mary could well understand her deep-seated fear.

"I don't want to risk anything happening which would prevent me from arriving safely in Britain and joining my husband," Ruth said. Then caressing her slightly swollen abdomen, she added,. "Me and my expected baby."

Mary placed her hand reassuringly over Ruth's and gave it a squeeze. "We shall make it. I promise you that," she declared. "We must ... for Andrew's sake."

"I never realized before how much Andrew meant to you," Ruth said. "I can't believe the sacrifices you have been willing to make and the risks you have undertaken for him and myself and our baby. What a devoted friend you have been!" Ruth reached out and took both of Mary's hands in hers. "When we were in England and you were my student – an indifferent one, I must admit – and I had no idea of the courage and selflessness you possess. It's no wonder that Andrew is so fond of you, Mary."

Mary looked down, still ashamed of everything that had transpired, especially knowing that her selfishness could have ultimately ended Ruth's life.

It was clearly apparent that telling Ruth that Andrew was no longer alive was going to be an exceedingly difficult thing to do. She agonized about when and how to tell her. For the time being, she felt that the stress of their escape was enough for the pregnant, frightened and malnourished young woman to endure. Later, somehow, somewhere, she would have to summon the courage to let her know the truth.

Leaning against the window, Ruth mused, "Andrew often said that you were the little sister he never had."

Little sister, indeed! Mary thought to herself, momentarily experiencing a twinge of indignation.

Chapter Twenty-six

Mary and Ruth dined on what remained of the Swiss cheese and rye bread Mary had purchased in Berlin's Hackesher Markt. After feeding Ruth before they set out from Berlin, she had stuffed what was left into her suitcase for their escape from the country.

"It would be pleasant if we had something to drink," Mary said, then, "Oh! I just remembered … !" and hopped up on the seat to retrieve her suitcase from the overhead rack. Inside, she withdrew a small package of tea.

Ruth stared at the package, shook her head and said, "Sometimes you amaze me, Mary."

"Now all we lack is some hot water and cups," Mary said. "Perhaps if I ring for the porter, he may be able to accommodate us."

"It's nice to have some time by ourselves without Helga and Franz," Ruth said. "They keep staring at us – especially me – watching every move we make, listening to every word we say. They make me very uncomfortable. I'm concerned about what they might do."

"I'll take care of them for you," Mary promised, a sly smile on her lips. Ruth was baffled. "How?"

"You"ll see."

While Mary and Ruth were waiting for the porter to respond to Mary's ring, Helga and Franz returned from the dining car.

"Well, I see that both of you are eating after all," Helga commented.

"Just sandwiches," Mary said with a shrug. "We're waiting for the porter to bring us some hot water and cups for tea. You know how we English do love our tea." Turning to Ruth, she said, "Don't we, Maria?"

"Oh, yes," Ruth responded, going along with the identity ruse. "I look forward to tea-time every afternoon."

The porter, an aged man and apparently not eligible for the German army as most of the train's male employees seemed to be, supplied a carafe of hot water and four cups, as Mary had requested, and she set about brewing tea as soon as he left.

While Helga and Franz kept their gaze fixed on Ruth, Mary, her back to the group, secretly took a small bottle of a dark red liquid from a small compartment in her suitcase and dispensed a few drops of it in two of the four cups. Mary was careful to present the two cups containing the drops to Helga and Franz.

"Mmmm, this is very nice tea," Helga said.

"It's a very special blend," Mary explained. "From Ceylon."

Franz wrinkled his nose. "It tastes a bid odd – not unpleasant, just odd."

Helga brushed aside her husband's comment with a wave of her pudgy hand. "Everything from Ceylon tastes odd," she said.

⊰⊱

Bouncing along in the open side-car near the city of Cologne, Heinzi, wearing only a thin jacket over his Hitler Youth uniform, was shivering from the cold wind blowing off the waters of the Rhine river. The motorcycle, a favorite Nazi means of transportation, had been designated for the mission by the Gestapo High Command with the assurance that they would be able to arrive at the border before – or at least simultaneously with – the train from Berlin. It was estimated that this older train would require a minimum of twelve hours to reach the border between the two countries.

The Gestapo agent, firmly gripping the handlebars of the motorcycle with his gloved hands, wore a heavy leather jacket which Heinzi envied during the long ride from Berlin which was proving longer and far more taxing than he had imagined. His past camping expeditions to the Alps with the Hitler Youth had not adequately prepared him for the rigors of this current excursion. He hoped that they would arrive at the French-German border near Karlsruhe where train passengers from Germany were required to pass through a German Customs Station prior to boarding the French train to Paris in time to apprehend Mary and Ruth.

Heinzi tolerated the hardships of the journey by repeatedly convincing himself that he was demonstrating his devotion to the Third Reich by helping to intercept a fleeing Jew and her British accomplice.

———

Helga and Franz had fallen into a deep sleep after drinking Mary's laudanum-laced tea.

"I can't believe how soundly they're sleeping," Ruth said, glancing at the snoring couple on the opposite seat.

"I'm not surprised," Mary replied. "I put double the usual dose of laudanum in their tea."

Ruth was shocked. "Why would you do such a thing?"

"So you could relax," Mary replied with a grin.

Ruth was puzzled. "Where did you get it?"

"I brought it with me from England to help me in case I had difficulty sleeping," Mary replied. "The doctor prescribed it to help after the death of my horse Blue Bonnet."

Ruth managed a smile. "You're a very clever girl, Mary – more clever than I would have imagined," she said, undoubtedly referring to Mary's performance as a former student. "And you've done so much for me. I shall never forget it."

On the outskirts of Mannheim, the train came to a sudden stop, jolting the German couple awake.

"What's happening?" Mary asked, turning to Ruth.

Her face pressed against the glass peering out the window, Mary observed a trainman operating a switching mechanism intended to divert their train from the main rails to a side-track.

An announcement in German by the engineer was broadcast throughout the train.

Without thinking, Mary turned to Ruth and asked, "What did he say?"

Hearing her, Helga and Franz snapped to attention and once again eyed Ruth suspiciously.

Immediately realizing the serious blunder she had committed, Mary forced a laugh. "Oh, how silly of me! You wouldn't know any more than I do, would you, Maria? You barely remember your Italian. Why would I ever expect you to understand German? Forgive me."

Ruth made no response, but Franz, slurring his words somewhat, which Mary attributed possibly to the laudantum, spoke up, explaining, "The engineer said he was forced to make a temporary stop on the side-rack so that another train behind us could pass."

A few minutes later, another train approached on the parallel main track. At first Mary paid no attention to it, assuming it was just an ordinary freight train until she happened to observe that the central door of one of the cattle cars was open. Expecting to see a heard of cattle on the way to market, instead she was shocked to realize that men, women and children were crowded together in the latticed cattle car. Their faces appeared gaunt and frightened at the prospect of the death camp to which they were being transported.

Stunned, Mary exclaimed, "I can't believe it! There are people in those cattle cars!"

"Those people are the enemies of the Third Reich being expelled from German society," Franz commented, a note of smug satisfaction in his voice.

Ruth stared out the window. A man visible through the open cattle car door bore a striking resemblance to her father. Startled, she was shaken to her core.

"Swine! All of them are swine – lower than swine," Helga ranted. "Jewish swine!"

With Helga's words, Ruth suddenly turned away from the window, and Mary realized that tears were streaming down her face. She hoped that Helga and Franz were too drugged to observe that she was crying.

"What is wrong with your friend?" Franz asked Mary, indicating that he was not as sedated as she had hoped.

Aware that Ruth had undoubtedly considered the possibility that her physician father might well be among those being hauled off to what was likely their ultimate doom, Mary put her arm comfortingly around Ruth.

"Maria is a very sensitive soul. She cannot abide, nor understand, cruelty. It's revolting that certain humans are being treated like animals," Mary said, gesturing toward the passing train, each cattle car crammed with human beings. Unable to restrain her feelings of outrage, she added, "As Germans, you should be ashamed."

Helga and Franz made no reply and, instead, merely grunted contemptuously and, once again, fell into a deep sleep.

Mary was relieved that the laudanum was resuming its effect.

❦

As the sun rose in an uncharacteristic blue sky filled with fluffy white clouds, the train reverted to the main track and slowly resumed its journey. When the aged conductor slid open the compartment door and made an announcement in German, the couple on the opposite seat were still sleeping, Helga snoring loudly.

With both Helga and Franz asleep, Mary felt it was safe to ask Ruth what he had said.

"He announced that the train will be reaching the French border in a few minutes and that we should get our passports and visas in order and prepare our luggage for Customs," Ruth explained.

❦

The train stopped at the Border Control Station, a drab building surrounded by a chain-link fence topped with multiple strands of barbed wire on the German side of the border.

On the French side of the fence, Mary was relieved to see that the Paris express train was awaiting the transfer of passengers. The delay of the German train near Mannheim had not disrupted the schedule.

A uniformed Customs agent ordered the passengers to form a single line in front of the door of the Border Control Station and enter one by one.

Mary and Ruth, carrying their suitcases, filed off the German train with the other passengers. Helga and Franz lagged behind, their gait stumbling from the effects of the laudanum.

Instead of joining the line that was forming outside the Border Control Station, Mary pulled Ruth into a dense grove of pine trees and whispered, "I think you'd better give me that velvet dressing gown in your suitcase. There's plenty of room in mine since we finished the food I brought with us. I probably have a better chance of getting it through Customs than you do. You're more badly shaken from witnessing those people in cattle cars than myself. You might generate too much suspicion in your present state of nervousness."

Hesitant at first, Ruth looked all around to be certain that nobody could see them, then opened her suitcase and transferred the dressing gown with the heirloom jewelry to Mary's.

As they left the pine grove and got into line, an announcement in German was issued over the loudspeaker. The only part of the message Mary could decipher was the name 'Maria Leonetti Hopkins'.

Alarmed, she turned to Ruth for a translation.

"They say I must report to the head of the Border Control Station immediately," Ruth replied, looking apprehensive.

"I'll go with you," Mary offered.

"No," Ruth refused. "It's better if you stay and hold our place in line."

Ruth left the line and reported to the station where she was directly escorted into the office of the head of the Border Control Station. A wooden plaque on his desk bore the name 'KAPITAN OSCAR EKHARDT'. He did not rise as she entered, but instead pointed to a hard wooden chair in front of his desk.

"Your passport, please," he said to her in English.

Opening her purse, Ruth passed it to him.

After studying the document a few minutes, he raised his eyes and said, "So, Mrs. Hopkins, you were born in Italy?"

"I was," Ruth affirmed, struggling to remain as calm as possible. She kept her hands clasped tightly together in her lap to conceal their trembling from Ekhardt.

"Are you not nostalgic for your homeland?" he asked, squinting at her suspiciously behind his black-framed glasses.

"Not at all. I was very young when my parents emigrated to England. I remember almost nothing of Italy."

"But, surely, you must admire Signor Mussolini?"

"I have no interest in Italian political matters."

Ekhardt leaned back in his chair, exposing the thick roll of fat around his mid-section.

A well-fed Nazi, Ruth thought contemptuously.

"You were in Berlin recently visiting friends, were you not?" he asked.

"I was."

"What was your address while you were in our capital?"

"I don't recall my friends' address. German addresses are difficult for me to remember."

Ekhardt merely nodded then turned his attention to her passport once again. "There is something irregular about one of these stamps," he said. "Can you explain it?"

"I know nothing of matters such as that," Ruth replied, becoming fearful. Was this man playing a cat-and-mouse game with her?

Ekhardt grunted. "No, you wouldn't, would you, Mrs. Hopkins?" After some moments of deliberation, he returned her passport to her, affixed a 'Passed' sticker to her suitcase and pointed to the exit door. "You may go now."

"What about Customs?" she asked, referring to her suitcase which she had placed beside her chair.

"That won't be necessary," he replied without an explanation as he shifted papers in preparation for his next interview.

Ruth left the office feeling relieved, although still wondering what had prompted the interview and also why she had not had her luggage subjected to inspection. She now regretted that she had transferred her dressing gown with the hidden jewelry to Mary.

Mary, now separated from Ruth by a fence which divided those who had passed the Customs inspection from those who were still waiting, received a 'thumbs-up' signal from her former tutor on the other side, indicating that she had successfully passed the inspection.

When it was Mary's turn to submit her suitcase to the rather gruff-appearing Customs agent, he ordered her in English, "You will empty the contents of your suitcase, Miss."

Mary complied, and the agent quickly dismissed the usual items of clothing, focusing instead on the velvet dressing gown containing Ruth's jewelry sewed into its lining causing Mary's heart to pound. He calmly slashed the silk lining with a knife, and the half dozen or so rings, bracelets, brooches, necklaces and a gold pocket watch tumbled out onto the counter. The gem-encrusted items glittered brilliantly even in the dim light of the inspection station.

Mary's heart was now in her throat.

Outside the whistle of the French train sounded, signaling that it would be soon departing, striking fear into Mary that she would be retained and miss it.

"Whose jewelry is this?" the agent demanded.

"Mine, of course," Mary answered indignantly. "Who else would it possibly belong to?"

"And you purchased these items in Germany?" he continued.

"Don't be ridiculous," she scolded. "These pieces are heirlooms which have been in my family for centuries."

"Why are you traveling with so many valuable pieces, and why are all of them concealed in this garment?" he persisted, eyeing her suspiciously and pointing to the dressing gown.

"Well, you see," Mary began, "I assumed it would be safer to have my friends' maid sew them into the lining of my dressing gown rather than carrying them loose on my person."

Puzzled by her answer, the agent frowned, "'Safer'?" he repeated.

"There are so many thieves in Berlin these days," she said.

The agent raised his eyebrows. "Yes, the damned Gypsies," he nodded. "But we Nazis are rounding them up and sending them to labor camps where they will have to give up their thieving ways for hard work."

"That serves them right!" Mary said, hating herself for going along with his bigoted ideas, but the desperate nature of the situation made her willing to agree with anything.

Returning to his interrogation, the agent asked, "Why did you bring all this valuable jewelry to Germany?"

"I was the guest of Graf and Graefin von Rhorsbach in Berlin. Perhaps you may have heard of the Graf? He's quite prominent in German banking."

The agent shook his head. "No. I have not."

"Anyway, I thought there might be special occasions such as balls, parties, the opera where fine jewelry would be *de riguer,*" she continued, using a French phrase she had learned from Mademoiselle Fouchet.

"This is wartime," the agent snapped as he selected a solid gold wedding band and squinted to read the engraved inscription inside it.

Mary held her breath.

Scowling, he said, "What are you doing with a wedding ring with Hebrew writing?"

Mary forced a laugh. "Don't be silly, sir. That's not Hebrew writing at all. It's ancient Celtic, the language of my Scottish ancestors. It's similar to the old Irish Gaelic."

The agent seemed baffled by her explanation.

Outside the train whistle sounded once again.

"Please, sir," Mary pleaded anxiously. "Give me back my things so I may leave. I can't miss my train."

Instead of responding, the agent summoned Captain Ekhardt from his office and confided something to him in German.

"You are being retained, Miss," Ekhardt said.

Inwardly terrified, Mary, nevertheless, gasped indignantly. "What!? That's absurd!"

Backing down somewhat in the face of her outrage, Ekhardt said, "Unless, of course, you can prove these jewels are yours and that you brought them from England with you." He and the agent exchanged a sly, conspiratorial glance.

"How can I possibly do that?" Mary demanded. "I never carry documents for my jewelry when I travel."

Ekhardt selected the wedding band with the questioned inscription from the collection. "Quite simple," he said. "You will simply place this ring on your finger."

Mary immediately realized that Ekhardt could see that all the rings were obviously too small for her fingers. Panic-stricken, but fiercely determined, she pretended to cough and, covering her mouth with both hands, managed to inconspicuously wet her ring finger. She then seized the wedding band and forced it, with great effort and the aid of saliva, over the knuckles of the fourth finger of her left hand. "My hands always swell a bit while traveling." She grinned triumphantly and waved the ring on her finger in front of the head of the Border Control Station.

Ekhardt, however, was unimpressed. "All of these rings, please, Miss," he calmly insisted.

One by one, Mary similarly forced the seven remaining rings on her seven remaining fingers with even greater difficulty, then boldly displayed her bejeweled hands to Ekhardt. The rings were squeezing and compressing her flesh to the point of agony, but she stubbornly suppressed any outward expression of pain.

"There now! Are you quite satisfied, sir?" she said.

Outside the train whistle blew for what Mary feared might be the last time.

Shaking his head in dismay, Ekhardt shoved the remainder of the jewelry and the velvet dressing gown back into her suitcase and had the agent stamp it 'Passed'. Then, he waved her toward the exit.

Although suffering severe discomfort from the constricting rings, Mary grabbed her suitcase and handbag and hurried outside to join Ruth.

Looking at her red and rapidly swelling hands, Ruth was distressed. "I'm so sorry I put you through all that just for the sake of my jewelry," she apologized.

Ignoring the apology, Mary said, "We've a train to catch," and the two of them rushed toward the gate which was guarded by a pair of German sentries, each armed and restraining a German shepherd dog on a leash.

On the other side of that gate, both Mary and Ruth knew that their goal – France – lay. Only the sentries and their dogs stood between them and freedom.

Looking disheveled and dusty, Heinzi burst into Ekhardt's office. Seizing the Border Control Station chief by the lapels of his Nazi uniform, he blurted in German, "A German Jew in her mid-to-late twenties, and her younger British friend are escaping!"

"We've already gotten a cable about them from headquarters, but we have processed many passengers today. You can be sure that we have not let any unauthorized German escape our attention," Ekhardt replied, shoving Heinzi away.

"But you don't understand," Heinzi continued. "Both are suspected spies, and the Jew has false documents!"

Although not alarmed to the same degree as this Hitler Youth individual standing before him was, Ekhardt, nevertheless, suspected that one of the young women to whom Heinzi was referring was likely the young Brit whom he had just interrogated and cleared.

That very well could have been Hebrew writing in the ring, he thought, realizing that he may have made a serious error in judgment.

Ekhardt immediately notified the pair of sentries at the gate separating Germany from France to apprehend the two young women now approaching them.

As Mary and Ruth were about to file through the gate, the young sentries unleashed their German shepherd dogs on them.

"Run!" Mary cried to Ruth as she saw that the dogs racing toward them.

The German shepherds caught up with the pair just a few steps from the gate. Frightened, Mary threw her suitcase at the snarling dog nearest her, but that didn't prevented it from sinking its teeth into her calf, forcing her to the ground. As she lay on the pavement, the dog pounced on her and continued its mauling.

The second dog clamped its teeth on Ruth's arm, pulling her down into the pavement beside Mary.

On the French side of the fence, that country's border guards were appalled by the sight of two young women viciously set upon by dogs, but were restricted by law from intervening.

The Nazi border guards called off the dogs and approached Mary and Ruth, both of whom were bleeding from the dog bites, their clothing dusty and torn. The sentries roughly yanked them to their feet and hustled them back inside the Border Control Station to face Ekhardt.

Upset and indignant, Mary ignored her bleeding injuries and angrily confronted the head of the station.

"See here, sir, you have no right to treat British subjects, whom you have already cleared, in such a brutal and dastardly manner."

"'British spies', you mean," Ekhardt corrected.

"Mrs. Hopkins and I are not spies," Mary insisted emphatically.

Focusing his attention on Ruth, Ekhardt said, "And Mrs. Hopkins, we have been informed, is not British at all, nor is she 'Mrs. Hopkins'. We have reason to believe that she is a Jew by the name of Ruth Herzog."

Panic-stricken, Mary mustered every ounce of courage she could and demanded, "What is the source of such false and damaging information?"

"I'll let you meet him," Ekhardt said with a grin as he opened the door of his office and ordered Heinzi to come forward.

Swaggering into the room, Heinzi reeked of arrogant confidence.

Mary gasped, flabbergasted to see him. She feared that all that she and Ruth had been striving for and endured was now lost.

Indicating Mary and Ruth, Ekhardt addressed Heinzi using his Hitler Youth rank, "*Scharfuehrer* von Rohrsback, are these the two young women you denounced to Gestapo headquarters in Berlin?"

Heinzi looked at Mary, who was bleeding from dog bites and abrasions suffered when she was attacked and dragged to the ground by the German shepherd. Her limbs bore impressions of canine teeth, her clothes were ripped and her hands grotesquely swollen.

Ruth was in a similar state.

Mary glared at him with utter revulsion and disdain while Ruth, in contrast, appeared terrified and defeated, fearing that her life and that of her unborn infant were now doomed.

Heinzi remained silent and seemed nervous and dazed as though thinking, *What on earth have I done?*

Losing patience with him, Ekhardt, demanded, "Speak up, *Scharfuehrer* von Rohrsbach. Are they or are they not the pair of young women you denounced?"

Stammering nervously, Heinzi muttered, "I've … I've made a mistake … a serious error. These young ladies are not the ones I described to Gestapo headquarters in Berlin. Please, sir, forgive … forgive me for this inconvenience."

Exasperated, Ekhardt shook his head in disgust. Scowling at Heinzi, he said. "This is more than an 'inconvenience', *Scharfuehrer* von Rohrsbach." Jumping to his feet, he pointed to the door. "Get out of here! Get out of here at once! I shall report this incident to the Gestapo High Command and see that you are severely disciplined for your impulsive actions."

Outside the train whistle sounded for – what Mary was sure – was the final time before its departure. She and Ruth exchanged looks of disbelief and enormous relief, grateful that they had narrowly escaped arrest and probable death.

At last they would be aboard the Paris express.

Chapter Twenty-seven

The journey on the Paris Express proved to be a far more pleasant experience than the German train. There were no longer Gestapo agents for Mary and Ruth to fear nor did they have to share their first class compartment with anyone, and, in addition, it offered the additional perk of a tiny adjoining bathroom.

In the close quarters of the compact bath, Mary stood at the sink, holding up her blonde hair and wincing as Ruth attended to the abrasions on her back from her fall and the dog bites on her leg suffered at the German border control station, cleaning them with cotton balls and hydrogen peroxide provided by a sympathetic French conductor from the train's first aid kit.

"I'm still absolutely stunned that Heinzi declined to identify us," Mary said.

"I don't think anyone believed him," Ruth commented.

"I'm sure his actions will put his future in jeopardy with the Nazi high command," Mary speculated. "Perhaps there is a shred of decency in Heinzi after all. His parents would have been proud of him. His devotion to his Hitler Youth group completely baffled them."

When Ruth finished caring for Mary's wounds, they switched places, and Mary treated her former tutor's injuries. For Mary, it was a more difficult task because of her swollen and painful hands. When they first realized that their compartment had an adjoining bath, Mary had tried using soap and water to remove the rings from her fingers but was unsuccessful. Later, Ruth obtained some olive oil from a member of the dining car staff but that, too, proved ineffective.

"I'm afraid you're going to have to get along without your rings until we get to London and, hopefully, find someone who knows a way to remove them. Whatever it is, I'm afraid it may damage your beautiful rings," Mary said, apologetically.

"I'm far more worried about your fingers than I am about my rings," Ruth replied. "They're becoming increasingly swollen and discolored. We must find a way to remove the rings even if they have to be cut off."

"You're not talking about my fingers, are you?" Mary joked, able to find humor in the painful situation.

"No, of course not," Ruth answered. Then, suddenly becoming deeply serious and looking Mary squarely in the eye, she asked, seemingly out of the blue, "Andrew is dead, isn't he?"

Mary was too stunned to answer her question right away.

"Tell me the truth, Mary," Ruth implored. "I have to know. I can tell by the sadness that comes over you whenever his name is mentioned that something is the matter. You always look away and change the subject as if -- were we to continue talking about him – you would burst into tears. I know that you don't want to be the bearer of sad tidings, but, as heart-breaking as it will be, I must know the truth. You must tell me. I have to know."

"All right," Mary consented with a sigh. "I'll tell you everything. Andrew was aware that time was running out for you in Germany. That's why he risked that first desperate – but unsuccessful -- attempt to rescue you."

"I know that," Ruth murmured.

"But that didn't prevent him from trying again. His goal was to get you – and your father, if possible – out, regardless of the risk. Even if it cost him his life, he was willing to take that chance. That's how determined he was. He made a second attempt using an unauthorized RAF plane that went down in a heavy fog over the North Sea. There are those, such as Nicholas, who speculate that the Germans detected his plane on their radar and shot it down with one of their fighter planes. We'll probably never know what really happened. The only thing of which we are certain is that Andrew is gone."

"The one thing which sustained me during those horrible days in that rat-infested former convalescent home where those around me, including my own father, lived constantly under the threat of being taken away in the middle of the night to one of those nightmarish Nazi labor camps was the firm belief that Andrew would find some way to rescue me and his unborn child and get us to England," Ruth said. "I never would have guessed in a thousand years that he would enlist you to be the one to help me escape in the event of his failure to accomplish his goal."

Mary smiled. "Is that because you perceived me as a pampered, spoiled little aristocrat whose debutante season with a presentation at court would be the highlight of her life?"

"Exactly," Ruth agreed.

"But you were wrong, weren't you?"

"I was," Ruth admitted with downcast eyes as she reached out and embraced her former student.

Chapter Twenty-eight

Jane and Lucy shared the stern of the twenty-five foot sailboat with Trevor who was manning the tiller. Oliver Longwood, who had been at Harrow with Trevor and was the boat's owner, skillfully managed the sails in accordance with the winds in the Solent between the Haslar marina in Gosport, where the boat was moored, and the Isle of Wight.

"Oh, what a delight be be out on the water amid this glorious fresh sea air which, incidentally, does wonders for a lady's complexion," Jane said, brushing her smooth cheek with her fingertips. "It's such a welcome change from the exhausting whirl of the Season with its almost nightly balls and the races at Ascot and tennis and parties and late night suppers and the Embassy Club … " She paused a moment to catch her breath and push a stubborn lock of her lustrous red hair from her face. "Don't misunderstand me; I love every delicious moment of it, but one does need a respite now and then."

"And I'm happy to provide it," tall, sandy-haired Oliver said as he tightened a rope controlling the main sail.

Jane said, turning to Lucy and patting her arm, "I'm so looking forward to your sister's ball."

"We all hope that Mary returns from Germany in time," Lucy replied. "Our parents are terribly worried about her."

"Yes, I've been concerned about her as well," Jane said. "Thank goodness for the endless distractions of the Season."

"Mary is a clever girl," Trevor remarked. "I'm sure she can take care of herself. In the meantime, Lucy, it's nice to have you aboard as your sister's surrogate."

Flattered by his attention, Lucy smiled and murmured, "Thank you."

"You fellows have no idea how difficult it was for me to persuade Lady Celia to allow Lucy to join us today. I had to convince her that you and I were acceptable chaperons, Trevor," Jane said.

"Your brother is a bit of a rogue," Oliver teased.

"You're the rogue," Trevor responded. "I've already warned my sister about you."

"There's nothing wrong with a man who's a bit of a rogue," Jane said.

"In that case, perhaps we should have brought Nicholas Buckford along for you?" Oliver jokingly suggested.

"No, no," Jane said, shaking her head and smiling at Oliver. "I'm quite satisfied with the present company."

"I rather fancy Nicholas," Lucy remarked, causing Trevor to react with a look of disappointment.

"You'll be doing the Season next year, will you not, Lucy?" Oliver asked.

"If there is a Season," Trevor commented.

Jane frowned at her brother. "What do you mean?"

"I'm talking about the probability of war and its consequences," Trevor replied.

"Trevor's right," Oliver said. "In fact, I suppose that in a way one could say that Andrew's death is the first war casualty among our crowd."

"I imagine there will be many more casualties among those we know as things get worse," Oliver speculated with a sigh.

"Speaking of Andrew, I'm glad for the family that his body was recovered," Trevor said. "It must have been a terrible ordeal for them."

"Indeed," Lucy agreed.

Chapter Twenty-nine

When the Paris Express pulled into the Gare du Est, Mary and Ruth got off and were stunned to encounter none other than Nicholas on the platform waiting to greet them.

Vigorously waving, he called out, "Mary! Ruth! Over here!"

Overjoyed to see him, Mary flew into his arms.

More restrained, Ruth waited until Mary released him before she stepped forward to receive Nicholas' embrace as well.

Smiling, he addressed her as, "'Sister-in-law!'"

"Are you aware that you're going to be an uncle?" Ruth asked.

"Yes," he replied and tenderly kissed her forehead. "Andrew confided that bit of good news to me."

"How did you know Ruth and I would be on this train?" Mary asked.

"I didn't. I just took a chance. Actually, I've been meeting trains and looking for you for days," Nicholas replied. "Your mother's cousin Anne managed to get through on the telephone to your parents the day you left Berlin and informed them that you were traveling by train to Paris. Lady Celia then related that information to me and – *voila!* – here I am." Then backing up a little, he inspected both young women with a worried frown. "My God, what happened to you? You look like you've been in some kind of hideous accident or something – all those cuts, bruises, bandages and torn clothing."

"It's a long story," Mary said. "Heinzi von Rohrsbach denounced us to the Gestapo as spies."   Nicholas scoffed, "Absurd!"

"But later, he recanted his story, but only after the Gestapo guards had set their dogs on us," Mary continued.

"That's how we got all these cuts and scrapes and dog bites," Ruth said, raising her sleeve to reveal the canine teeth marks on her arm.

Nicholas shook his head in disgust. "That little bastard Heinzi! Even as as lad, he was rotten."

"Later, when he was asked to identify Ruth and myself at the German Border Control Station, he retracted everything," Mary said.

"With regard to Heinzi I could imagine anything," Nicholas replied with a contemptuous sneer. "Allow me to take your bags, ladies. Each of you has only one, so it's not worth the bother trying to engage a porter."

As Mary passed him her suitcase, he glimpsed her swollen and discolored hands.

Shocked at the sight, he asked, "Good Lord, Mary! What happened to your hands?"

"I'm afraid that's another long story," Mary replied.

Home after an exhausting week at parliament, Simon returned to Lammersley and prepared for bed with the help of his valet Fitzsimmons who unstrapped his prosthetic leg.

When the valet had departed, Antonia, in her night clothes and robe, opened the door between their adjoining bedrooms and joined her husband.

"Did you assign one of the maids to our new guest?" Simon asked.

"Ruth is not our 'guest', as you say. She's our daughter-in-law, the widowed wife of our elder son," Antonia corrected. Her tone was matter-of-fact, revealing neither joy nor empathy. "Not only that, I found out from Nicholas that she's carrying Andrew's child – our grandchild."

Simon was stunned. "You don't say! Really?"

"Yes, really," Antonia affirmed.

"Well, she seems pleasant enough and is certainly well-educated. Nicholas said she has had a ghastly time of it in Germany, poor girl."

"She's Jewish, you know."

"So Nicholas mentioned. He's welcomed her, and so must we," Simon replied. "I don't see what difference it makes. That American ambassador fellow to the Court of Saint James – Kennedy – his daughter … what's her name?"

"Kathleen," Antonia supplied. "Everyone calls her 'Kick'. She's been enormously popular with those participating in the Season."

"Eventually, Miss Kennedy persuaded her rigidly Catholic family to accept the protestant Marquess of Hartington. I see no reason why we can't follow their example with someone of the Jewish faith."

Antonia shook her head in dismay. "I suppose so, but it's going to take some adjusting."

"Life is one adjustment after another, and we must make the best of whatever situation it presents us with. Our challenge is to go on and, at the same time, honor Andrew's memory. As we both know, he was a bright, righteous and determined young man. He was also brave and loved this young woman Ruth enough to die trying to rescue her. It's our challenge to accept and love her, too."

"Yes, I imagine it is," Antonia reluctantly conceded.

"Andrew is going to live on through this child Ruth is expecting. That's why we must accept and love her," Simon continued. "The child, whether a boy or girl, will be our reward if we meet this challenge in the proper manner."

Antonia contemplated her husband's words for a few moments before replying, "Throughout the many years of our marriage, Simon, you have never failed to enlighten me on countless matters and open my mind to new ways of thinking. This is one of those times."

Delighted by her response, Simon beamed and patted the bed next to him. "Come and join me," he invited. "I think we will need the comfort of one another more than ever in the days ahead."

Wordlessly Antonia slipped out of her robe, laid it carefully across the foot of the bed and crawled under the covers with her husband, resting her head on his chest, his arm around her.

"Yes, more than ever," she agreed.

Chapter Thirty

Nicholas decided that the condition of Mary's hands was too serious to wait until they arrived in London before seeking treatment . Prior to leaving Paris, he took her to the American Hospital where a young American physician used a special instrument to cut through the base of the rings and remove them, assuring her that the redness and swelling of her hands would most likely be gone by the time of her ball. He also cleansed her dog bites, and Ruth's as well, to prevent infection which he claimed was a greater threat than rabies.

"The one thing you can say for the Gestapo is that they take good care of their German shepherd dogs. I seriously doubt that there's ever been a case of rabies among them," the physician commented as he bandaged Mary's hands.

After a brief stopover in Paris, the three traveled by train to Calais where they boarded the ferry to Dover.

"There have been times lately when I thought I might never see these beautiful white cliffs again," Mary said wistfully, standing beside Nicholas at the railing around the ferry's deck as it approached the Dover pier. Ruth had remained below deck during the brief voyage because of apparent 'morning sickness'.

In London, Nicholas picked up his car which he had left in charge of Dunsmuir at the Ashmore's Regents Park home. The three of them climbed into the vehicle and headed for Surrey.

Although Mary invited Ruth to stay with her family at Stagsbridge, she opted instead for Nicholas' suggestion of Lammersley.

"Well, why not?" he confided to Mary when they were alone in his car, stopped by the side of the narrow road for a few minutes in a rural area between London and Surrey. Ruth, still queasy, pleaded with Nicholas to allow her to get out of the vehicle to walk around a bit in the fresh country air, hoping it would quell her nausea. "After all, when one gets right down to the heart of the matter, that child of hers and Andrew's – if it's a boy – will be the master of Lammersley one day."

"What about Lady Antonia? What will she say?" Mary asked. "I don't think she would be keen on the idea of Ruth living in her house."

Nicholas shrugged. "Ruth's presence, and the future presence of her child at Lammersley is simply something to which Mother will have to become accustomed. I would hope they get on well, but if they don't, the damned place is large enough for them to avoid one another if they so choose."

On Ruth's first morning at Lammersley, Nicholas rose earlier than usual to join her for breakfast, aware that the servants would have to have time to adjust not only to her presence in the great house, but to her status as Andrew's widow and mother of his offspring as well. Antonia had withheld the news of Andrew's marriage to Ruth from the household staff for reasons which had their roots in her personal disappointment and prejudice.

"How are you feeling today, Ruth?" he asked.

"Better," she answered with a smile. "It was the first decent night's sleep I've had in a very, very long time," adding, "And on a feather mattress."

"Is the staff taking good care of you?"

"Oh, yes," Ruth nodded. "I informed the cook that I wanted only a soft boiled egg, a piece of plain toast and tea this morning and that's what I was served. My stomach is still a bit uneasy."

"Would you like me to call the doctor?"

"Oh, no, no no. That's not necessary. I'll be all right in a bit," Ruth replied. "But I would like to ask one favor of you?"

"What's that?" he asked as one of the kitchen maids placed a plate of sausages, fried eggs with beans and fried tomatoes plus several slices of toast before him.

"I remember from my days as Mary's German tutor at Stagsbridge that someone mentioned a family cemetery here at Lammersley," Ruth said. "Is that correct?"

"It is," he answered, slicing off the end of a piece of sausage. "It's behind our chapel. Buckfords have been buried there for centuries."

Glancing at him uncertainly, Ruth asked, "Is Andrew buried there?"

"He is," Nicholas replied. "His body washed ashore on a rocky beach in East Anglia along with pieces of his plane wreckage. My brother was brought here to Lammersley for burial."

"I'd like to visit Andrew's grave. Will you accompany me there this morning?"

Looking apologetic, Nicholas said, "I'm sorry, Ruth, I can't today. I have an important meeting in Suffolk." He glanced at his wristwatch. "I have to fetch Lord Arthur from Stagsbridge in a few minutes. He's going with me today. You can walk there if you like. It's not far from the house."

"Is the chapel difficult to find?"

"No, it's very easy," he said, dipping a corner of his toast in an egg yolk. "It's a small stone building with a steeple and a cross on top of it."

Later that morning, Ruth set out for the chapel, stopping on the way in a meadow of grazing sheep to pick a bouquet of early spring wild flowers.

The Buckford family cemetery lay behind the gray stone chapel and was enclosed by a wrought iron fence. Opening the creaking, wrought iron gate, she entered and wandered among the ancient gravestones, glancing at the engraved – and sometimes faded – names of Andrew's ancestors. She mused that these antecedents of her late husband would be – her unborn child's ancestors as well.

Noticing a rectangular plot of freshly overturned earth with a freshly carved tombstone, she approached it and ran her fingers over the engraved words the marble stone bore which brought tears to her dark eyes.

ANDREW GEORGE BUCKFORD
BORN 1910 DIED 1939
BELOVED HUSBAND OF RUTH

With tears rolling down her cheeks, she lay the bouquet of wild flowers on the grave and sobbed uncontrollably for Andrew, for her mother and for her father.

Eventually recovering, she dried her eyes on the sleeve of her jacket and began reciting the *Kaddish*, the traditional Jewish prayer for the dead.

Ruth was so deeply caught up in her praying that she failed to hear the creaking of the cemetery gate behind her as it was opened. Only when she felt a hand on her shoulder did she realize that Antonia had entered the burial ground and was standing behind her.

"Please, don't stop praying," the older woman said quietly.

"It's a Jewish prayer," Ruth felt compelled to explain. "It's the only sort of prayer I know."

"A prayer is a prayer," Antonia said as she knelt beside her. "Hopefully God hears them all, no matter the source," she added and, with her hands clasped, began her own Anglican prayer which blended with Ruth's in a strange ecumenical harmony.

When they finished praying, the two women left the cemetery together.

"I heard from Nicholas that you're expecting Andrew's child. Is that correct?" Antonia asked.

Placing both her hands on her rounded abdomen, Ruth proudly replied, "I am."

"In that case, I would like to help you raise him in the Jewish faith," she offered.

Ruth reacted with surprise. "I always thought that it would be important to me," Ruth replied. "But I'm not sure any longer. My people have been through so much. Perhaps it might be better for him to be raised in the Church of England, as his father was."

"No," Antonia countered. "It's important that your child be raised Jewish and that you carry on the traditions with which you were raised. You should be proud of who you are, Ruth, and the many strengths and accomplishments of your people." Chuckling softly, she added, "Who knows? Perhaps when my grandchild grows up, he or she will marry one of the Rothschilds. I say, now wouldn't that be lovely?"

Chapter Thirty-one

A chilly wind was blowing off the North Sea as Nicholas sped along the narrow road to Bawdsey in his turquoise sports car with Arthur, hunkered down against the cold in the passenger seat.

"I don't understand why you are bringing me out here, Nicholas," Arthur said.

"I want you to see the results of your investment," Nicholas replied.

"Investment in what? Polo ponies? Scrap metal?"

"You'll see, sir," Nicholas promised as he stopped before the gate at the Air Ministry site.

A sentry emerged from the guard station and greeted Nicholas. "Good morning, Lord Ashmore."

"Good morning," Nicholas replied.

Surprised, Arthur remarked, "They know you here."

"They do," Nicholas said, driving onto the grounds of the facility, eventually passing the brick manor house and stopping before the former stables which had been converted into a research laboratory.

Getting out of the car, the two men proceeded into the laboratory where Arthur was thoroughly perplexed to find himself surrounded by banks of electronic equipment.

A horde of scientists and technicians were busily engaged, many of them monitoring glowing electronic screens with rapt attention. A repetitive beeping sound seemed to be emanating from one of the screens displaying three dark, moving images which captured Arthur's attention.

"I say, what is all this about?" Arthur asked, looking around.

At that moment, Robert Watson-Watt, in his usual gray laboratory coat, approached and greeted the two visitors.

"Here's the gentleman who can answer that question much better than I," Nicholas said.

He then performed the introductions of the two older men to one another, and they shook hands.

Pointing to the screen, Watson-Watt explained, "What you're seeing on the oscilloscope screen, Lord Ashmore, are short pulses of radio energy." Then turning to Nicholas, he said, "We've got them all right, Lord Buckford." Although a usually calm man, there was excitement in the physicist's voice.

"'Got what', may I ask?" Arthur questioned.

Watson-Watt pointed to the radar screen in front of them. "Three aircraft. They're those three dark images you see on the screen."

Turning to Arthur, Nicholas asked, "Do you understand what this means, sir?"

Frowning, Arthur replied, "No, I'm not sure I do.'

"It means that not a single aircraft can get within five hundred miles of Britain's shores without being detected," Nicholas explained. "That gives the RAF time to get our Spitfires and Hurricanes into the air and repulse an enemy attack."

"I'm impressed," Arthur said.

"You'll be even more impressed when you go up on the cliff outside and see what Lord Buckford's generosity and belief in me have helped to create," Watson-Watt promised.

Permitting the noted physicist to return to his work, Nicholas led Arthur up the steep grade to the cliff over-looking the ocean where a pair of towers -- a two hundred and forty foot wooden receiver tower and a three hundred and sixty foot steel transmitter tower – rose high into the gray, cloud-covered sky.

"These are the initial radar towers in a network of nineteen similar towers referred to as the 'Chain Home' system which will soon be in operation along the entire southeastern British coast. This system will detect in-coming German planes in time to stop them before they can inflict any damage on us," Nicholas explained. "It's rather ironic when one realizes that Britain will be protected by the research of a German-Jewish physicist and engineer by the name of Heinrich Rudolph Hertz at the end of the nineteenth century. Hertz discovered that radio waves are reflected off of metal objects and their presence can, therefore, be detected. Robert Watson-Watt, whom you just met today, elaborated on Hertz's discoveries and perfected radar, which we have put into action for the defense of our country."

"With a nasty war with the Germans looming on the horizon, I dread to think what Britain's fate would be without the work of these men," Arthur said.

"We'd be bombed into submission by the Nazis without radar, that's what," Nicholas responded. "It took a lot to convince Whitehall of the value of radar for Britain's defense, but they finally agreed and gave us the funds we needed to construct the network of radar towers. That was only after their effectiveness was unequivocally demonstrated to the Air Ministry during the Daventry Experiment in Northhampshire."

"I'm proud of you, Nicholas, very proud indeed," Arthur beamed. "I dread to think what Britain's fate might be without this invention of radar."

"There will always be an England," Nicholas assured him, then adding with a grin, "As the song goes."

Chapter Thirty-two

In order to properly prepare for Mary's ball, Mary, Celia, Arthur and Lucy, in addition to some of the Stagsbridge household servants, temporarily relocated to their London residence. Charles, although home from boarding school, remained behind with a tutor, considered too young at thirteen by Arthur and Celia to attend the ball.

Before leaving, Mary made a special request of her younger brother. "Promise me, Charles, that you will see that Sable is well cared for and exercised daily while I am in London," she said. "You'll like her. She's a lovely horse. I haven't been able to ride her properly, nor as much as I would have liked, with my hands this way." He looked down at her hands still swathed in gauze and adhesive tape. "The Harley Street physician with whom Nicholas arranged a consultation has assured me that I can discard these bandages by the time of my ball."

Because he was busy administering the complex affairs and mainte-nance of Stagsbridge, Arthur had not seen the results of Celia's redecorating efforts prior to their arrival at the London Regents Park home on the day of Mary's ball.

Arriving early, the elegant couple stood at the entrance of the ballroom.

"Splendid! Splendid, my dear!" Arthur proclaimed as he took in the beauty of the home.

The hardwood floors were freshly polished, the walls, doors and decora-tive moldings sere newly painted, and the décor was breathtaking. The bal-cony-like mezzanine encircled the entire ballroom. allowing its occupants a view of the action below. It was accessed by a grand, sweeping staircase which rose upward from the ballroom.

The vast room was a bustle of activity as a legion of servants and contractors prepared for the ball that evening. Some placed tables set with fine china, gleaming silver and Austrian crystal around the edge of the dancefloor while others prepared the bar at the far end of the room. A florist, trailed by a small army of assistants, arranged banks of flowers at strategic locations while caterers readied trays of hors d'ouvres and other refreshments.

"Yes, the workmen did an excellent job," Celia agreed, pleased by her husband's compliment. "I'm so glad that Nicholas will be Mary's escort."

"I doubt if you would have said that a few months ago," Arthur reminded her.

"Nicholas has redeemed himself quite admirably," Celia replied.

"He's a clever lad, that Nicholas," Arthur said. "He's made a considerable contribution to our country's defense with his indispensable help in the development of radar."

"Which he kept quite secret," Celia remarked.

"For national security reasons, I'm sure – as well as modesty, perhaps," Arthur said. "Quite frankly, I'd be proud to welcome him to our family."

"That's ultimately Mary's decision," Celia responded. "I don't think she is ready to make any sort of important decisions right now, given everything else she's experienced recently."

"Yes, it's been a difficult time for her," Arthur concurred. "And she's handled things well for a girl of her age."

"Indeed she has," Celia said. "Her coming-out ball is apropos in more ways than one."

Lord Simon Buckford had been so absorbed in affairs of state at Parliament, preparing Britain's declaration of war against Germany, that there was some question whether he and Antonia would be able to attend Mary's ball.

"I won't be able to do much dancing anyway with my leg," he said, referring to his prosthetic limb. "I've been on my feet so much lately that it's been giving me trouble. With this damned new war on the horizon, I wonder how many other young men are going to lose their limbs. I tell you, Antonia, there's simply got to be another way for nations to resolve their differences."

"Well, when groups of individuals are viciously persecuted, it makes war the inevitable course of action," his wife replied. With a heavy sigh she added, "My heart goes out to Ruth. I'm proud to call her my daughter-in-law."

⸺ ⸺

At Thurstonbury Hall, Jane was having difficulty deciding which of Mrs. Kazanjian's gowns to wear to Mary's ball and decided to seek her brother's opinion. Trevor had returned from Oxford especially for the ball.

Finding him in the library pouring over the latest copy of the *London Times,* she displayed two gowns, one on each arm, an aquamarine and a white one trimmed in silver, and asked, "Which dress shall I wear tonight?"

"What difference does it make? You'll look smashing no matter which gown you wear," he answered indifferently, continuing to read despite his sister's presence.

"Are you bitter because you're not escorting Mary?"

"Lord and Lady Ashmore have relegated me to escorting her little sister Lucy," he responded with a sneer.

"There's nothing wrong with Lucy. She's quite pretty and reasonably clever," Jane said.

"Lucy Ashmore is a child, for God's sake!" Trevor complained, tossing the newspaper aside. "Besides, all this ball business is not that important with the prospect of war looming. I reckon that half the chaps at Oxford will be volunteering, myself included."

"Oh, don't say that, Trevor," Jane responded with a slight gasp. "Mother and Father and I will miss you terribly if you're off to war."

"When one's country calls, one must respond," he said. "Duty is duty."

"Mary's ball is important, too," Jane insisted. "This year will be the last Season for the duration of the war – possibly forever. God only knows how long the conflict will last. That's why we must make this Season a memorable one. I feel obligated to look my best and, therefore, need your opinion on a gown."

"Wear the white one with the silver trim," he said. "It won't clash with your red hair."

⚜

From the balcony-like mezzanine overlooking the ballroom, Mary looked stunning in her robin's egg blue satin gown. A group of female relatives, nannies and miscellaneous chaperons were seated at tables around the edge of the mezzanine. Mary's fellow debutantes were enjoying the evening with their elegant escorts, several now in military uniforms in place of tuxedos, dancing to the music of a large orchestra surrounded by banks of fresh flowers.

Despite the glittering gaiety below, Mary felt wistful.

Accompanied by her parents and her sister Lucy, Mary had stood in the receiving line earlier, dutifully greeting her guests as they arrived. As soon as everyone was assembled in the ballroom, she retreated to the mezzanine once again and awaited her escort Nicholas. He had agreed to substitute for his deceased brother, but was distressingly late, apparently delayed by his involvement with the Bawdsey radar project. For that reason, Mary excused him.

As she contemplated descending the staircase and returning to the dance-floor to fulfill her promise of a dance with Trevor, she spotted him enjoying Lucy's company, making her genuinely smile for the first time that night. Looking out the window, she saw Nicholas behind the wheel of his open Delahaye 135Ms in the now familiar brilliant shade of turquoise. He had just finished changing his clothes and was looking in the rear view mirror as he straightened his white bow tie, then grabbed his formal black jacket from the back seat and jumped out, racing to the doorway.

Although his gleaming, raven-wing black hair was wind-blown from his open car, Nicholas looked handsome and dashing in his expertly tailored tuxedo as he made his entrance.

After politely greeting Arthur and Celia, he surveyed the ballroom. Perhaps clued by Celia, he glanced up at the mezzanine and spotted Mary. As their gaze met, he broke into a broad smile.

Weaving his way through the dancing couples, he headed for the stairs and joined Mary on the mezzanine.

"Why aren't you down there dancing?" he asked. "It's your ball, after all."

"I was waiting for you," she replied.

"Well, your wait is over, my lady," he said with a bow. "Your prince has arrived."

Mary laughed, her spirits soaring for the first time since her return from Germany, grateful for his warmth and entertaining presence.

"Let's take advantage of this occasion and dance, shall we?" he suggested, adding with a more serious tone, "God only knows what tomorrow will bring. But, hell, we might as well enjoy life while we can. We've got to maintain our traditions, such as this ball and the Season. Correct?"

"Correct," Mary agreed as she gazed into his dark eyes. "After all, it's our traditions that make us who we are."

"And we Brits are damned good, if you ask me," Nicholas said as he gently took Mary's gloved hand in his.

"We are indeed," she agreed.

Together they descended the stairs to the dance-floor and joined the others, gazing affectionately at one another as they gracefully whirled about the ballroom to the strains of the Johann Strauss, Jr. waltz, *Voices of Spring*.

Mary nestled her head into Nicholas' broad shoulder and began to weep softly.

Nicholas knew, perhaps better than anyone else, that the world weighed heavily on her ivory shoulders.

"As a wise woman once said, '*a dark storm is descending upon the world*', but I believe that we must try to find a ray of sunshine among the clouds," Nicholas said. "So, please, Mary, don't cry on your special night," he pleaded.

"These are tears of joy," she responded.

Puzzled, Nicholas frowned. "'Joy'?" he repeated.

"Well, for one thing, Ruth is safely out of Germany."

Nicholas nodded in agreement. "Yes, that is a very good reason to be happy. What you did makes me proud. Know that I will always be here for you."

"You always have been," she replied. "It just took a while for me to realize it."

Lowering his head, Nicholas kissed Mary, passionately yet tenderly, a kiss he had been yearning to bestow for a very long time.